Bonded

The low growl was the only warning
that she had, before two hundred pounds
of fur and muscle pounced.

Mountain lion!

She crashed to the ground with the cat
on top, screaming and trying to shield her
face from the furious beast, but although
the huge paw with its deadly claws
brushed the skin of her neck, there was no
pain. She felt a brief tugging sensation as
the amulet came free, and then the world
rushed in.

The web crashed down on her like an
avalanche, hammering her into the ground
as it thundered through her mind.

Also available from Impulse Books UK

The Devan Chronicles

The God Decrees
The Power That Binds
The Warrior Within
Dragon Dawn
Destiny's Pawn*

The Merkiaari Wars

Hard Duty
What Price Honour
Operation Oracle
Operation Breakout
Incursion!*
Countermeasures*
No Mercy*

The Shifter Legacies

Way of the Wolf
Wolf's Revenge
Wolf's Justice*

The Rune Gate Cycle
Rune Gate
Chosen

* Forthcoming from Impulse Books UK

These and other titles available from Impulse Books UK
http://www.impulsebooks.co.uk

Chosen
by

Mark E. Cooper

Published by Impulse Books UK

Published by Impulse Books UK November 2014
http://www.impulsebooks.co.uk

PUBLISHER'S NOTE
The characters and events in this book are fictitious. Any similarity to real persons living or dead, business establishments, events, or locales is entirely coincidental and not intended by the author.

Books are available at quantity discounts. For more information please write to Impulse Books UK, 18 Lampits Hill Avenue, Corringham, Essex SS177NY, United Kingdom.

Cover design: Ravven www.ravven.com

A CIP catalogue record for this book is available from the British Library.

ISBN: 978-1-905380-49-7

impulse
books uk

Printed and bound in Great Britain
Impulse Books UK

Acknowledgments

Special thanks go to Dave Milne, Bill Mcenzie, Irene Blackburn, Barbara Bonshor, Thom Fitzgibbon, and John Bradley for all their help in making this series better than any one person could alone.

Thanks for everything.

1 ~ Rune Gate

Cold blackness. A total absence of light and sound. Was she breathing? Was there even anything to breathe in this place? Alex screamed... she thought she did, but there was no sound. She was running, falling, jumping... it was all in her head. She was doing none of those things. She couldn't be. With that thought rationality began to return.

She had a seemingly infinite amount of time to think it through. She was between worlds on her way to Inari—Douglas' world. He'd never mentioned the trip would be like this. He hadn't talked about it at all, she realised. Perhaps his confusion when they first met wasn't all due to the accident.

Douglas! Where was he? Was he all right? What about Sandy and Michael? Panic began to take her again, but she mastered it. There was nothing she could do for them now. She had to try and keep her wits about her. She would need to get back through the gate, and there was Karel to think of. She tried to feel him near but she couldn't. She couldn't feel her own body let alone Karel's choking grip upon her throat.

One moment she was drifting through the void, a place of utter darkness with no references for her mind to grasp, the next she was bursting into a world of dazzling sunlight. The sudden assault upon her senses, was overwhelming. Her ears popped painfully as she staggered away from the gate. She was only dimly aware that Karel wasn't with her as the world rushed in.

The light was wrong and too bright to her sensitive eyes, and sounds too loud after her deprivation in the void. A gentle breeze rustled leaves and tree branches groaned, making her jump and spin around in fright. Dizziness took her, and she fell to her knees, retching. Still on her knees, she looked blearily around. There were mountains in the distance and a forested valley that stretched for as far as she could easily see. The scent of wet leaves and good soil was heavy upon the air. The sun was high and its light illuminated her in beams filtered by tall trees. It looked bloated, bigger than it should be, and yellow-orange in colour. She was on her knees partway down the slope of a hill surmounted by standing stones. It was a stone ring like the one she saw in Doug's memories. The same one? What had he called it? Dun something... Dun'Velkomen? She looked around at the trees shrouding the land and decided it wasn't the same place.

Where was Karel?

She looked fearfully around at the encampment set up among the stones. She could see the remains of a campfire still smouldering not far away, and about a half dozen small tents set up in the shadow of the tallest stones. A rope had been stretched and tied off between two of the monoliths and she counted ten horses picketed along it. Karel was nowhere in sight. The camp was deserted.

She ran for the concealment that the trees offered. Lucky she did, for as soon as she went to ground and looked back up the slope, Karel appeared through the gate. He nearly fell as she had done, but after a second or two, he forced his knees to hold him up. He cut his palm, smeared the talisman he still held with blood, and began chanting. He made odd gestures and shapes in the air with the bloodied knife, passing it over the talisman repeatedly and naming them in an emphatic voice.

He was trying to close the gate!

She climbed back to her feet, preparing to run back and dive through the portal before it closed, when Mardus and two of his henchmen tumbled in a heap at Karel's feet. The wizard took no notice. Lloyd was the next one through, followed by a dishevelled looking Alison. They took one fearful look at Mardus where he lay puking upon the ground, and bolted into the trees. Again, Karel took no notice and continued chanting. She wanted to shout to her friends, but she didn't dare call attention to herself.

The gate was closing—it was definitely smaller.

She gasped in relief when Douglas tumbled through the gate. He had her gun! He fell to his knees, but he was ready for the disorientation after experiencing it before. He raised the gun and squeezed off two shots at Karel.

"Gah!" Karel yelped in shock and danced back holding his hand. One of the bullets had hit the talisman he'd been using and knocked it from his grasp. "You fool! You don't know what you're doing!"

But Douglas did know. He fired again, this time directly at the talisman where it lay in the grass, and he didn't miss. It shattered with a blinding flash of blue tinged white light. The gate shrank to half its size in an instant, and Karel collapsed as if poleaxed.

Mardus climbed shakily to his feet.

Douglas aimed at him, right between the eyes. "Drop your weapons, and order your men to do the same. Do anything else and I will kill you," he said flatly.

Mardus hesitated but the look on Douglas' face was enough to make him reconsider. He threw down his sword and dagger. His men did the same; among them was the man carrying Douglas' sword.

"Now walk away," Douglas said.

"And go where? We're in the middle of nowhere!" Mardus said angrily.

"And that concerns me how?"

"What about him?"

Douglas glanced at where Karel lay semi-conscious from the backlash of his shattered spell. "His life is forfeit. Ask one more question, and so is yours."

Mardus swallowed and backed away. When he reached the tree line, he turned and fled hotly pursued by his men.

Douglas shakily lowered the gun.

Alex quickly scrambled from her hiding place and joined him just as Tomas tumbled head over heels out of the gate. Seconds later, Michael and Sandy staggered through. Both sank to their knees in shock at what had happened.

"The Goddess blast all fools!" Douglas cried, reaching for Michael where he lay panting upon the ground. "Get up! Quickly you fool, or you'll be trapped here! Alex, get Sandy. Heave her back through if you must, but hurry!"

"I think it's too late for that," she said as the gate flickered unsteadily and shrank to the size of a basketball. "It's too small."

Douglas cried out in dismay dropping Michael and running back to the gate already reaching toward it as if he might hold it open by main strength. There was nothing he could do. The gate flickered once more and snapped shut in his face. He looked back at her in stricken silence. They were here to stay.

"Drop the gun, Skeldon," Tomas croaked from where he knelt. His aim was unsteady, but the look upon his face was determined. "You're under arrest."

"It's not loaded," Douglas said and threw the now useless gun aside.

"What are you doing?" she said in exasperation. Didn't he realise how much trouble they were in? Mardus and his men were less than a few minutes away, and the gate was gone, maybe forever.

Tomas ignored her. "Down on your face, hands behind your back."

Douglas shook his head. "Now you go too far."

"He's on our side!" she cried.

"He killed two men. I saw it myself."

She turned to Douglas. "Did you?"

Douglas shrugged. "It was a fight. They would have killed Michael and Lloyd. Me as well given the chance."

"There see. He had no choice."

Tomas kept his gun out and aimed. "He gave them no warning. He shot one twice in the back and the other in the back of the head. Ask him."

She winced.

"I don't deny it," Douglas said. "It was a fight. I'd be foolish indeed to offer a formal challenge under such circumstances; neither would they have expected it. Besides, there wasn't time. Karel was trying to close the gate against me—I had to get though before he stranded me on your world."

"You can tell it to the judge," Tomas grated.

She sighed. "Don't be ridiculous, Tom. You're not arresting him or anyone. You do realise we're not on Earth any more, right? I think you're a little out of your jurisdiction."

He thought about that for a minute. He finally took the time to look around and lowered his gun. He shook his head at the sight of the mountains in the distance, and then at the huge stones surmounting the mound they occupied. The orangey-yellow sun had him staring for the longest time. He swallowed then nodded at some decision he had made.

"As soon as we get the… the whatever it is, open again, I'm taking you back to face charges."

Douglas shrugged, unconcerned.

She thought it best not to mention that Douglas had just

destroyed the only way to open the gate. Even if there was another talisman like the one Karel had stolen, there was no guarantee it would open a gate home. Douglas had explained back at the farm that there were many artefacts created during the War of Power. Most had long since been discovered and destroyed. Those deemed benign, or of sufficient benefit to the kingdom, were held in trust by the Guild. No one but the Guildmaster himself had access to them.

Karel groaned and mumbled something.

Alex began to kneel beside him to see if he was alright.

"Get back!" Douglas yelled in sudden panic, and pulled her roughly away. She almost fell as she staggered backward.

"He's hurt," she protested.

"Not enough. Not nearly enough," he said grimly and retrieved his sword. "Best we kill him now."

"We can't do that!" she gasped at the same moment Tomas bellowed, "Drop it!"

"Listen to me both of you. This man is wanted by the Guild, by the Queen, and by every lord from the Vale of Dreams in the east to the western sea. There's a huge price on his head. He has stolen, murdered, and committed treason so many times, a thousand death sentences wouldn't begin to cover it. He's your killer, Alex, the one you called Shadowman. He killed that woman you told me of… Sharon Brydon? He's killed many other women in his time."

She bit her lip. He didn't feel evil. If he was Shadowman, shouldn't he feel evil? Maybe not. Maybe it wasn't actually him that she'd felt, but his magic. It really might be best to kill him, but they couldn't just murder him.

"You'll kill him over my dead body," Tomas said coldly. "I'm a police officer no matter where I happen to be standing. Does this place—"

"Inari. We're in the kingdom of Inari," Douglas said.

"Inari then. Inari has laws I suppose?"

"Of course," Douglas said indignantly.

"Then we take him to where he can stand trial."

"That will take days or even weeks! We can't hold him, Tomas. Please believe me, and have done. No one can hold a rune speaker against his will for long. Let me do this for all our sakes."

Muscles bunched at Tomas' jaw. "You're not killing him or anyone as long as I'm close enough to stop you."

Douglas' grip on his sword tightened. "Then leave!"

"So you can murder him? No."

Douglas' hissed in frustration. He slammed his sword back into its sheath and held out a hand. "Your manacles."

"He means handcuffs," she translated.

Tomas removed them from his belt and handed them over.

Douglas handcuffed Karel, and then he hurriedly searched the camp for what he needed. He tore a strip of material from a cloak that lay discarded within one of the tents, and used it to blindfold and gag Karel. He withdrew his *taufr* from the pouch on his belt, touched it to Karel's head for a moment, and grunted in satisfaction when the man fell into a deep sleep. He used more strips of cloth to bind Karel's fingers together into a useless lump, muttering about fools and risks all the while.

"Don't you think you're being a little petty now?" Tomas said in amusement.

Douglas rounded on him, almost hissing in rage. "If Alex or the others are hurt by what you force me to do here today... if *anyone* is hurt by it, I will hold you fully accountable. Do I make myself understood? *Do I?*"

Tomas' eyes narrowed. "Don't threaten me, mister Skeldon."

"Threaten?" Douglas' eyes flashed with his fury. "You mistake me, sirrah. I simply warn you. You seemed to think me churlish for not giving a warning to those men in the warehouse. Well then, for what it's worth, take my warning and be satisfied."

"Doug!" she hissed, shocked by the intent she heard hidden in his words. "He's just—"

"You have no idea what we risk letting him live, Alex! You know nothing of Inari or our situation, which is dire, yet you hem me in with your rules of what you'll allow me to do. What right have you to dictate to me in my own land? You could at least have the courtesy of learning the situation before deciding that I'm some kind of felon."

Tomas looked at his shoes for a long moment in thought, and then nodded to himself. "Fair enough. I'll listen to what you have to say before I make up my mind."

"Good decision, but first we have to pack up and get out of here before Mardus finds his courage and returns with more men."

"He said we're in the middle of nowhere," she pointed out.

"That might be so," Douglas said over his shoulder as he checked the condition of the horses. "But Karel opened the gate to your world from here for a reason. I don't know what that reason is, but I can guess. He'll be back with more of Wallace's men. Count on it."

"Wallace?" Tomas asked.

"That's Duke Wallace," she explained. "Karel works for him. Doug was spying on him when he caught Karel sacrificing a woman at another of these stone circles."

"Like the Brydon girl and that guy in the warehouse?"

"Karel killed her to open a gate back here, the man too."

Michael and Sandy joined them. Watching the tree line fearfully, Michael said, "has anyone seen Lloyd or Alison?"

She groaned; she'd forgotten about them! "I did. They ran into the trees, that way," she pointed off to the right.

"I'll go look," Michael said reluctantly.

"No!" Douglas hurried back from the horses. "No, Michael. Tomas and I will go. I want you and Sandy to help

Alex saddle the horses—all of them. We leave none behind for Mardus. Use the spare mounts as pack horses. I want four of the tents, any food you can find, weapons, water bags… pack up anything you think might prove useful. We can sort it out later. Do it fast. I don't want the night to catch us here."

"Done."

Douglas cocked his head at Tomas and they trotted off in the direction Lloyd and Alison had taken.

* * *

2 ~ Inari

Douglas stopped and crouched to examine the trampled ground. "Someone fell here." He pointed to the tell-tale scuffs. "I can't tell who, but he or she went that way."

Tomas peered through the trees. "What's down there?"

"I've no idea."

They set off again. Lloyd and Alison had a good head start on them and could be miles away by now. If that was the case, long before they found them, he would have to turn back. They were here because of him, and he was reluctant to leave them unfound, but he would do it for the sake of the others.

"They're circling around," he said in relief a few minutes later. "Lloyd has a brain in his head. It's my guess that he's doubling back for a look at the situation back at the camp."

"Which way?"

He pointed.

"Isn't that the way Mardus and his friends went?"

He nodded uneasily. Mardus and his men were unarmed, but that didn't mean they weren't a danger. With Tomas on his heels, he dodged in and out of the trees following the grade down and toward the east. Now and then, they stopped to verify they were on the right track, and then pushed on. It was Tomas who saw it first.

"Camp," Tomas gasped, panting for breath. "There see it?"

He crouched to better conceal himself, and moved behind the massive trunk of a tree. He peered ahead trying to estimate the distance and number of men.

"A mile, maybe less."

"They're not trying to hide. Who do you suppose they are?"

"Travelling people... you know, tinkers?"

"Gypsies?" Tomas offered.

He shrugged. "If that's what you call people that live in wagons like those down there, and travel from place to place, then yes, they're gypsies. We call them tinkers."

Tomas' confusion reminded him that his spell-learned English wasn't perfect. Although Alex had gained Inarian in exchange for his knowledge, the others would be helpless on their own. When there was time, he would cast the spell on each of them.

He turned his attention back to the tinkers. There were only four brightly painted wagons in the camp, each with a four-horse team. Tinkers took great pride in their homes, which were as individual as their owners. Some were painted with pictures of bright flowers, others with fanciful creatures like flying horses. He'd seen some that mimicked life with landscapes or dragons. No two were alike.

"They're like giant-sized barrels," Tomas said, sounding delighted.

He smiled at the sheriff's childish delight. Tinker wagons did look like barrels in a way... if a barrel could have a door in one end, windows in the sides, lacquered paintwork, and four wheels under it.

"Maybe we should warn them about Mardus. What do

you think?"

Douglas didn't answer right away. There was something not right about this. He stared down at the tinker camp trying to find the source of his unease, and stiffened when he noted the lack of women. Tinker women always dressed in bright colours and wore skirts that flared from the waist. There were none that he could see. The men looked right. Tinker men always wore black, brown, or dark grey for some reason. It made the women stand out like peacocks among sparrows.

"Something's wrong."

"Like what?" Tomas said scanning the area intently.

"I see only men. Where are the women and children? And why so few wagons? I've never seen tinkers travel in parties of fewer than a dozen families." His eyes narrowed. "Wallace's men, they have to be. That's why there are no women among them."

"Undercover?"

"Soldiers pretending to be tinkers," he explained.

Tomas frowned. "That's what I said. What are they hiding from?"

"Who, not what, Tomas. If a certain person learned of their presence in Dun'Moore, their lives wouldn't be worth spit."

Henry Moore, whose land they currently trespassed, had a feud with Wallace, but it wouldn't simply mean a skirmish should Henry learn of the pretend tinkers. Rhiannon could well become involved, and she had decreed that tinkers were under her protection in Dun'Moore. There had been a lot of speculation about why, and he didn't know the truth of it, but he suspected that the Reverend Mother was using them as her eyes and ears in the countryside. If true, Rhiannon had done them a disservice announcing her protection. It made everyone suspect them of spying whether they really did or not.

The wagons down there had been confiscated from tinkers, that much was obvious. Whether the tinkers were imprisoned or simply killed he didn't know, but the men were wearing tinker clothes. That was suggestive in itself. If Rhiannon found them, they would beg the Duke's mercy before the end. It would not be forthcoming.

Tomas frowned at the scene. "If your friends went down there, we have no chance of getting them back. There are too many for us."

"They didn't."

"How do you..."

He pointed off to his right. Lloyd and Alison were lying in the undergrowth watching the camp. "Follow me quietly. Don't spook them."

He led the way and quickly joined the wayward pair. When Lloyd saw him, a look of relieved welcome replaced the worry on his face. Alison seemed the happiest to see them, especially Tomas and his gun.

"Mardus went down there," Lloyd said. "We saw him."

Alison nodded. "He had some friends with him. He looked angry."

"I'm sure he did," Douglas said. "I've seen enough here. Let's rejoin Alex and the others. I want to be gone before that lot decides to pay us a visit."

Back at the camp, he was pleased to find Alex had all the horses saddled and most of the packing done. He immediately began helping with that. In short order, everything was ready and he led the way westward out of camp.

West wasn't where he wanted to go. If he was right, Hardenburg was south from here. He didn't know precisely where he was, not for sure, but the mountains to the east gave him a rough idea. If he was right, he was somewhere in the duchy of Dun' Moore—about as far as it was possible to be from Hardenburg and still be in Inari. It could have been

worse. He could have found himself in the middle of Dun'
Wallace.

He led the party followed by Lloyd and Michael. Lloyd
had never ridden before, but Michael could after a fashion.
He said he'd had lessons from Alex years ago. Both men sat
their saddles uneasily, and neither was good for a gallop, that
was for sure, but they could at least keep each other from
falling off. They would learn. They would have to—there
were no trucks in Inari or anywhere in the world. Each man
led one of the pack horses on a long rein.

The three women came next in the column. Alex was a
fine horsewoman—completely at ease. Alison was a liability
and knew it. Alex had taken the embarrassed woman up
behind her, while Sandy swayed in her saddle and rode
beside her. Tomas came last leading one of the pack horses
with Karel tied face down over its back—an uncomfortable
way to travel. It was a shame Karel was asleep; he would have
enjoyed the traitor's discomfit. Apart from Alex, Tomas was
the only one that he could rely upon in a mounted fight.

For protection, he had armed the men with swords, all
except Tomas who still had plenty of bullets for his gun.
Tomas had also taken charge of Alex's gun to keep it out of
Mardus' hands, but it had no ammunition left and was useless
for anything more than clubbing someone unconscious. The
women had a dagger each, but they would be little use in a
fight... well maybe Alex would be. Her use of compulsion
spells could easily sway the outcome of any battle. A dagger
for each of the ladies was simply a gesture, and anyway, it was
his goal to avoid fighting. Hence his haste in leaving the area
as quickly as possible, and the pace he had set to do that. As
it was, Tomas had already delayed them overlong with his
foolish questioning, and his insistence on not killing Karel.

Thoughts of Karel were uneasy ones. Handcuffs were not
enough to hold any rune speaker let alone one of his stature.
A gag and blindfold were only basic precautions. He'd tied

the man's fingers together ignoring all protests, and still he knew it wasn't enough. He should have executed him, but Tomas wouldn't allow it and he carried the only gun.

Binding fingers was a common practice designed to prevent hedge wizards from using ritual gestures. Doing that was an insult to the man, implying he needed such basic gestures to work magic, but insult wasn't why he'd done it. Karel was a runemaster, the highest order of wizard in the Guild. Gagging prevented him from voicing his runes, blindfolding hopefully prevented him finding a target for his magic, and tying his fingers stopped him drawing runes and using lesser magics.

That was the theory, and still it worried him.

As he rode between tall trees from light to shadow and back into light, he tried to come up with a plan. They had weapons and horses, such as they were, and supplies enough for a few days travel, but that wouldn't be enough. He needed to find a town, or at least a village, where he could trade a pair of the horses for proper clothing and more food. What the other men were wearing would raise a few eyebrows, no more than that. What the women were wearing however, especially Alex in her borrowed miniskirt, would send blood pressures soaring.

Finding a town then was a priority, but not *the* priority just now. That honour fell to losing any pursuit Mardus could scrape together. He knew they were leaving a trail an untutored child could follow, but he could do nothing about that until they were a little farther along. He knew some spells of concealment that might help if Mardus didn't have a wizard with him. The spells were simple things of misdirection; they could easily be overcome by the lowliest of hedge wizards, but Karel might have been their only magic user.

He frowned uncertainly. His tricks wouldn't fool everyone equally; a ranger's forestry skills alone would be enough to tell him he was riding in circles, when by all appearances he was doing no such thing. But again, maybe Mardus didn't have one.

Such spells worked best when set to encourage a pursuer's natural inclinations. At a crossroads say, or at a point where direction was in doubt, a pursuer could be made to think his quarry had taken the easier of two routes—a natural assumption reinforced by the spell—when in fact the quarry had taken the more treacherous of the two. Setting the spell here though would be useless. Anyone with sense would know that all routes led downward from a hill.

He led the way down the slope, and then picked a meandering route through the woods westward. He avoided a game trail he ran across, and chose instead a random course that had them all ducking under low branches, and urging the horses over treacherous root-infested ground.

"Hold here," he said and dismounted when he judged the time was right for his first trick.

He pulled a hair from his horse's tail, and made his way back, ignoring enquiring looks from the others. He took a moment to check on Karel before continuing along their back trail a short distance. When he reached the game trail, he crouched to examine the ground.

As expected, the ground had been trampled. Glancing around, he judged this a good spot for what he had in mind. He chose to use a simple misdirection spell cloaked within a *you-see-me-not* spell. If it worked, Mardus wouldn't even detect the misdirection. If he did somehow break it, he might miss the spell it concealed.

He gathered a few simple things together: a twig snapped by one of the horses hooves, some crushed leaves, and a little soil from a hoof print. Using the mud, he made a fist-sized ball and poked the leaves inside it. He tied the broken twig to the outside with the hair from his horse, and knotted it three times. Concentrating on the *taufr* in his fist, and on the effect he desired, he chanted the cantrip he had been taught as a boy.

> *"O Lord of places wild and free,*
> *Please help us now as we flee,*
> *Confuse and confound those who pursue,*
> *As I will, so let it be."*

The spell took hold, and he smiled in satisfaction. He carefully placed the activated charm in the depression left by one of the horses. It was good to feel his powers at their peak again. Although he was a weak wizard as such things were judged in Inari, it was reassuring to be able to rely on the few tricks he knew how to do. It had been unsettling for him when he found himself bereft of much of his strength on Alex's world. He'd found himself constantly testing his magic, trying to judge if his weakness was worsening or not.

> *"Dragon's breath, chameleon sight,*
> *I command the shrouded sea,*
> *I blend the mist, I mix the light,*
> *To bend all around thee."*

The charm shimmered and disappeared… or rather, it seemed to. Instead of a hoof print as before, the ground where the charm sat looked undisturbed. That was as it should be. With luck, no one would find it. Anyone coming this way over the next few days would find themselves turning aside and following the game trail without realising it. Made of mud as it was, the first heavy rain would likely destroy the charm, but that was more than good enough. The weather seemed set to remain dry for a while.

He retraced his footsteps and mounted his horse. "I've left a present for Mardus," he said to his companions. "In an hour or so, I'll leave another, and then one more before we camp for the night. That should be enough to see us safely away."

Alex smiled vaguely at him, and he frowned. She'd been quiet and was probably tired. They had awoken early at the farm, and now here they were facing another long day without sleep between. He wondered how it was possible to have two days without a night between them like that, but then he shook his head. It didn't matter now. He pointed westward and led the way.

* * *

3 ~ The Web

Douglas led a meandering course through the woods, seeming to know where he was going. Alex was sure the others believed that he did, but she knew him well enough to doubt it. She couldn't read his thoughts, he had tightened his shields after her attempt to compel him at the warehouse, but she knew his expressions, and he was worried.

She breathed deeply of the perfumed air, and smiled dreamily. There was something about Inari that really appealed to her. It was as if she'd been here before, or maybe she'd dreamed of it. She didn't think it was Douglas' tales—he had spoken more about his family and hardly anything about the land itself.

Maybe it was sharing his memories that first night that made everything seem so familiar to her, because everything she'd seen here looked different to things she knew, even the trees. They were not quite oaks, but something very like them. Their leaves looked almost right, but their trunks were huge in circumference and the trees were very tall. They were far taller than any oak she had ever seen—more like redwood in height. Whatever they were called, she decided that she liked them.

She thought that perhaps, just perhaps, she was taking all this too calmly. She had been kidnapped, and forced through a magical gate to another world by a murderous magician, yet she found herself riding along without a care. Not so the others.

Tomas was obsessing about Jenn. She would have to take his place as sheriff, at least she would until he got back. He was thinking nasty things about Sheriff Larson too. Larson had apparently delayed him when he drove to Westwood. He blamed that delay for their current situation. Michael was thinking about his wife as usual. Lloyd was thinking how weird Inari felt to him.

She concentrated on his thoughts.

Something's not right about that. I felt what he did back there. How can that be? I never felt that at the farm when he showed us his tricks... or did I? I did feel something, didn't I? Was that him? No, it couldn't have been. I felt it on the drive out to Alex's farm as well. There's something strange about Susanville. No, that's not right. Not the town. I didn't feel it at the hotel, it was on the drive to the farm...

...there's something in those trees. About halfway to the farm. I wonder where that girl was killed. Was it in those trees? Maybe I just felt something left over from the gate. Could be, but I've never been that sensitive before. The others always laughed at me. I tried the hardest and they just laughed. Everything came easy to them, even Michael smiles when I try to raise power.

Don't think about that! Think about what Douglas is doing. There's something he's not telling us, I know there is. Something isn't right. It feels like I'm being watched...

Alex smiled when Lloyd noticed her watching him. He smiled back uncertainly, and then frowned at Douglas' back again. She was coming to suspect something that would explain his discomfort. Douglas had felt his powers were weakened when he found himself stuck on Earth, and realised that magic must be stronger in Inari, or perhaps its source was closer. She knew she should be worried about that. She could hardly control her gifts back home; what would it be like here? She frowned; nothing seemed different. She still couldn't block people's thoughts, but that was normal for her.

The web was very strong here. Very strong indeed. The difference was like comparing the sun to a candle flame. The trees here were old. Old didn't begin to cover it. They were ancient, easily over a thousand years old. She couldn't possibly block the web when it was so strong; she didn't want to, and hadn't tried. It buoyed her up as it never had back home. It was like floating in a warm bath. It was peace and contentment. It was power and the glorious strength of wild things untamed.

Without thinking about it, she found herself following the web back to the stone ring. Mardus and a dozen other men were scouting the mound. She smiled dreamily when the soldiers began tracking. She watched them coming, and grinned when they turned onto the game trail.

"Alex?" Alison said.

"Hmmm?"

"Are you going to get down?"

She blinked stupidly at the woman, trying to understand what she meant, and the web receded slightly. It was enough for her to realise it was dark, and that everyone had dismounted. All of them were watching her worriedly. She had dreamed the day away—no, the web had stolen it. It had trapped her into watching Mardus and his men riding in circles. The moment he entered her head, the web surged up, and she was back watching him again. He was backtracking, looking for the charm Douglas had left, and he was *pissed!*

"Alex?"

"Hmmm?"

Douglas reached up to help her. She clutched his arms, and he easily lifted her down. He was wonderfully strong. Lloyd did the same for Alison, but her legs nearly gave way when he released her. She was unused to riding. Douglas led her to his chosen camping ground and made her sit on a rock. She complied without fuss, and he frowned worriedly. She smiled and blinked at him slowly. There was really nothing to worry about. Everything was fine. Wonderful. Inari was a very fine place.

"What's the matter with her?" Michael said worriedly.

Douglas shook his head uncertainly.

"I think I know," Lloyd said. "I've been feeling it too."

"Feeling what?" Michael said.

"Magic… or power anyway. Haven't you noticed?"

Michael frowned. "I noticed it, but what has that got to do with anything? Douglas told us his magic is stronger here…" he spun to look at Alex. "Oh crap! What are we going to do? She can't control it."

"I'm fine," she protested and giggled. They just didn't understand how great Inari was. "I feel wonderful!"

"She's drunk," Douglas said and then frowned. "Well, not really drunk, but it's very like it. Although the ungifted would dispute us, we all know that using magic is tiring. It *is* work, no matter what they believe. Without a shield, she can't shut it out."

"It must be overwhelming."

"She's high on magic, like an overdose. Is that what you're saying?" Tomas said. "How dangerous?"

"Very," Douglas said grimly. "She needs to shield herself, but she can't, can she?"

Michael shook his head.

"I know what she needs. I'll see to it. Someone sit with her, and make sure she doesn't wander. The rest of you set up the tents and build a fire—a small one. I need to find something."

"But where are you going?" Michael called as Douglas left.

"The river. Just set up the camp like I said. I won't be long."

Alex thought the river sounded like fun. "Can I come?"

Sandy patted her hand. "No dear. You sit here and keep me company, all right?"

"Okay."

* * *

4 ~ Ward

Skeldon disappeared into the trees and Tomas sighed under his breath. Why did that man rub him the wrong way so easily? He glanced at Alex where she sat grinning next to Sandy, and sighed again. He knew why, dammit.

"Come on," he said. "Our lord and master has spoken. We better set the tents."

Lloyd nodded.

"Maybe we shouldn't stop here," Michael said, peering uneasily into the trees. "We have Mardus and his soldiers to consider. They might catch up."

"They might," he agreed. He almost hoped they would, because passively following Skeldon's lead didn't sit right. A little action sounded good right about now. "I have my gun, but I don't think it's likely. Their horses need rest the same as ours do."

"Right. Okay, you're right."

He clapped Michael on the shoulder and pointed to the pack horses carrying the tents.

"What about him?" Alison said, nodding at Karel, still face down over his saddle.

"I'll get him down. Scout around for some firewood,

would you?"

Alison nodded.

While she did that, he went to retrieve their sleeping bad guy. He carried Karel on his shoulder to the centre of camp, and left him there still sleeping, before helping the others to raise the tents.

Getting everything ready for the night didn't take them long, and they were soon gathered around a cheery fire. It was small and smokeless as Skeldon had wanted, but welcome. It wasn't cold yet, but the flames gave them light, and that was reassuring in an unfamiliar forest at night.

Sandy helped Alison put together a savoury stew from the makings they found in the packs, and they ate, grateful for something hot. He cleaned his plate and wondered what they would do when the supplies ran out. They would only last a few days. No doubt Skeldon had a plan; he just wished he knew what it was.

"What do you think he's doing out there?" Alison said, spooning a little stew into Karel's mouth. She massaged his throat to make him swallow. "He's been gone hours."

Tomas shrugged.

"It only seems like hours," Lloyd said. "Anyone checked a watch lately?"

Watch? He took a moment to check his, and frowned at the blank display. He grunted in annoyance. "Needs a new battery."

"So does mine," Lloyd agreed. "That's what I meant."

"Hey, mine too," Sandy said.

"Yes," Alison agreed looking at the blank display on her wrist.

"Mine works," Michael said a little smugly, and brandished the analogue watch he wore. "It's an automatic. Not battery powered."

"Does that mean batteries don't work here?"

Michael shrugged. "I've no idea, sheriff. It could be

something to do with the gate. Maybe it drained them. Guns work."

"Guns are mechanical, like your watch."

"But bullets are chemical, or the propellant is anyway."

"Who cares!" Lloyd said in annoyance. "I want to know what the hell we're going to do. Douglas might have run off and left us here for all we know."

"He wouldn't do that," Sandy said glancing at Alex.

Alex smiled dreamily. "I haven't got a watch."

Sandy grimaced.

"He'll be back," Tomas said, a touch grimly. "He'll need his horse if nothing else."

But it was Alex he was really thinking of. Skeldon and Alex meant something to each other. He didn't like that, but it was obviously true. Skeldon would no more abandon her than he would.

He watched Alison caring for Karel and brooded upon what had happened. He wondered what Jenn thought of his disappearance. She and Meeks had been right behind him when Larson gave the order to storm the warehouse. They would have seen him tackling Skeldon and falling through the gate. He didn't know what Larson and the others saw, but his disappearance would take a hell of a lot of explaining, and that was a fact. Jenn would do okay as sheriff. She was more than qualified, and the mayor thought highly of her. No, Jenn didn't need him to hold her hand. Alex didn't either, but he was determined to do it regardless.

"Three moons," Lloyd said, staring up at them through the branches of the trees. "I guess that makes it official. We're the first Americans to set foot on another inhabited planet. One small step for man, and all that."

Everyone chuckled uneasily.

"The constellations are different too," Michael said. "I guess that follows."

"Any way to know how far away Earth is?" Sandy said.

Michael shook his head. "I don't see how. Maybe a fully equipped observatory could tell you. We could be in another galaxy entirely for all I know."

"Or another reality," Lloyd said. "Science can't explain the gate. Instantaneous travel across light years, or as near to it as makes no difference? No way."

"We're living proof it can be done."

"Magic can't be explained by science. It just *is*," Alison said, crossly. "If this world is just one of millions in our universe, why would it have people like us? Ever heard of evolution? I think another reality is closer to the truth, if not *the* truth. And do you know what? I think this world leaks. The only reason we have magic back home is because it leaks from here to there. That's why it's stronger here."

He laughed. "It leaks?"

Michael smiled. "It could be true. Almost anything could be true somewhere, especially if this is another reality. Where there are two realities, there will be more. Maybe every conceivable possibility is real somewhere—in its own reality I mean."

"The gates," Alex said vaguely.

Sandy leaned toward Alex. "What did you say?"

"Take no notice," Alison said. "She's rambling."

"I am not!" Alex said indignantly. "Douglas told me about them. During the War of Power, there were lots of things made with magic. Weapons, and tools, and—oh all sorts of things."

"Gates?" Michael asked.

Alex nodded eagerly. "A lot of things were seized and destroyed, but some were lost in the chaos. What if one of them was a gate and it's still active? Magic could be leaking into our world through it even now."

"I don't think so," Lloyd said uncertainly. "Someone would have stumbled upon it by now. If not someone from here, at least someone from Earth."

"I don't know," Michael said thoughtfully. "There are some striking similarities between Douglas' beliefs and ours. It could be true. Maybe it's in a really remote location, or hidden under ground like in a cave or something."

"That's Bermuda Triangle stuff," Tomas protested. "Your theory belongs in the woo-woo section of the library."

"*Thank you*, sheriff," Michael said sarcastically. "Maybe all those missing boats and planes are here somewhere. Ever thought of that?"

He snorted.

Lloyd looked thoughtful.

Tomas shot to his feet at the sound of someone slogging through the trees. He motioned everyone to be quiet while he went to investigate, gun in hand. He used one of the trees to protect his back and went to one knee. It might be Skeldon returning, but if it was, he had chosen to circle around and approach the camp from the south. The shadow moved carefully among the trees, and then froze.

"It's me," Skeldon said before approaching again.

Tomas rose to his feet and holstered his gun. "Took you long enough."

"I had something to attend to."

"Something?"

"Another of my tricks for Mardus."

He grunted not sure that he knew what to say about that. He was the only one in the group not able to sense magic. He didn't doubt it existed, not anymore. The gate had cured him of his pessimism. Not being able to sense it put him at a disadvantage; it made him the odd one out. He didn't like the feeling of separation from the others it caused in him—especially separation from Alex. Skeldon was entirely too close to her as it was.

They headed back to camp.

"Did you find what you need?" Michael said.

Skeldon drew his dagger and bent to examine one of the

packs. Everyone watched as he vandalised the pack for its leather strings. He produced a smooth oval of stone from a pocket and used the strings to create a pendant. It wasn't pretty, but the stone seemed securely held in its makeshift setting of leather.

"A ward stone amulet," Skeldon said holding it up.

"Ward?" Tomas asked.

"A form of protection against attack," Michael explained. "Like a magic shield."

Skeldon knelt before Alex. "I made this for you. Put it on."

Alex took the amulet. "What will happen?"

"Nothing that will harm you. It won't hurt, but it will be uncomfortable at first. You'll get used to it."

Alex raised it over her head and let the stone slip under her clothes to nestle between her breasts. Her eyes flew wide in shock, and she made to remove it, but Skeldon captured her hands before she could.

"Let go!"

"Wait. Just wait. Trust me, Alex. It will get better."

Alex struggled for a moment longer, but then she stilled. "I can't hear them anymore," she said in wonder, but then she fidgeted and smiled anxiously. "My magic is gone. I can't sense the web. It's gone."

"Not forever, don't worry. You're shielded as long as the stone rests against your skin. It can't replace proper shields and training, but it will stop the voices."

"She can't hear us anymore?" Lloyd said intently.

"I can't sense anything," Alex said. "It's like my head is stuffed with cotton wool. Everything is muffled, like my ears have been stopped up."

"I know it's uncomfortable," Skeldon said, "but it's the best I can do. I have another for Karel, but I don't know how long it will last. He's very strong."

Alex seemed distracted as if trying to hear something

too quiet to make out. "It's wonderful," she said, not very convincingly. "Thank you."

"You're welcome." Skeldon climbed back to his feet. "Is there anything to eat?"

"I'll get you some," Alison said, leading him back to the fire.

Tomas crouched before Alex to look her in the eyes. "Are you really okay?"

She smiled and took his hand—she took his hand and nothing bad happened!

"I'll be fine now," she said with a smile.

* * *

5 ~ Adventurers

Alex groaned and rolled over. "Go away."

Sandy shook her again. "Come on sleepy head, its dawn."

"Tired," she said plaintively.

"*You're* tired! Just think about how poor Alison is feeling. At least you knew how to ride before we came here. The only horse she had ever seen was on TV!"

She snorted uncharitably and pulled the blanket over her head.

"Come *on!*" Sandy dragged the blanket off again. "Doug has been up ages."

She propped herself up on her elbows and glared. "He was on watch. Of course he's up!"

"If you want something for breakfast, you had better get dressed."

Alex shuddered at the thought.

"You still don't eat in the mornings?"

"Never have, you know that."

"Breakfast is..."

"...the most important meal of the day!" she parroted. "I know, I know, but I can't face food this early."

Sandy nodded at the ward stone nestled between Alex's breasts. "How are you feeling now?"

She thought about that for a minute.

There was real silence in her head for the first time in many years. Even when she blocked out people's thoughts, she could usually hear a buzz of indistinct voices like background noise. Now there was silence, but it wasn't a comfortable one. Douglas had warned her it would be uncomfortable, and he was right. Her head and ears felt stuffed up as if with a heavy cold, but she wasn't ill. It felt as if she'd gone deaf, but no amount of yawning to clear her ears would equalise this pressure. There *was* no pressure. The stone just damped her powers, buried them deep and out of reach. It felt like she was suffocating at first. If he hadn't restrained her last night, she would have thrown the stone as far from her as she could.

"Fine," she lied. "I feel good. I could do with a shower though."

"Couldn't we all."

"What about a quick dip in the river?" She dressed quickly in her borrowed and rumpled clothes. "I wish we'd had time to change before coming here. Susan might be my size, but this stuff isn't my style. Give me jeans over skirts any day."

Sandy smirked. "I bet Doug likes it though."

"Let him wear it then."

"A mini definitely wouldn't suit him," Sandy said with a grin. "I wonder what they told Susan about us. Would your friend tell her, do you think?"

"Jenn you mean? I think she probably would, not that she really knows what happened to us. I know she'll look after the farm for me." She frowned, remembering her cat and the horses waiting for her. "Jenn will take care of it."

"Don't take this wrong, but I'd swap places with her in a hot second."

"Can't blame you for that," she said, following Sandy out

of the tent.

Douglas was crouched by the fire, stirring something cooking in a blackened pot that smelled vaguely edible. Michael and Lloyd were watering the horses, while Alison had taken it upon herself to care for their prisoner again. There was something about Alison's attentiveness to Karel that made her uncomfortable. Someone had to see to him she supposed, but Alison had seemed almost eager to do it last night, and now here she was doing it again. Karel was awake and sitting propped up against the trunk of a tree. Alison was holding a plate and occasionally spooning something into his mouth. His gag hung loosely around his neck.

She stumbled to a shocked halt.

"Oh don't worry about him," Sandy said noticing her sudden fear. "He's got an amulet like yours, and Douglas used his whammy on him when he got lippy this morning."

"His what?"

Sandy raised a hand and wiggled her fingers in a vaguely magical seeming way. "You know, he spelled him—took his voice."

"If he could do that, why didn't he do it last night?"

Sandy shrugged and they walked on. "The spell needs constant attention apparently, and it doesn't last long. Karel was really pissed when he woke up, I can tell you that. Scares me being on the same planet with him."

"Yeah." She wrenched her attention back to where they were going before she tripped. The look on his face hadn't been pleasant. "Where we going?"

"You said you wanted a dip in the river."

"Oh... oh yeah... that would be great. Shouldn't we tell Doug though?"

"He already knows." Sandy nodded across the camp. "Look, here comes our watchdog."

She turned in time to see Tomas leave Douglas' side and head their way. She sighed. He didn't look happy, but he rarely did anymore. Determined not to wait, she urged Sandy on.

The river wasn't what she was expecting. She had thought it would be more stream than river, but that wasn't the case. The Ilse was wide and placid; it promised to become a major waterway further west. The current was calm, an indication that it was deep. She wondered if there might be boats further downstream. Probably there were, and with them towns.

"I'll stand over here. Just yell if you need me," Tomas said holding back to give them privacy. He would be out of sight but within shouting distance.

She stripped quickly and dove into the river. The water was icy cold, and it shocked a gasp out of her. Sandy was slower at diving in, but not by much. She surfaced just in time to get dunked again. Before Sandy could do the same to her, she launched herself onto her back and stroked away, laughing at the spluttering and dire threats sent her way.

"Isn't this great," she said a while later, as they floated on their backs beside each other. "What a place."

"Yeah, what a place," Sandy said sourly. "You haven't forgotten how we ended up here have you?"

"Of course not, but Inari isn't the only place with men like Karel. The States has its share of problems—more than its share of some."

"You'd know better than I."

"Hmmm," she agreed, remembering all the crime scenes she had been called to attend. "I know Inari isn't a paradise, but this little part of it is. Can't you feel it?"

"I feel it, but I don't let it blind me. This place is dangerous in ways we've never thought of. Doug and the others aren't wearing swords for show."

She frowned. Michael and Lloyd didn't know how to fight using their swords, so they *were* wearing them for show, but she took Sandy's point. She ducked her head one last time then stood to wring her hair dry.

"I wish we had some soap and shampoo."

"Mardus' men weren't big on baths."

They climbed the riverbank back to their clothes. "Maybe we have time to rinse our stuff?"

"I wouldn't think so. Doug will want to make up some time today."

She nodded and dressed with clothes clinging to wet bodies, they retraced their steps to collect Tomas. They found him sitting attentively on a rock not far up slope from where they had been bathing. She looked back at the river with narrowed eyes, but she couldn't decide if he'd been peeking or not. Not, she decided after a moment. Tomas might be many things, but a voyeur he was not.

"Better?" Tomas said as he escorted them back to camp.

"Much," she agreed. "Did you and the others...?"

"Doug let us go in shifts."

She frowned at his sour tone, but at least he wasn't using Doug's last name anymore. "He has his reasons."

"I guess he must have. I just think it's time we knew what they were."

Douglas was still by the fire when they returned to camp. He was staring into the flames unseeing, while Lloyd and Michael finished packing the tents. Karel looked up sharply when Tomas wandered over to talk with Alison. He'd been unconscious when Tomas came through the gate, but he obviously knew what the uniform and badge meant. She watched him assessing what, if anything, Tomas' presence meant to him.

She joined Douglas by the fire. "Tomas wants to know what you plan to do next," she said quietly. She picked up a twig and poked the fire. "I admit to wondering about that myself. You should fill us in."

Douglas nodded.

"In case something happens to you. Not that anything will, but it would be better if we knew what to do if... well, if we get separated or something."

"I understand. You don't need to explain. It's my fault you're all stuck here."

"I didn't mean it like that," she protested. "No one blames you. I just meant... look, you know everything there is to know about your world—"

Douglas snorted. "Hardly!"

"—but we don't even know its name!"

"Its name? Rune masters call it Othala after the first rune, but to everyone else it's simply the World."

"Okay. Where in Othala are we exactly?"

The others gathered to listen. Alison said something to Karel then joined the group. Douglas checked the position of the sun and seemed satisfied that there was time to explain a few things. With a smouldering stick taken from the fire, he began drawing a rough map in the dirt. He drew a long line of Xs first.

"The Ilsethorn Mountains east of here," he explained, and then drew a wavy line from the Xs westward. "The River Ilse that we're following west. This area..." he drew a meandering line along the mountains, then westward, then back north, and finally connected it to the line's origin. "...is called Dun'Moore. South of here is Dun'Wallace. The stone ring where we arrived is called Dun'Morogh."

"What's special about it? Karel must have chosen it for a reason," Tomas said.

"Dun'Morogh is one of three stone rings in Dun'Moore. All of the great rings are places of power no matter where in Inari they happen to be, but the three in Dun'Moore are the oldest. They're revered by Daughters of the Mother, by witches, as sacred to the Goddess. What's important about that is where Dun'Morogh is located. It's right on the border with Dun'Wallace, which is a place I dare not go."

"Could it be one of the others?" Alex said. She knew why he couldn't set foot upon Duke Wallace's lands.

Douglas frowned. "I don't think so. Dun'Laoghaire is in the west of Dun'Moore and the mountains would not be visible from such a distance. That leaves Dun'Vulan, but I can't believe Karel would dare cross the witches so blatantly. Dun'Morogh is one thing—he could have fled back across the border, but to reach Vulan, he would have to cross most of Dun'Moore and pass within a few miles of the motherhouse at Dehra. I can't believe Rhiannon would allow that. No, the river we're following *must* be the Ilse, and that means the circle was Dun'Morogh."

"Rhiannon?" she said.

"The Reverend Mother."

"She's a witch?"

"Rhiannon is..." Douglas paused for thought. "The Daughters of the Mother keep their secrets close, Alex. They don't seem to have ranks, or if they do, I don't know what they are. The witches call Rhiannon first among equals, and yes, she is a witch—a very *powerful* witch. To everyone else, she's the Reverend Mother, and accorded the respect due a queen."

"And this queen of witches lives here in Dun'Moore?"

"In Dehra, yes. It's said that Dun'Moore is the ancestral home of the witches—they certainly act as if they believe it and who better to know? Their motherhouse is at Dehra, which is Duke Moore's ancestral seat. Henry Moore, all the dukes of Moore come to that, always support the Reverend Mother in whatever she chooses to do. In return, Clan Moore and its dukes enjoy a special relationship with the witches."

"As interesting as all this is," Lloyd interrupted impatiently. "You still haven't explained how we get home."

Douglas frowned.

She answered for him. "That's because he doesn't know how."

Alison gasped. "What do you mean he doesn't know? I thought he was taking us somewhere safe to open another gate!"

She shook her head pityingly. "You haven't been listening, have you? Karel had to kill someone to open a gate. Who did you have in mind for your sacrifice?"

Alison paled. "I didn't... I mean I don't... I would never..."

"It's worse than that," Douglas said. "I destroyed the talisman Karel used. I make no apology for that. It was an evil thing and dangerous. I tried to keep you all out of this. I tried to keep the gate open long enough to send you back—Alex was witness, I did try."

"He did," she agreed.

"What good is that now?" Alison cried angrily. "We're stuck here!"

"You *are* stuck here," Douglas agreed. "But perhaps not forever. It depends."

"On?" Lloyd said.

"On whether or not we reach Hardenburg before Wallace tries to take the throne, on whether or not the Guildmaster has another gate talisman, and on whether he can use it."

"Karel found a way," Tomas pointed out.

"Karel stole the one he used from the Guild years ago. Why do you think he never used it before this year?"

"Because he couldn't," Alex said.

Douglas nodded. "He didn't know how. He told me back at the warehouse that he spent years studying it. I have no doubt he sacrificed many lives to learn what he needed. Now, it may well be that the Guildmaster already knows the way of it. He's not Guildmaster for nothing, but that is speculation not fact. Either way, our best course is south to Hardenburg."

"South." Tomas nodded at the crude map. "We're heading west."

"I'm aware of that. Dun'Wallace is south from here. I cannot go that way, and neither can you if you want to live to reach Hardenburg. We go west, and then south when I deem it safe."

"What's west?" Michael said.

Douglas sketched in more of his map. "The lowlands and eventually the fen. The fen is mine as part of Dun'Morgan, and beyond that is the sea. If we follow the river west, we'll find villages and towns aplenty."

"And you think we'll find a welcome there?" she asked.

"I'm not without means. I know it might seem that way, but let me get us to a decent sized town, and I can call upon people of my acquaintance to obtain what we need. I'm not unknown in Inari, as you must realise."

She nodded thoughtfully.

"You mentioned a place called Hardenburg," Michael said.

Douglas stabbed the stick in the ground, well to the south of what they now knew was Dun'Moore. "The capital of Inari is the centre of power in Dun'Harden. It's there we must ultimately go. I must warn the queen of Wallace's treachery, and you need to learn whether the Guild possesses another talisman capable of getting you home. It's a long journey from here; a month at least, and more probably two because of the route we must take."

"Dun'Wallace is between Dun'Moore and Dun'Harden," Lloyd said watching as Douglas slowly filled in the map. "What's east of Dun'Wallace?"

"The Vale of Dreams. Disputed territory, and the source of many of Inari's woes. It's the gateway into the Sawai Empire."

"Who does it belong to?" Tomas asked.

"It forms part of Dun'Wallace. It was once a very rich land, but the War of Power changed that. It's an uncanny place now and well named. Men have gone mad trying to pass through it. Caravans hire the Guild to protect them, but not everyone can afford to do that. There are plenty of fools willing to risk the danger for the profits the empire can offer. The land itself has no value any longer except as a route for trade, but that's enough to make it worth committing treason for."

"I've been meaning to ask. Why are you Duke Skeldon and not Duke Morgan?" Michael said curiously.

Douglas shifted uncomfortably. "That's a tale for another time. Come my friends, daylight is wasting. We are not so far ahead of Mardus that we can afford to dally here. Do you feel up to a riding lesson, Alison?"

Alison nodded.

"Come then," Douglas said rising to his feet, and kicking the remains of the fire apart. "Let me attend to that as we ride this morning."

With that, the meeting broke up.

As promised, Douglas undertook to tutor Alison in the basics of riding her horse. He was a patient teacher, and Alison quickly learned how to move with her horse rather than against it. Although still tentative, it wasn't long before she was riding beside him, capable of anticipating what her horse would do.

Karel rode astride his horse this time, with his blindfold and gag firmly in place. Douglas wouldn't hear his protests, and had ended them with a firm ultimatum. Wear them, or be spelled asleep and travel thrown over a saddle. Karel wore them. Tomas led his horse using a long rein.

Alex rode beside Sandy trapped in the silence of her thoughts, and probing the empty place in her mind where the web should be. It was not pleasant, that sense of something missing. It was like a phantom pain... perhaps this was how an amputee felt. The web had been a constant irritant upon her mind for so long, that now it was silenced, she felt like a part of her was missing.

They travelled steadily west following the river's course, and Douglas seemed well pleased with their progress. He became ever chattier as the hours fled by without a sign of Mardus or other pursuit. He ordered a short rest at midday and sent Lloyd to refill the water bags while he taught Michael the basics of fighting with sword and dagger. Tomas watched the lesson with a keen interest, and when Michael called for a rest, panting with exertion, Tomas removed his gun belt and took his place.

Douglas had stripped to the waist, and was gleaming with sweat. Tomas was modest and kept his shirt on. Both men were concentrating hard upon besting the other. Douglas held himself back because Tomas was new to the sword, but he didn't make it obvious. He allowed Tomas to get close any number of times, and this seemed to spur him on. In the end, both men were grinning and panting.

Douglas was full of praise for the effort Tomas and Michael had put in. He assured them that by the time they reached Hardenburg they would be able to hold their own against anyone they were likely to fight. Nowhere was completely free of brigands, he said, but with work they would be fine.

Lloyd shook his head. "Look at them. They're just lapping it up."

She frowned. "What?"

"Douglas says jump, and they say how high. They don't even realise it. Haven't you noticed that when he says something, everyone stops to listen?"

"I guess so, but what's your point?"

"That *is* my point. He's a lord, and he's acting like one."

"This is his country. You can't expect him to act like a tourist, and besides, we need a guide. Who better to lead us than him?"

Lloyd shook his head and stomped off.

She shrugged and went to join Sandy as she prepared a meal of hard bread and cheese for everyone. She sat next to her friend and took the hunk of bread offered to her, broken from one of the loaves found in the packs. They were the size and shape of a dinner plate and were about two inches thick. The bread was quite tasty when soaked in some stew like last night—it had nuts and other fruit in it, but it was almost impossible to eat like this. It was hard as concrete and dry as sawdust. She looked at it with distaste for a long moment before gnawing upon one corner. It was like eating dust.

"Here," Sandy said offering her a lump of cheese.

She sighed. "I used to like cheese."

"Yeah," Sandy agreed glumly and nibbled on hers.

Alex took a sip of water to wash the dusty bread down. "Listen to us. We've only been here two days and already we're complaining. Maybe the rest of the world is right. Americans really *are* decadent."

Sandy snorted. "I challenge anyone to enjoy eating this stuff."

Just then Douglas walked up. "A challenge is it?" He held out a hand and Sandy gave him his ration, but rather than eat it straight away, he fetched some water. "Watch carefully."

He softened his bread with water, and used his dagger to cut it into two slices. Next, he shaved off some of his cheese and sprinkled it between the slices of bread. Finally, he thrust a stick through the entire thing and held it over the campfire for about a minute to toast.

He took a bite of his toasted cheese sandwich. "Delicious!"

She grinned. Sandy didn't notice, she was concentrating on toasting her own sandwich to the exclusion of all else. She was a fast learner.

Douglas sat next to Alex and watched her make her own dinner. "Don't hold it in the flames or it will scorch. Try a handspan above them."

"Thanks," she said and raised her food a little higher. "I didn't know you were a cook too."

"A soldier who cannot cook won't eat, at least not very

well. Besides, this is nothing. Journey bread makes poor fare, true, but I've been in situations where I've blessed it. It will keep you alive, though perhaps not happy to be so."

She grinned and took a bite of her sandwich. The melted cheese was hot, and she had to chew quickly.

"If we weren't in such a hurry, I could have set a few snares last night, or if Mardus' men had carried bows, I could have hunted for meat. You would've eaten a meal fit for the queen."

"Tomas has his gun."

Douglas looked shocked. "For hunting? He does better saving it for Mardus, rather than wasting it upon a full belly. Besides, there are other dangers out here. He must save his bullets in case of attack."

"Is that likely, for us to be attacked I mean?"

Sandy turned to listen, her food half eaten and momentarily forgotten.

His face settled into grim lines. "I'm afraid it is, yes. We are few, and half our number are unarmed women. We have Mardus on our trail, that's bad enough, but any kind of travel through the wilds is dangerous if not prepared. By rights, we should be travelling in a well-guarded caravan. Small parties like ours risk being waylaid by bandits. That's one reason I'm keeping to the trees. Bandits and robbers tend to haunt the roads looking for their prey."

"I wish I had more bullets for my gun," she said. "I could help then."

"I could make you a bow. I could make each of you one in time, and teach you how to shoot. Many fine ladies choose archery over hawking for sport, but I think our time is better spent reaching a village where we might purchase what we need, rather than delay out here making poor second-rate weapons."

"I doubt anything you do is second rate."

Douglas blushed. "I thank you," he said, inclining his

head solemnly. "I shall relieve Tomas of his guard duty. Perhaps you would be kind enough to show him our secret journey bread recipe."

"Of course I will."

Douglas rose to his feet and trotted off to take Tomas' place guarding Karel.

"Be careful," Sandy said around her sandwich. "Don't fall too far or too fast."

"I know what I'm doing."

Sandy shrugged and concentrated upon her food.

* * *

6 ~ Betrayed

Lloyd lay awake staring into the darkness. Events had finally conspired to give him an opportunity that he would be a fool not to act upon, but getting started was hard. It would be a betrayal of the others. He sighed, forcing his thoughts away from his guilt and onto what he needed to do. The decision was already made, and besides, they wouldn't be hurt by his choices; he would see to that. He liked Alex and her friends. It was Douglas he had the problem with.

He had bided his time until tonight for a number of reasons. Alex's magic had been the biggest one, but now that she wore the ward stone pendant, she wouldn't know anything unless she took it off. Secondly, he had needed a night that Douglas wasn't standing watch. That man took his responsibilities too seriously to risk trying anything while he was awake. Thirdly, there was Karel himself to deal with. The answer had fallen in his lap only that morning when Douglas had given Karel a choice to ride gagged as usual, or be spelled asleep and thrown over a saddle like luggage. Alex had suggested Karel swear an oath on his powers—something Douglas had told her about apparently—but Karel had steadfastly refused. Michael had asked why anyone would refuse when it was obviously better to swear than be gagged, and Douglas explained that the Goddess herself bore witness and punished oath breakers harshly. An oath breaker cursed by the Goddess never lived long. Karel was insanely dangerous. There was no way he could be trusted to deal fairly unless forced. Just as Douglas forced him with handcuffs, gags, and spells, he planned to coerce Karel with an oath that he would accept but never break.

It will work, I know it will.

It wasn't time for him to stand watch, but he couldn't wait any longer. His few belongings were in his pack ready to go, and sleep was beyond him. He crawled quietly out of the tent, careful not to wake Tomas and looked around. It was pitch dark, but the banked campfire gave enough light for him to make out Michael. He was sitting cross-legged with his sword across his knees, staring into the trees. He had his back to the fire to preserve his night vision, and seemed to be taking good care to stay alert—he kept his head moving, not letting himself zone out with staring too long.

"Hey," Michael said, keeping his voice low.

"Hey," he replied. "I couldn't sleep; I thought I might as well take over from you."

Michael nodded, but not in agreement. "I could use the company. I'll sit with you a bit."

"No need. Why don't you get some rest?"

"Nah, I'm good for a couple more hours, but thanks."

Lloyd gritted his teeth. Damn! He chose a spot near the fire and sat. "You think Mark knows about any of this?"

"I've thought about it, but I can't say I know what the police would tell them. I mean, think about it. They aren't in the habit of telling civilians things at the best of times, and this is something out of the ordinary."

"Off the charts," he agreed.

"Exactly. Alex seems to think her friend, that deputy..."

"Deputy Hale."

"That's her. Alex thinks Deputy Hale would tell him what she knows, off the record so to speak, but what does she know? If she saw anything at all, and it's a big if, she could tell them that she saw us go through the gate. That would be enough for them to guess *where* we are, but not much else, and Doug left some bodies behind. The police will be investigating that, and I don't think all of Karel's men got back here. When we get back, we'll have a lot of explaining to do."

"I'll pass thanks," he said dryly. "I'm planning amnesia."

"Good plan, I might join you."

"No seriously, we should do it that way. All of us need to have the same story and stick to it. They don't have anything on us. We didn't shoot anyone, but they might try to pin it on us anyway."

"Not with Tomas with us. When we get back, he can sort it out. He saw Doug shoot those men. Not that I blame him for it. It was self-defence, absolutely."

The conversation lapsed into companionable silence, but his frustration was going to boil over if he had to wait too much longer. He stared into the darkness imagining what he would say to Karel when it was time. The man had to agree, he had to. A couple of horses and the pack he'd left just inside the tent would be all they took with them. They would be long gone when Douglas woke and all hell broke loose.

"I wonder where we'll be in a week's time, or a month," Michael mused. "Doug has told me a few things about the places we'll see. Hardenburg sounds fascinating don't you think?"

"I can't wait to visit the Guildhall there. You heard him describe it?"

"The dome and columns theme sounds a bit like the Basilica in Rome. The palace towers sound special too, but then, converting a fortress into a palace is hardly a new idea. I can't wait to see them though. You know, you have to wonder about things when a completely new world throws up similarities like this. Is it something innate within man that makes us yearn to build things on such an epic scale? It can't just be sociological. This world is too different."

"Castles are about defence. I'm no expert on architecture like you, or battles like Doug, but it seems to me certain tactics will always be better than others will—castles and fortresses at strategic points for example. They're big because they need to be that way. They have to be hard to attack, and they have a lot of people inside. But if you're talking churches and cathedrals, I'm not sure it applies here."

"Architecture used to pay homage to the divine is widespread," Michael insisted.

"Not here, not that I have heard."

"Hmmm. You know, you're on to something there. Doug told me the Goddess and her consort are worshipped exclusively in Inari. He says that it's the same in every country—even in the Empire where they're less devout. And we *know* the Goddess is more at home in a forest glade than in stone buildings, grand ones or not."

He nodded. Fundamentally, the Goddess and the god were embodiments of the life-force manifest in nature. Together they represented balance. Ironic really, because many covens back home honoured the three aspects of the Goddess alone and paid no attention to the horned god, her consort, even though traditionally he represented nature in its truest form—the wilderness and the life and death cycle of the hunt. Silver Mist—Michael's coven—was more traditional and would fit right in here. Silver Mist had it right as far as he was concerned. He was a believer in balance, and always tried to give the god his due in rituals he took part in.

About an hour went by as they talked about what they would see on their way to Hardenburg, before Michael finally stood, ready for bed.

"I think I'll leave the rest of the night to you if you don't mind."

Lloyd felt like cheering. "Okay, see you in the morning."

"Good night."

"Night, Michael."

Michael slipped into his wife's tent and closed the flap. As soon as he was out of sight, Lloyd went to saddle two horses. He was practised at the task now, and it took him only minutes to complete. Next he gathered his pack from the tent he shared with Tomas, very careful not to wake him. Being caught with horses readied and a pack full of food in hand would be a disaster.

He took a deep breath to settle his nerves before entering Karel's tent. He shook the man awake and raised his knife so that Karel could see it clearly. "Make no sound, or I'll use this on your throat instead of the ropes."

Karel's eyes glittered in the meagre light, but he nodded.

"I'll help you escape if you agree to my terms. I won't budge on what I want from you, so don't bother trying to negotiate. Are you willing to hear them?"

Karel nodded again.

"I want you to teach me magic. I'll be your apprentice until I decide to leave you and join the Guild. I leave when I decide... when *I decide,* are we clear on that? Do this for me, and I'll free you. Agreed?"

Karel managed to convey his scepticism despite the gag.

Lloyd grinned. "You're right, there is more to it. I want an oath from you, sworn on your life and powers that you'll teach me as I said. You'll swear not to harm me in *any* way, and you'll swear not to harm anyone in this camp. Do this, and you go free. Agreed?"

Karel seemed to take an age to decide, but finally he nodded.

"Good. I'm going to remove the gag so you can swear. Try using magic on me, or say anything else, anything I don't like, and I'll slit your throat from ear to ear."

One final nod.

He held the dagger to Karel's throat and tugged the gag down.

"I swear by my life and powers to train this man in my arts. I further swear not to harm him in any way, or order him to be harmed..."

Lloyd swallowed sickly. He hadn't thought of that. Holy crap, what else hadn't he thought of?

"...and will not harm anyone in this camp. All this do I swear on my life and powers, may the Goddess bear witness!"

Suddenly the air felt thick with tension and magic swirled around them. Karel's face paled as the Goddess heard the oath and accepted it. The magic rushed into Karel, binding him, leaving him pale faced and sweating.

"*Loose me, apprentice!*" Karel hissed under his breath. "Quickly. Skeldon might have felt the binding."

Damn it all! Another thing he hadn't considered. He quickly went to work with the knife and cut the ropes binding the mage's legs. Karel held out his hands and Lloyd used the key he'd stolen from Tomas to remove the handcuffs. Lastly, he cut away the rags Doug had used to bind Karel's fingers.

"I have horses ready."

"Lead the way, quickly," Karel said ripping free the ward stone pendant he wore around his neck. He dropped it on the dirt floor.

Lloyd nodded and hurried to the horses. They didn't mount straight away. Instead, they walked them into the trees and out of earshot of the camp. Before mounting his horse, Karel hastily kicked a space clear of leaves and detritus on the ground until the bare earth was uncovered. He retrieved a broken branch and quickly used it to scribe a circle with himself at the centre. He threw the branch into the trees, and began gesturing and muttering to himself. Karel had sworn not to harm him, but he listened fearfully expecting the worst. Only a few words were familiar. With each unfamiliar word, Karel gestured and wove patterns in the air with his hands and fingers.

"By othala I conjure,
by luft and aed
by krellr I command you
Seek Mardus!"

Karel threw a handful of leaves into the air and a sudden gust of wind took them up and carried them into the trees. Karel nodded in satisfaction, obviously taking note of the direction they took, and broke the circle by erasing part of the line with a careless swipe of his foot.

"Come, apprentice. Mardus is not far, but we need to be away from here. Skeldon might decide to be adventurous, and chase me. I almost wish he would."

He swallowed at the hate he saw flash upon Karel's face. It was there only a moment, and then it was gone, wiped away by a frown and a small shake of the head. He turned toward his horse, ready to mount, and gasped in fright. Alison was standing there, watching them from the shadows. Karel heard, and spun already gesturing at the woman as she stepped forward leading a horse.

"No!" Lloyd gasped as Alison crumpled. He threw himself forward and onto the ground beside her, thinking to help somehow, but there was nothing he could do. "Oh no, no, no, no... this isn't happening. This isn't what I wanted. Please forgive me. I didn't mean this to happen."

Alison's frightened eyes found his, and she tried to say something. Her lips moved a little, but no sound emerged. Karel's spell had paralysed her body, even her chest. She had no breath, and already her lips were turning blue. He watched her dying, crying tears of guilt and shame, but he could do nothing for her. Alison blinked twice more and then stilled in death. Her stare would haunt him for the rest of his days.

He looked back at Karel mounting his horse. "How? You swore the oath. I felt the binding."

Karel smiled. "Your first lesson then, apprentice. I swore to harm no one in camp. We are not *in* the camp."

He groaned. "Are you going to kill me too?"

"The oath, fool, remember?"

He thought back and nodded. Karel had sworn not to harm him, or order it done, and location was not specified. He wasn't a threat to him.

"We can't just leave her like this."

"Best not I suppose."

Without climbing down, Karel muttered and gestured toward Alison, and her body slowly sank into the ground as if the earth had become water. Moments later the ground solidified leaving no sign anything had happened.

"Mount up, apprentice. You lead her horse."

He did as ordered, and followed Karel into the trees. He looked back only once before burying his guilt. One day soon, he would be the master of his own destiny again, and he vowed Karel would pay for his crimes.

* * *

7 ~ Escape

"Where is he?" Tomas shouted angrily. "Damn you, what did you do, fall asleep?"

"Let go of me!" Michael snarled. "I don't have to take that from you!"

"Tomas don't... Michael please..." Sandy pleaded. "He didn't mean it!"

Douglas groaned at the noise and the dream dissolved. He wanted to cry out in protest as his beloved Anna faded away, leaving him alone in their room at Skeldon. Moment's later, the room dissolved too and he opened his eyes.

He rolled over to stare at the shadowed roof of his tent. By the Goddess, he was tired. Surely it wasn't dawn already? Travelling with these people was like trying to herd cats—an impossible task. Just a week of riding with them and already he was tired of it. Their bickering had seemed amusing at first, but it had palled quickly. He was used to soldiers bitching, but this was different. They acted like spoilt children unless he gave them a task to complete. They didn't think for themselves. It always took a word from him to get them started. The chores he set were the same every time they camped, and *still* he needed to tell them what to do to get them moving!

Alex ducked head and shoulders into the tent. "Are you awake?"

"Who could sleep with that noise?"

"There's trouble. You better come."

He sighed and threw back his blankets to crawl out of the tent. He pulled his shirt on, but didn't bother to tuck it in. He had a feeling he would be crawling back under his blankets again soon.

As suspected, it was still dark. The Maiden was high in the sky and the Mother close to setting. He judged there were hours yet before dawn. Someone had stoked the campfire back to life, but it did little to brighten the area. Tomas and Michael had squared off with each other, but Sandy had attached herself to her husband's arm like a limpet. She wasn't letting go, and both men were reluctant to start anything with a woman in the way.

"What's the argument this time?"

Alex hesitated. "You're not going to like it. Please say you won't get angry."

"Tell me."

"Karel is gone. Lloyd and Alison went with him."

"The fools!" he barked, and Alex jumped. "How many times do I have to say it? Karel is dangerous!" He marched over to Tomas and grabbed his arm to swing him away from his confrontation with Michael. He felt the blood throbbing at his temples and his legs shook in reaction. "This is your fault!"

"Michael was on guard not me!" Tomas snarled back, but he couldn't meet his eyes.

He shoved Tomas away and turned to Michael. "What happened?"

"I was just telling this—" Michael began to say.

"*Then tell me!*" he roared.

"I was on second watch. He," Michael gestured at Tomas,

"had first watch. I relieved him and checked on Karel before sitting by the fire."

"I told you to stay out of the firelight."

"To save my night vision. I remember. I sat with my back to it, all right?"

He relaxed tight shoulders. "All right. Was Karel asleep when you checked?"

"Yes, but Lloyd wasn't. About an hour into my watch, he came out to chat. He said he couldn't sleep. We talked about this and that—about you, about where we were going, and what we would see. Then he says that seeing as he couldn't sleep anyway, he might as well take my watch."

"And you agreed." If he'd been Michael with a pretty wife in a tent not ten yards away, he would have been tempted as well.

"Not at first. It didn't seem fair to leave him out here alone, so we watched together for another hour. By that time it was almost his watch anyway, so I left him to it."

"What of Alison?"

Michael frowned. "What about her?"

"Alex says she's missing too."

"I didn't see her."

Douglas stared into the darkened forest as if expecting Lloyd and Karel to ride into view. He shook his head. Of course they did no such thing, and if truth be known, he was glad of it. Karel would be ready this time, and he didn't have Alex's gun to face him down. The next time they met wouldn't be pretty.

Sandy took her husband's arm again. "What are we going to do?"

"We go after them of course," Tomas said quickly. "We have to."

He frowned. "Do we? I'm not so sure."

"We can't just do nothing! What if Karel took them as hostages?"

He hadn't considered that possibility. He did so now, but he didn't think it likely that Karel would take hostages; they would slow him down. It made more sense that Lloyd and Alison had joined him voluntarily, though why they would make such a foolish choice was beyond him.

He beckoned Alex to follow him, and stepped apart from the others. "I hate to ask this of you, Alex, but I must. Can you use your magic to find Karel?"

Alex bit her lip. "If I take off the stone…"

"I know, but I am here. I'll watch and put it back if you falter. I must know if Lloyd and Alison are prisoners."

She nodded and reluctantly removed the ward. Holding the amulet by the stone, she reluctantly surrendered it to him. The moment it left her hand, her eyes went blank and her breathing slowed. He watched her for what seemed an age, but it could only have been a minute. He was about to put the stone back on her, when she blinked and took it from him. She took a deep breath and quickly hung the amulet around her neck.

"The web is so strong here," she said almost in wonder.

"Did you see Karel?"

"I couldn't find him. I couldn't find any of them."

He frowned as reasons for that began to occur to him. None were good. "Mardus?"

"No."

That was bad. He knew Mardus had no magic. Alex failing to find him meant he was closer than expected. More than that, it meant Karel had already linked up with him, and was using his power to hide the entire party. He glared into the forest. Karel could be watching them right now and planning to attack. They had to break camp, now, immediately. He went to tell the others.

"He can't have gotten far," Tomas was saying as Douglas rejoined him. "If we ride hard we can catch him before midday."

"How many times must I say this, Tomas, before you will heed me? Karel is dangerous!"

"I don't see the problem. We held him easily enough. I have my gun. We can catch him by surprise. Simple."

"The only thing simple about your plan is you'll be simply *dead!* As for holding him, you cannot know my sheer amazement that we were able to for so long. I will not risk trying the same again. No. I can't risk it. I must get to the queen with what I know, and you're all coming with me."

"I say we vote on it," Michael said.

"There will be no vote," he said quickly.

"You can't make this decision for us!" Tomas said, outraged.

"Yes I can. I'll not lead you after Karel. I will lead you to Hardenburg. Choose."

Alex took his arm. "I don't think…"

He shrugged her off. He couldn't let her persuade him to give in. "Choose!"

Michael looked helplessly at Tomas.

"I could probably find them," Tomas said, looking uneasily into the trees. "I'm not as good a tracker as you, but I reckon I could do it."

"And then do what? Assuming you don't get everyone killed, where will you go?"

Tomas sighed. "You win."

So he had. Why then did he feel as if he'd lost? He hoped Lloyd and Alison really had cast their lot with Karel. It was better than believing they were prisoners in need of rescue. He prayed they were safe, and forced himself not to consider them further. Whatever the truth of the situation, they were no longer his concern.

"Break camp," he ordered.

"Now?" Alex said in surprise.

"We dare not stay here. Karel may or may not turn around and come after us, but I cannot take the chance. We have to move, and move quickly."

"The road then?" Tomas said.

He grimaced. For the last couple of days they had paralleled the road at a distance to avoid meeting anyone. Now though, there was a need for haste, and the road would be far quicker than wandering through the woods.

"I think its best," he said.

"But the danger," Sandy said. "You said there might be robbers."

"And there might be, but I must weigh that possibility against the certain danger Karel poses. The road it is."

Alex and Sandy went off to saddle the horses while Michael and he struck the tents. Tomas would normally have helped them with the task, but with Karel unaccounted for, he thought it best that Tomas remain on watch with his gun ready. With fear to speed them on, they erased all traces of the camp, and loaded the pack horses. No one spoke as they worked, and all mounted their horses quickly.

He led the way through the trees with Tomas bringing up the rear. The nighttime noises of the forest were usually a comforting sound, but not this night. Everyone was jumpy. Michael pulled his horse up short when the hooting of an owl startled him. Douglas waved him on after pointing out the culprit in the branches of a tree.

Who... Whooo.

"Me, you silly bird," he said.

Michael laughed. It was a strained sound. "I've never seen one so big."

He looked again, but he'd seen larger. "The differences between our worlds might be greater than we assumed."

"Maybe."

* * *

Part II

8 ~ On the Road

Douglas cantered along the road with Alex by his side. There had been no sign of pursuit, but he didn't relax. In places, the trees encroached upon the road with branches entwined overhead creating leafy tunnels full of shadows. The sun was well up now, but failed to penetrate to the road. Instead, it speared the branches creating a multitude of insubstantial columns of light that did little to illuminate the way.

"It's beautiful," Alex said, enjoying the ride.

"It's annoying is what it is," he said. "I can't see a blasted thing."

"Don't be so grumpy. It's not your fault. You couldn't have known that Lloyd would do what he did."

That was true, and he didn't blame himself for that anyway, but he shouldn't have allowed Tomas to sway him from the proper course. He should have killed Karel when he'd the chance that day at Dun'Morogh.

"I know it's not my fault. I'm just impatient. After visiting your world, travel on horseback seems too slow. It never did before, and my mission is urgent." He turned to glance over his shoulder, but the others were keeping pace. "I worry that Wallace will carry out his plan before I can warn Isabeau."

"Is that the queen?"

"She is queen and regent for Erland—her son."

"What's she like?"

Trying to talk while riding like this was awkward. He looked for the sun to judge the time, but then sighed in exasperation. He couldn't see the sky for the trees.

"Let's walk them for a while," he said and raised his hand. He reigned in his horse, and the others followed his lead. "We'll give them half an hour," he called over his shoulder.

"We could stop and have some breakfast," Alex suggested.

"Not yet."

"Suit yourself. Why did the queen send *you* to find out what's happening in Dun'Wallace? She must have people in Hardenburg that she trusts."

"She didn't send me."

"But you said—"

"I said I went into Dun'Wallace to learn what was going on. I never said anyone sent me."

"What made you do it then?"

He grinned. "Someone sent me."

Alex sighed, but her lips slipped into a smile. "Okay, you don't have to tell me if you don't want to."

"In a strange way it was my brother who sent me."

"Edmund?"

"Not Edmund; my older brother, Theon."

"I didn't know you had another brother."

"I don't anymore," he said grimly. It still hurt remembering that. "He's dead now. Theo... he preferred us to call him Theo. He said Theon sounded too much like Theehan."

"Theehan?"

He tried not to laugh. "Your accent, sorry, you say it like this: Tee-hnn."

"Teehnn?"

"Close enough. The Sawainese dialect is a little hard to

master."

Alex said the word under her breath a few times. "What does it mean?"

"It's a cuss word, Alex. It means idiot. Sort of."

"Sort of?"

"Well, in your language it would be closer to whore's son I believe."

Alex burst out laughing.

He grinned. "You see now why he preferred Theo."

"What was he like?"

His laughter died. "He was the best man I ever knew, and the bravest. He was my brother, my best friend, my shield man, and I was all of those things to him. I would've given my life to save his without hesitation, but in the end I couldn't save him."

"What happened?" Alex said softly.

For an instant, he saw his brother as he lay dying upon the muddy ground. The memory was shockingly intense, and the pain was once again sharp in his chest. It felt like a knife driven into his heart. His throat closed as if preventing a wail of grief, but there was no danger of such here. He'd screamed his throat raw that day, two years ago, and then locked the pain away deep inside. Only the Lady and the dead had seen him cry for Theo. It would remain that way.

"Doug?"

He smiled sadly at Alex. "He died in battle. My father would have said we were up to mischief, and he would've been right. It was so stupid. Theo could have ridden with hundreds of men if he'd wanted. As chief of Clan Morgan, he could have raised his vassals and led them to war, but he didn't want to do that. He didn't want to cause the very thing he feared—civil war."

"Was he right to fear that?"

"Probably, almost certainly. The clans were at war with each other not thirty years ago. Skirmishes still occur from time to time. Raising his forces would have forced the others to do the same; Wallace for a certainty, possibly Henri Moore also. It depends. Rhiannon might have dissuaded him; again, it depends. Who knows what the Reverend Mother thinks about all this, I certainly don't."

Alex frowned in concern. "I had no idea Inari was so unstable."

"It's not," he shrugged. "Not really. The clans posture and threaten; a raid now and then to satisfy honour is about as far as it goes these days. Inari must remain united to oppose Sawai. The empire is landlocked, and everyone knows the emperor wants access to our ports."

"Sawai is on the other side of the mountains?"

"The Ilsehorns, that's right."

"So it was Theo who sent you into Dun'Wallace?"

He shook his head.

"What then?"

"As I said, Theo was my brother, but he was also my Duke and clan chief. He could have asked me to go, he could have ordered me, or anyone in the clan to investigate the rumours, but he didn't. He decided to look into it himself. As I said, it was stupid. He took a handful of men with him, and I was left behind."

Alex grinned. "But not for long I bet."

"You're right. I followed him for a while, and then joined his party when I judged he wouldn't send me away. We journeyed in secret, pretending to be mercenaries looking for work. There are always sell swords looking to become caravan guards and such."

"What did you learn?"

He shrugged. "Nothing, and we paid dearly for it. We were hardly over Wallace's border when bandits, or so I thought at the time, attacked us."

"You don't think they were bandits?"

"At the time I did. They wore bits and pieces of ill-fitting armour, and none matched. Some carried crossbows, others swords, still others used long bows better suited to hunting, but they'd known we were coming. They were waiting for us. Theo led us in a charge; it was the only thing to do."

"I would have galloped in the opposite direction," Tomas said.

Douglas started. He'd forgotten the others, and hadn't noticed them edging closer to listen. He should make them spread out again; they were nothing but a big target for archers riding in a group like this.

"So would I," Alex agreed.

He winced at the thought. "That would have been the quickest way to get an arrow, or a bolt in the back. Theo did the right thing. It was the only thing to do against so many men with bows. We had to get in close to use our swords and horses. The bandits were mounted on beasts little better than those we ride now."

"What's wrong with them?" Michael said in a puzzled tone.

"Nothing if you want to pull a wagon or a plough. These are little more than mountain ponies. Affectionate rogues, I grant you, and they have their place, but not in battle. We rode heavy horses—trained for war and battle tested. Such beasts are weapons in themselves. We were outnumbered, but even so, we killed half their number before the first of us fell. His name was Duncan—a good man, and one of my teachers in the sword. I didn't see Theo fall, but when the last of the bandits fled, I turned back to find him dying."

"What happened then?" Sandy said quietly.

"I was the only survivor. Theo lingered for a short time—I tried magic and binding the wound with herbs and bandages, but it did no good. He died later that day. I buried the others beside the road and took Theo home. It was all I could do."

"And then you came back alone," Alex said.

"Not right away, but yes I did. I promised Theo I would finish what he began." He took a deep breath and expelled it in a sigh. "So, now you know the story of how I killed my brother, and earned the name Red Hand."

"Oh come on!" Alex cried. "That's not fair. You didn't do anything wrong."

"I survived, my brother didn't. Fairness has nothing to do with it. It was my duty to protect my Duke. I failed, and took his place. I'm sure you can see the implications without me spelling them out."

Alex's mouth worked but nothing came out.

Tomas interrupted her attempt. "So that's why you're Duke Skeldon and not Duke Morgan? You would no more kill your brother than I would kill Alex."

He nodded. "Without the authority of clan chief, being Duke Morgan is an empty title. I prefer to use Skeldon, which is mine by right of birth. The last I heard, a new clan chief hadn't been chosen, but I've been away from things."

They rode along in silence for a while, but then he ordered a canter to make up some time. When he judged midmorning was approaching, they stopped for a short break. Alex and Sandy took their turn with the cooking, leaving Michael and Tomas to tend to the horses. He watched them working, and realised this was the first time he hadn't needed to tell them what to do. It was as if a cart he had been pushing up hill had suddenly crested, and now it was rolling down the other side without him.

He smiled.

Douglas listened to Michael practising his Inarian, and smiled when Alex laughed at a particularly funny mistake. Inarian had come easy to her. She was already proficient, and had been almost from the first. He could explain it to her easily enough, but he didn't need to. She didn't blame him for his actions that night. Alone and hurt in a strange land, she might well have spelled the first person to come along, just as he had done, or so she said. Despite his best efforts, Alex's fluency had not come as easily to the others.

With him spending all his waking moments teaching them about his world, and learning more about each of them—using Inarian exclusively of course—it was not surprising that he missed the warning signs. Alex had pulled slightly ahead as the others chatted, so she was the first to notice the road cresting yet another hill up ahead. They had ridden over many on the journey thus far, so she did not mention this one. The incline cloaked the road and terrain up ahead, the forest remained dense with trees and shadows beneath. All was peaceful as they crested the hill, but what awaited them on the other side was far from it.

"Doug!" Alex yelled.

He drew his sword and kicked his horse into a brief gallop to join Alex at the brow of the hill. What he saw below them on the road made him tense and dart paranoid glances all around. He found nothing hiding in the shadows beneath the trees, but that didn't mean they were safe. The wagons were still smouldering; the attack was probably only hours old. Wisps of smoke trailed leadenly into the sky, and the smell of burning wood—along with other less pleasant things—lay on the air. The slaughter was no more than half a day old. The bandits had used the darkness for their evil work.

"I'll go down and look for survivors," he said. "Keep a close watch on things from here."

"I'll come along," Tomas said checking his gun.

"No, Tomas. I need your gun here to protect the women. Perhaps Michael will come?"

Michael swallowed and nodded nervously. "I can do it."

"Good then. Let us go quickly."

The two of them rode down the hill, both studying the trees to each side carefully. As before, there was no sign of any danger lurking in the shadows. He began to feel a little easier. It was doubtful the bandits would have stayed in the vicinity longer than it took them to loot the wagons. They were probably many leagues distant by now.

Michael dismounted at the remains of the first wagon, and knelt beside the corpse of a woman. The arrow in her back was testament to how she died. "I wonder who she was?"

"She was a Tinker. They all were. No others use wagons like these or dress that way." He dismounted and tied the reins to an unburned wheel. "Check them all, but I think I know what you'll find."

"But why kill her?"

"Robbers don't usually like to leave witnesses to their crimes."

"No, I suppose they don't," Michael said, staring sadly at the young Tinker woman. She was Sandy's age or thereabouts. "We have to get home, Doug. *We have to!*"

"You will."

"It's too dangerous here! If anything happens to Sandy—"

"Calm down. Nothing is going to happen to your wife, not unless we do something stupid, like arguing here in the open with the Goddess knows who watching."

Michael took a shaky breath and nodded. "You're right."

Together they searched for survivors, but it soon became apparent that the bandits had been very thorough. They had left none alive. The Tinkers had died fighting their attackers, and had killed a few of them, but not enough. He examined the robbers' bodies and found raggedly dressed men, all dead from knife wounds to the throat or kidney area. Tinkers were never soldiers, but that didn't mean they were a gentle people. They knew how to live the itinerant life of the truly homeless, and when cornered, how to fight. Daggers and knives were their preferred weapons, and they used them well. Just not well or fast enough this time. The women had died trying to save the children; their pathetic remains were huddled in a circle around them. Thankfully, there were few of the latter.

"We have to bury them," Michael said.

He wanted to argue, but Michael was on the edge of rebellion already. He simply nodded, and went to call the others down to help.

* * *

9 ~ Tinkers

The men carried the corpses into the trees, and covered them with the soft loam found there—they didn't have the tools they needed to dig deeply in the root-infested ground. The women were spared the grim task, and Alex was grateful to Douglas for that, but on Sandy's behalf not her own. Death didn't frighten or hold power over her; she had seen too much of it. The living on the other hand, had always been a trial, but even that had changed with meeting Douglas. She was learning to live with people again, learning to be a part of the group. Despite the horrid amulet that she forced herself not to throw away each morning, and despite the situation they were all in, she was happy. It had been many years since she had felt that, or had any hope that things would work out for the best. It was wonderful.

Given the choice of going into the trees for firewood, or caring for the horses, Sandy had chosen the horses. Alex helped her friend unsaddle them at their chosen camp a short distance from the burned wagons, and then performed her own chores. It was up to her to gather the firewood, and she would need a lot of it. They wouldn't be moving on for quite a while. Despite the necessity of shallow graves, it would still take most of the day to finish the grisly job.

She collected an armful of dead wood from beneath the trees and built a tepee ready to be lit later, and then went looking for thicker branches that would burn longer to last through the night. About an hour of foraging let her build a good pile of wood, more than enough for their needs.

Douglas came back to the camp for a drink and to take some back for the others. He nodded at her woodpile. "I saw some things that we can use. There's food and other things in the wagons."

She regarded the burned mess doubtfully. "Real food?"

"I'll show you."

She followed him back to one of the wagons. Though burned like the rest, the wheels on one side had collapsed toppling the wagon onto its side, stifling the fire before it could do its work. Douglas knelt next to the burned wreckage and pointed inside. She scrambled into the wagon and started sorting through the mess.

"The tripod goes over a campfire," Douglas explained. "There should be an iron pot to hang on its hook."

She nodded and began dragging things nearer the entrance. The tripod and its hook were first; they hadn't found one at Mardus' camp. She found the pot wedged in a corner. It had been blackened by the fire, but it was made of iron and undamaged. When she looked up to show Doug, he was gone. She shrugged and pushed her finds outside.

The food he'd mentioned lay scattered all over the wagon where the brigands had thrown it, looking for better loot. Flour coated everything. She gathered the strings of onions and refilled the deflated flour sacks with vegetables. She left the spilled flour. It would take too long to collect, and she would need to sift the dirt from it. Besides, she doubted there would be time to make fresh bread, even if she found all the ingredients needed. She tossed aside bedding, clothes, and bits of furniture trying not to think about the people who had once cared for it all. They were gone, and her friends were in need.

She found some loaves of bread, but the real find came as she was about to give up. Two earthenware pots that when opened proved to be butter and honey. The fire had not reached them, and the pots were thick enough that they hadn't broken when the wagon fell on its side. She piled her loot into the cook pot, and struggling with the weight, carried it back to camp.

"We have bread, butter, honey, and..." she said as Sandy came to help carry the pot. "Tadaaaah!"

"Onions?" Sandy said, taking them and holding them up by their string.

"Well yeah," she said, feeling a little deflated by Sandy's reaction. "I found other things too. We can make soup or something."

"Onion soup?"

"I guess not, huh?"

"Not without something else to go with it, but the butter and honey are good."

She went back to fetch the tripod. She left it with Sandy, and decided to check out the rest of the wagons. The robbers couldn't have carried everything away. A smashed barrel yielded apples. The horses would love them, and her friends were getting desperate for anything other than cheese and journey bread. She used a blanket to create a makeshift sack, and filled it with the apples. Sandy was more appreciative this time.

Alex went back to the search, munching an apple.

There wasn't much to find; more bread, some cheeses, a few scattered piles of scorched vegetables and fruits, but anything else the Tinkers owned had burned. She took it all back to camp, and divided it evenly among the packs ready to be loaded on the horses in the morning. They wouldn't starve; Douglas had assured her of that, even before the finds she'd made today. He could set traps and hunt for meat if it came down to it. It was only their haste preventing him from doing that already.

With her chores done, she left Sandy trying to make a vegetable soup in their new cook pot. She'd offered to help, but Sandy had grumpily waved her away, muttering all the while about needing potatoes to go with the carrots and other things they now had. She didn't argue, and took the opportunity for a little quiet time.

She walked back along the road, trying to ignore the wagons that were beginning to weigh heavily on her mood, and tried to cheer herself with thoughts of the future. Where would she be in a year? Back at the farm with Katy, remembering Inari as if it were a dream; or would she be with Douglas at Skeldon Castle, or in Hardenburg maybe, looking for a way back for her friends? She knew which one she hoped for, but until recently, hope had been foreign to her. She shook her head. Thinking about her hopes and silly dreams, wouldn't make them more likely to come true.

She looked around and realised that she'd wandered into the woods. She turned back, but she couldn't see the road. Frowning at her stupid wool-gathering, she tried to find her own trail, but by some fluke of ill luck the ground was firm and it hadn't taken a print. She sighed in exasperation. The road couldn't be more than a few hundred yards away, but which way? She turned on the spot looking for anything to point her way back, but saw nothing familiar. There were trees in every direction she looked, and they were so numerous, that they became a wall after a few yards. A chill of unease ran down her spine. She couldn't even remember which way she'd been facing on the way in.

"Don't panic," she muttered, on the edge of panic already. "If you shout, the others will hear you. They can't be that far from here. You were walking for what, ten minutes? At most fifteen, right?" She swallowed nervously. "Right."

Lady she felt so stupid. If she shouted, Douglas would come running. He'd be nice to her. He'd say everything was fine, and not to worry, but all the while he would be silently calling her an idiot. She just knew it. She groaned inwardly. Things had been going so well, why did this have to happen to her? She didn't want to cause a fuss. She certainly didn't want him thinking she couldn't look after herself! So that's what she would do. She would find her way back on her own. She would show him that she could do things, and not be a burden, and maybe... just maybe, he would ask her to stay with him when the others went home. Rather than hope for it to happen, she would *make* it happen.

Goddess, please hear my plea. Help me find my way.

She smiled, suddenly feeling much calmer. Closing her eyes, and trusting that the Lady was watching over her, she turned and began walking. When she tripped over the tree root, she laughed at herself. Yes, the Goddess did watch over her, but she wouldn't do all the work. She helped best those who helped themselves, and well she knew that lesson. Keeping her eyes firmly on her footing this time, she forged ahead.

The low growl was the only warning that she had, before two hundred pounds of fur and muscle pounced.

Mountain lion!

She crashed to the ground with the cat on top, screaming and trying to shield her face from the furious beast, but although the huge paw with its deadly claws brushed the skin of her neck, there was no pain. She felt a brief tugging sensation as the amulet came free, and then the world rushed in.

The web crashed down on her like an avalanche, hammering her into the ground as it thundered through her mind. It filled that place so long empty, but it wasn't satisfied. As if berating her for being so long away, it forced more and more of itself into her, until she felt she would burst apart.

She howled as the strain built beyond anything she'd ever felt. She reached out for something, *anything* to help her contain it, and her hands encountered soft fur sheathing hard muscle.

The cat was waiting for something, to eat her? She felt its amusement coming strongly through the contact, but she couldn't think of that now. She couldn't do anything but hold on and ride the rapid flow of power through her. She forged a link to the cat stronger than steel, hoping it would anchor her to its world if not her own, but the effort left her even more drained. She struggled, trying to force the web away, but it hammered her back even harder for her temerity. She was weakening under the constant pain of its attack. She couldn't direct it; she couldn't wall it away.

She was so tired of fighting. She let it take her.

* * *

10 ~ Lost

It was mid-afternoon before they finished burying the tinkers. Douglas silently cursed his luck. More time lost. Everything he'd done, every decision he'd made since choosing to venture into Dun'Wallace, had led to disaster and more bad decisions. It was as if the Goddess had cursed him—he crossed his fingers and made the sign to ward off evil luck. He sighed, knowing it wouldn't work. It was just peasant superstition, not magic. Not that magic would work either of course. If the Goddess truly wished to curse him, he would *be* cursed, and no two ways about it. She rarely did that to anyone but oath breakers, such curses usually led to a quick death.

"Let's get back," he said after they used some of their water to wash the stink of death from their hands. "Sandy will have food for us."

Michael made a face. "I don't think I can eat after this."

Tomas grunted, looking back at the grave mounds. "Me neither."

"I know how you feel. I feel the same, but the road is long, and we need to keep our strength up." He turned to head back to the road, and Michael followed.

Tomas held back. "Shouldn't we say something over

them? Leaving like this doesn't feel right."

He hesitated, but then walked back. "You're right. Do you want to do it?"

"I thought maybe you'd do it. This is *your* world, Doug."

He nodded, thinking for a moment. "Goddess mother of us all, please comfort the souls of these tinkers. They died like warriors, bravely defending those they loved. Judge their misdeeds lightly, saving your wrath for those who murdered them," he couldn't think of anything else to say. "So let it be."

"Amen," Tomas said with a sharp nod.

Michael regarded him doubtfully. "So let it be."

Douglas led them back to the road, and on toward their camp. He could smell food cooking. Sandy had the cook pot that Alex had found set up over a fire. Michael kissed his wife, and made a show of how good the food smelled. He didn't have to try too hard. It *did* smell really tasty.

"I used your spell stone to light the fire. Hope you don't mind," Sandy said.

"That's what it's for."

He'd left his firestone with Alex. She must have given it to Sandy when she went looking for more food. He took the stone, dropping it in his pouch with the others, and looked around for Alex. They'd picketed the horses only a short distance away, but she wasn't tending them.

"Where's Alex?"

Sandy nodded up the road toward the wagons. "Looking for stuff we can use."

"No, we just came that way."

Sandy stood, looking at the wagons, and then turned to the horses as he'd done. There was no sign of her. "Where the hell is she then?"

Without needing to discuss it, Tomas went back along the road to double-check the wagons. They might have missed her if she'd been inside one of them. While Tomas did that, Michael went in the opposite direction, and continued up the road beyond the horses. She might have been curious about what lay over the rise in the road. Douglas stayed where he was with Sandy, watching first one man, and then the other, but neither found her.

Tomas trotted back to the camp. "No sign of her—"

"Doug!" Michael called from atop the rise. He waved urgently.

He ran to join Michael. "What is it?" he called when he was close enough.

For an answer, Michael pointed into the distance. "Riders."

He shaded his eyes, trying to make them out. He counted twenty riders, all on powerful looking horses bred for war. Each man wore helm and armour, and carried sabres hung from their saddles. Lance points gleamed wickedly above their heads. The bannerman unfurled his charge, and raised it high.

Tomas had his gun out. "Did they kill the tinkers?"

"No," he said. "These are lancers not robbers. That's the banner of Dun'Moore. Put away your gun. They may not be here for us."

Tomas reluctantly holstered his weapon.

"Doesn't seem likely," Michael said. "Look at them. They know we're here. Someone must have sent them."

Oh, they knew they were being watched all right, why else unfurl the banner at such a distance? He waited for the lancers to arrive, wondering what it meant. They could simply be patrolling the road, but it was far more likely that someone had reported the massacre, and these men had been dispatched to deal with those responsible.

The lancers halted at a command from their officer, and he dismounted to approach them. He stopped a few paces away, and removed his gloves, pulling them neatly through his belt. He regarded them all, assessing each separately. His eyes lingered thoughtfully on Tomas and his gun belt, and then he searched beyond them to the camp where Sandy waited for news of Alex.

Finally, he spoke, addressing himself to Douglas. "Captain Arlen at your service. Do I have the honour of addressing Lord Skeldon?"

Douglas grunted. That answered one question at least. The lancers had come to meet him, not to deliver justice upon the murderers of tinkers. "You do, Captain. My companions are Tomas and Michael," he said indicating each with a gesture.

Arlen came to attention, and inclined his head briefly to each of them. "I am ordered to escort you to the Duke at Ilsehaven. I'll have some of my men help you pack your gear. There's plenty of light left for travel."

"But what about Alex—"

Douglas raised a hand to silence Michael. "We don't need an escort, Captain. We plan to stay here tonight, and move on in the morning."

"I'm sorry, my lord. Perhaps I didn't make myself clear. I'm not offering to escort you. I'm telling you that my men and I *will* escort you."

"Now listen," Tomas said angrily. "You heard what he said, we don't need you and we don't want you. Turn around and ride away."

Arlen ignored the outburst. "I'm informed that two women ride with your party. I see only one."

"That's Sandy, my wife," Michael said.

"And the other is where?" Arlen said. Everyone looked to Douglas. "Where is she?"

"We were looking for Alex when we sighted you," he said, reluctantly.

"Her name is Alex, and she's missing?" Arlen said, and Douglas nodded. He turned to his men. "Sergeant!"

A man quickly dismounted and joined them. "Sir?"

"We have a woman missing. I want her found. Have the men comb the woods either side of the road, but hold back two to care for the horses, and another two to help break camp ready for travel. All clear?"

"Yes, sir," the sergeant said, and things began happening.

Arlen insisted upon meeting Sandy, and then accompanying Douglas. Tomas and Michael teamed up to search, and chose to take Sandy along, perhaps not trusting the new situation. Arlen's troops meanwhile had doused the fire by pouring Sandy's soup over it, and then they rapidly loaded the horses ready to move out.

He indicated the burned out wagons. "We found them this morning. There were bodies all around here. Tinkers, all dead. We stopped to bury them."

Arlen nodded. "We've had some trouble with banditry this season. I'll report this when we get to Ilsehaven."

"Why is Henry residing at Ilsehaven, and not at home in Dehra?"

"He's accompanying the Reverend Mother to Hardenburg for the coronation. My men and I are a small part of their escort."

He paused in surprise. His time was even shorter than he'd thought. Wallace would be desperate to act before the prince was crowned, and able to call the clans to arms.

Arlen frowned. "You didn't know of the coronation. How can you not? Everyone is talking about it."

"We've been away from things for some time, Captain. You and your men are the first we've met to hear the news."

"The roads are thick with traffic," Arlen protested. "All the lords are travelling to Hardenburg for the coronation, and many of the commons as well."

Thick with traffic? He wondered what Arlen would have made of Alex's world and its huge freeways. "We saw no evidence of that. As I said, you are the first travellers we've seen."

They stopped near the wagon he'd shown Alex earlier, and looked around. Where would he go in her place? That was easy, he would've gone back to talk with Sandy, but she hadn't done that. Where else would she go? He turned to look into the trees upslope. No, too much effort, and they'd buried the tinkers there. Down and into the trees then.

"My guess is that she went for a walk and got lost, Captain."

"Out here in the wilds?" Arlen said incredulously.

"I should explain that Alex and the others are... *unused* to travel. She wouldn't have feared to walk in the woods. She wouldn't know there is reason to fear."

"City born and bred?"

"Something like," he agreed. "Let's try down slope a little way."

* * *

11 ~ Bonded

Alex opened her eyes. A leafy sky welcomed her. How long had she been asleep? Were the others worried for her, looking for her? She felt the cat's contented purring through the vibrations under her hand, through the evidence of her ears, and in her mind. The link had held then. She tried to examine it, but it slipped away from her awareness, already becoming an integral part of her. That was wrong. That had never happened when she linked with her horses or Katy back home. How would she dissolve it? She was too tired now to worry about it. She was so tired of running from herself, so tired of fighting. She would wait here and let the cat eat her if it wanted.

The web flowed smoothly through her, holding her gently like a mother cradling her child. It still filled her to bursting, but there was no pain now. It had found all her secret silly wants and desires, and had washed them all away, leaving behind peace and contentment. It was amazing, the strength of wild things untamed, it was freedom…

"You are free at last. I have waited long, but you seemed unready for me."

"Are you the Goddess? Am I dead?"

The presence laughed. **"I am not Her, and you are not dead, Chosen."**

"Chosen? My name is Alex."

"I am your chosen and you are mine. You may call me that, or Shieri if you like."

"Your name is Shieri?"

"Some know me by that name, yes. My given name is Shieriraneth."

"I think I'm dreaming all this, but I'm glad to meet you Shieri."

Shieri laughed, except it was more a feeling of laughter than a sound. She supposed that made sense as much as anything. If a talking cat as big as Shieri could be real, she could certainly talk and laugh however she liked.

"Why do you call me your chosen?"

"We are bonded, now and forever, as She wills."

"Does She?"

"Of course. I knew from the first moment that I sensed your coming, that we would bond, but then you hid yourself from me. Why did you do that?"

"I wasn't trying to hide from you. I didn't even know you existed. I was trying to stop the web."

"Why try something as foolish as that?"

"Because I cannot control it."

"Do I control the trees or the mountains? No. Does it stop me from using them to hunt my prey? Again no. Why is control so important to you, when no one and nothing controls the web of all life?"

"I can't explain. It just is that's all."

"Of course, you cannot. Foolishness is ever hard to explain."

Alex sat up, looking around. The web still filled her with its strength, supporting and comforting, but the amulet lay broken upon the ground nearby. Biting her lip, she carefully pulled her hand away from the cat, ready to put it back if something should happen, but nothing did. Her link remained steady and strong.

"Of course it did. You are my chosen. Only death can separate us."

"You hear my thoughts?"

"Only when you send them to me."

But she hadn't been sending them, or had she? She realised that she could've been doing it all along. She'd never needed to guard her thoughts from anyone before, but she made the effort now. It gave her a new appreciation of how hard it was for Tomas to hide his thoughts from her. She wondered if Shieri could still hear her, but when the enormous cat didn't react, she decided that she couldn't.

She climbed to her feet, and Shieri used the opportunity to stretch lazily. She watched in fascination as the cat flexed every part of herself before joining her. Shieri was the biggest mountain lion she'd ever seen, but *was* she a mountain lion? She doubted it. She was huge for one thing; almost big enough to ride now that she was standing. Her pelt was a very pale grey, almost white, with the barest suggestion of darker grey stripes like a tiger. The long fangs descending from her upper jaw, on display even with her mouth closed, gave the cat an aggressive visage no mountain lion could match. Those huge teeth cinched it in her mind. Shieri was a flaming sabre-tooth tiger or something! She was no ordinary cat.

"I'm an extraordinary cat!"

She snorted. *"Every cat ever born thinks that!"*

* * *

12 ~ Chosen

"Do you know the way back to the road, Shieri?"

The cat leapt away and into the trees. **"Follow."**

"Wait!" she yelled, hurrying to catch up. "I'm not as fast as you!"

"No one is as swift as Shieriraneth."

Or as modest I bet, she thought.

Shieri dropped back to walk by her side, and Alex rested a hand on her back to steady herself as they negotiated the incline together. It felt exactly right, being with the cat like this, but she wondered what the others would say about it.

They picked their way over the root infested ground, but Alex didn't recognise anything. *"Are you sure this is the right way?"*

"Of course it is," Shieri said disdainfully.

"But it seems an awfully long way. I'm sure I didn't walk this far earlier."

Shieri's rumbling growl and her sudden stillness, were all the warning she needed that things were not right at the camp. She knelt on one knee beside the cat, and tried to make out what was going on. Through the trees, she could make out the road and the camp just beyond it. Shieri had brought her back to her friends, but then she saw the two unfamiliar men. Soldiers. She watched them saddling the horses, and loading the packs. Where were Douglas and the others? Could these two be some of the people who killed the tinkers? She feared they might be.

"I don't know who they are, Shieri."

"I smell old blood, a lot of it."

"Many people were killed here. You don't smell any fresh blood do you?"

"No."

That relieved some of her anxiety, but not all. If her friends were safe, where were they? They wouldn't have left her behind, not voluntarily at least. She watched the men at their chores and tried to decide what to do. What would Douglas do? That was easy; he would take out his sword and confront the men to demand answers. She couldn't do that; she didn't have a sword or any other weapons. Wait, she had the web.

"Can you knock one of them down? I don't know if they're enemies or not, so can you just hold him?"

"Easily."

"I don't want to kill anyone," she warned, trying to project her thoughts with a stern edge to them. *"Just hold him down while I deal with the other."*

"Then tell him not to struggle."

Shieri moved silently away, circling the camp. When she was close enough, she pounced on the man farthest from the horses.

Alex couldn't believe how fast she was. The man screamed, and fell under the snarling cat, trying to fend her off. The horses erupted in panic, trying to pull away from where the danger lay, but the ropes were securely tied, and they couldn't get free. They stamped and tugged to no avail.

As soon as the cat made her move, Alex reached out to the web through her link to Shieri, and captured the other man. The sword in his hand fell from suddenly nerveless fingers. With a thought, she put him to sleep. He dropped on the spot, and she ran into the camp. She stared down at the sleeping man. Never had it been so easy to push someone. The guilt hit her then, making her shake. What was happening to her, what was she becoming?

Shieri's snarling growls snapped her back to the present.

"Stop struggling or she'll rip your throat out," she said, trying to make her voice sound threatening, and not as shaky as it really was. The cat had him by the throat already, so he believed her. He went still. "Let him up, Shieri, but watch him close."

With a last snarl, the cat backed up.

The man touched his throat, and wiped Shieri's drool from his skin. He looked at his fingers, checking for blood and found none. Relief blossomed on his face. He watched the cat warily, but when she made no further move toward him, he sat up. He searched the camp with his eyes, not daring to stand, and found his friend lying motionless not far away. His eyes darkened at the sight.

"Don't worry about him. He's just sleeping. You should start worrying about yourself."

"We mean you no harm, my lady."

"I'll be the judge of that if you don't mind. Who are you?"

He gestured at his tunic. It was a flamboyant red with two rows of golden buttons running down the front. If it was supposed to mean something, it was entirely lost on her. Her eyes lingered upon the bugle he carried hanging from a white braided cord looped across his chest. He was a soldier, she had already known that, but on what side? If he was Wallace's man, Douglas could be a prisoner, and her friends with him.

"So you wear red. Does that mean something? I want answers."

"But all know the colours of Dun'Moore," he said in

confusion.

She sighed. "All right, let's start with simpler questions. Name?"

He climbed to his feet, keeping a wary eye on Shieri, straightened his tunic, and came to attention. "I am Flynn, 2nd Dehra Lancers, at your service, my lady." He placed his right palm over his heart and bowed. "It is my honour to serve the Goddess and her chosen daughters."

"He means you, Chosen. You are a Daughter of the Mother."

Her jaw dropped at Shieri's explanation.

Flynn took it as a sign she didn't believe him. He hurried to reassure her. "Escorting the Duke and the Reverend Mother—blessings upon her—is a very great honour. My regiment won the right at the last games. It was a close thing—"

She raised a hand to cut him off; it was too much information too soon. Now that she had time, she could tell he was very young, certainly no older than mid teens.

"Why are you *here*, and not with your Duke?"

"The Reverend Mother…" he began, but something behind her distracted him.

Shieri growled and moved to stand between her and a new threat.

Alex saw a flash of red moving through the trees, but before she could think of running, Douglas stepped out of the woods and into the light. Relief suddenly turned to fear as Shieri charged to attack.

"Shieri no, he's a friend!" she screamed.

Shieri tried to stop and went down, going tail over nose, yowling in complaint at the undignified tumble. She got back to her feet, shook herself free of leaves and dirt, and growled angrily. Douglas had drawn his sword, and moved between her and Alex. The red-coated soldier, eyes intent and wary, circled to get behind Shieri with his sabre ready for mayhem.

Alex threw herself onto her knees next to Shieri. "You leave her alone! If you try anything, I'll *do* something to you!"

"Come away, Alex!" Douglas cried, shocked by her sudden move. "Our cats are not like the ones you know. That's not Katy!"

She rolled her eyes. "Duh! I *can* tell the difference. Shieri belongs to me, and I belong to her."

The soldier straightened at hearing that, and sheathed his sabre. He stepped away and circled wide around them to rejoin Douglas. He whispered something to him, and Alex narrowed her eyes. What were they up to? She couldn't hear what they said to each other, but Douglas sheathed his sword. That was an improvement.

The soldier bowed. "I am Captain Arlen, Lady Alex. My men and I will escort you and your friends to Ilsehaven."

"Just call me Alex, everyone does."

"I would be honoured to do so."

Arlen sounded as if she'd done him a favour. Perhaps she had. She didn't know Inari's customs, but Douglas had always been informal. Maybe that was just his way.

"Where is Ilsehaven?" she asked. "And why would you want to escort us there? And what about Shieri? I'll not leave her behind!"

Arlen patted the air as if to soothe her. "Ilsehaven is a river town not far from here, and your familiar is welcome to come, of course."

"She's my chosen, and I am hers. She told me so."

"They are very insistent about that, or so I hear."

"Only Daughters of the Mother call a familiar their chosen," Douglas said. "Does she really speak to you?"

She nodded firmly.

"You're bonded then—you're absolutely certain?"

"What's wrong with that? Shieri and I do talk, and we are

linked, but it's not a bad thing. It's wonderful!"

"I'm sure it is," Douglas said sadly.

He didn't sound sure, but before she could pursue it, he turned and walked away. She watched him go, feeling his pain, but not what caused it or what to do about it. He was shielding his thoughts. She decided to let him alone for a while. It wasn't as if she couldn't weasel it out of him on the journey. They had plenty of time to talk.

"Flynn, sound recall," Arlen said.

"Yes, sir!"

Flynn raised his bugle to play a short tune, and red uniformed men came out of the trees all around the camp. Alex counted twenty of them including Arlen, Flynn, and the sleeping man. She woke the soldier and apologised to him. He accepted the apology, but he seemed very relieved to escape, and get back to his companions. She heard his friends laughing with him about sleeping on duty. He laughed along with them, obviously happy to have a good story to tell.

Tomas and Michael appeared last with Sandy in tow. Sandy rushed toward her, but Shieri growled a warning, and she skidded to a stop.

"Where the hell have you been?" Sandy said, panting with fright at the sight of the huge cat. "And what the bloody hell is that?!"

She grinned. "Hi guys, I'm okay thanks for asking. This is Shieri, my chosen. That's a familiar apparently."

"I am not a familiar," Shieri said indignantly. **"You are not a hedge witch!"**

"Oh hush. She doesn't know the difference."

"It seems she is not the only one. You are a Daughter of the Mother and my chosen. Do not ever forget that, or let others tell you different."

Sandy blinked in surprise. "Well I… I mean I guess… hello?" Shieri stepped forward and buried her face in Sandy's crotch. "Hey, stop that!"

"Shieri!" Alex gasped, embarrassed for her friend.

"I must gather their scents to remember them."

"She says that she's memorising your scent. She won't hurt you."

Sandy stopped trying to push Shieri away, and waited red-faced while the cat got a good lung full. The cat did the same thing with each of their friends. When she was satisfied, she wandered away to find Douglas. She wondered what he would say when the cat tried the same thing with him.

"We were worried. Where did you go?" Tomas said. "We couldn't find you anywhere."

"I'm fine. I just went for a walk."

"A walk out here?" Sandy said in disbelief. "Are you nuts? We just got done burying about a hundred people who probably just went for a walk."

"It wasn't a hundred."

Sandy threw her hands in the air. "Who cares how many it was? They're dead and you could have joined them. What's the matter with you? It's dangerous out here. We could have lost you."

She couldn't be angry. Without the pendant blocking her friends' thoughts and feelings, it was easy to feel Sandy's fear for her. Before she'd bonded with Shieri, such strong emotion would have overwhelmed her, but she had a measure of control now. The bond buffered and filtered the web, opening possibilities she wouldn't have dared to dream before; she was so very grateful. She wanted to explain to Douglas how she felt, and what Shieri meant to her... to them both.

"I'm sorry, guys. I didn't think about it. I promise I'll be more careful."

Sandy hugged her, and she stiffened expecting bad things to happen, but again the bond with Shieri stood as a filter between them. It worked as well as the pendant had done to protect her, but without the horrible side effect of cutting her off from the web and her magic.

She hugged Sandy back, hard. *"You're a gift from the Goddess, Shieri."*

"That is what being chosen means," Shieri said wryly, but she sounded pleased.

"I love you," she whispered to Sandy. She raised her voice for the others. "I love all of you."

Michael smiled. "Of course you do. I'm a lovable kind of guy."

Tomas didn't speak, but his feelings were obvious, and they troubled her. She had loved him as more than a friend once, but that was long ago. He destroyed what they'd had, destroyed it so thoroughly that he might as well have killed her. He had in a way. She was no longer the same person. Her time in LA had changed her, and meeting Douglas had changed her more still. Her bond with Shieri had given her life back to her, and made it possible to pursue her dreams at last. Tomas was the past, and she wouldn't live in the past.

They headed for their horses.

"Why is Arlen here?" she said curiously as they joined the bustle. Everyone was in a hurry to mount up.

"He was sent to escort us to some town up the road," Tomas said. "But he admitted he wasn't giving us a choice. He asked where you were."

"He knew my name, how?"

"No, but he knew we had two women with us. When he saw Sandy he asked about you."

"Okay, but he's one of the good guys, right?"

Tomas shrugged.

"Right?" she said, more insistently.

"I don't know, but Doug hasn't tried to kill him yet, so Arlen can't be that bad."

She winced at the sarcasm. "It was self-defence! Dammit, Tom, when will you see that he had no choice?"

Tomas did not answer.

She mounted her horse, and threaded her way carefully

through the milling soldiers toward Douglas. He was on the road already, obviously impatient to be moving. She brought her horse to a stop next to him, and felt Shieri shadowing her. The cat was keeping to the trees, downwind of the horses. She didn't need to look; she knew exactly where she was through the bond.

"Should I be scared?"

"What?" he said, startled out of his reverie. "No, why?"

She nodded at the soldiers as they mounted their horses. "Are we under arrest?"

"Not arrest but…" he frowned. "All right, I admit I don't like being forcibly escorted like this, but Arlen is within his rights. This is Dun'Moore, not Dun'Morgan after all."

"Okay, I can see that, but he didn't just stumble upon us. I bet he doesn't insist on escorting every traveller he meets. So why us?"

"Not every traveller he meets happens to be a Duke, and the coronation has been announced. That's why Arlen was in the area and available to escort us. I think—I don't know it for fact you realise—but I think the coronation is why Karel did not pursue us after he escaped. No doubt Wallace will want him there to cause mischief."

"You'll stop him."

"I'll try, certainly. I shall pay my respects to Henry at Ilsehaven and see what can be done."

"Who?"

"Henry Moore. Remember I told you that he's Duke of Moore?"

She nodded. "He lives at Dehra with the witches."

"Not with them, but they live there too. Henry is passing through Ilsehaven on his way to the coronation. I'll prevail upon him for funds to take passage downriver. With luck, I'll be in Hardenburg before Wallace can carry out his plan."

"You mean *we* will take passage."

He looked away.

"What is it? I know there's something wrong. I feel it. Is it Shieri?"

He shook his head. "When we reach Ilsehaven, I'll leave you and the others with Henry. He'll see you safely to Hardenburg."

"*But why?*" she cried. "I don't understand. Have I done something wrong?"

"It's nothing like that," he began, but then resolve hardened his features. "You want to know what's wrong? I'll tell you. You slow me down. You and your friends hold me back when I should be half way to Hardenburg already!"

He didn't wait for her to scream at him, he urged his horse away from her and joined Captain Arlen.

She stared at his back in silence. If Douglas had known she was no longer wearing his pendant, he wouldn't have tried to lie to her like that, but he didn't know. His shield might be strong enough to stop her hearing his thoughts, but it wasn't strong enough to keep such strong emotions from her. She wouldn't tell him that she'd felt his pain as he pushed her away, but she had felt it. He didn't want to leave her behind. That knowledge should have made her happy, but she also knew, despite his real wishes, that he would leave and she didn't know why.

If he wouldn't tell her what was going on, she would have to ask someone who would. Henry Moore seemed a likely candidate. She wouldn't let go of her dreams, not now that she'd been given her life back. She sat straighter in her saddle, determination hardening. She would fix this.

* * *

Part III

13 ~ Ilsehaven

Captain Arlen had described Ilsehaven as a river town, and Alex supposed it was from a certain point of view, but as she cantered towards its tall wooden gates, it looked more like a city to her. It was certainly bigger than her imaginings had painted it. Michael excitedly pointed to the high towers and crenelated walls, built he said, to withstand sieges. He eagerly questioned Arlen about it. When was it built and why here? Had it ever fallen to an invader?

Arlen knew some of the answers, but he wasn't nearly knowledgeable enough to satisfy Michael's insatiable curiosity. He was an architect, and had worked in modern construction for years, but he'd never lost his passion for historic architecture just like this. Arlen smiled tolerantly, though he obviously didn't share Michael's excitement. To him, Ilsehaven was just another river town, one of many he'd seen in his life.

Alex stared hard at Douglas' back. He had walled himself off from her and their friends. It was as if he had already left them behind. He took no part in the discussion. She left him alone with his thoughts, and let him think his lies had worked.

"The foundations must go very deep," Michael mused. "I would love to have been here when they dammed the river."

"How do you know they did?" Sandy asked.

"They must have." He pointed at the walls. "See how they go into the river? There are probably tunnels to let the water pass through when the river gates are closed. There would have to be something like that, or the stress could topple the walls. Besides, the river would flood. They couldn't have built the foundation under water. There are places in Europe like this, built on canals I grant you, but the principle is the same. They must have diverted the river. I wonder if I can find where they moved it."

"A quest for another time," Arlen said.

Michael nodded reluctantly.

The gates were open to river traffic. Boats of all shapes and sizes were entering and leaving. Small fishing boats with a single mast, vied for space with much larger merchant craft as they passed through. She could see masts towering high over the roofs, moving by behind the houses. It looked very odd. River traffic seemed sparse upstream, only smaller vessels ventured out of the gates on that side of town. Downstream was much busier. She watched a big three masted sailing ship leaving, and marvelled at the tiny figures of the crew scampering into the rigging to set the sails.

"I do not like walls."

"Just between you and me, I don't care much for them either."

"Then let us leave this place."

"If you're that uncomfortable, you can wait in the woods."

"No, where you go I go."

She glanced aside at Shieri where she walked beside her horse, and smiled at the grumpy sounding cat. Getting the horses to tolerate her was a neat trick, one she was determined to learn when they had more time. According to Shieri, horses were never chosen; she thought they were too stupid, but that didn't mean that they didn't understand her. Apparently, all she'd done was convince them to accept her as part of their herd, just as they accepted the soldiers were part of it. Alex had a feeling there was more to it than a simple chat. Whatever the means she used, the horses accepted Shieri now as perfectly normal.

The same could not be said for the population of Ilsehaven.

People stared as the column made its way through the streets, the road clearing ahead as word of their coming spread. People lining the street exclaimed at the sight of Shieri, and the shameless cat took full advantage. She turned her normal economical walk into a regal slinking march, turning her head to stare down the onlookers, and letting them marvel at her huge fangs. She added to the thrill with low cough-like roars, and the audience responded with oohs and aahs.

She enjoyed the attention immensely.

"Battle Cat!" voices whispered in awe. "Goddess bless, is there war?"

"She's huge..."

"Bless us, Chosen. Bless us!"

"She's so beautiful..."

A little girl tugged at her mother's sleeve urgently. "Lift me up, momma! I can't see!"

"Never seen one before... rare as dragon spit they is... watch it, she's looking this way!"

"Battle Cat..."

"Is war coming?"

"Battle Cat..."

"It's a huge one too. Battle Cats fought in the last war they say."

"The Goddess sent her. She's so pretty!"

"Why do they call you a Battle Cat?"

"We have many names. They call us Battle Cats for

the wars we fought beside our chosen long ago. On the other side of the mountains, the cub slayers name us Fanged Demons for the way we stalk those who come to steal our fur. In some places, we are Sabre Cats. It's all the same to us. Chosen is the name we honour above all—the Goddess summons only those she deems worthy and bestows it."

"And what name do you use among yourselves?"

"Swift-silent-death-hunting-high-cold-place-that-kills-the unwary."

She laughed. *"I can see why they call you Battle Cats. The high-cold-place-that-kills-the-unwary would be mountains?"*

"High places," Shieri agreed. **"High places so we can see far and hunt. There are no walls there. Nowhere for enemies or prey to hide."**

She nodded thoughtfully. People would shun such inhospitable places. Probably the reason cats like Shieri were rare down here where people lived. A good thing too. She didn't like the sound of the cub slayers.

Arlen led them to the docks and they dismounted.

Ilsehaven didn't have bridges, but it did have boats—lots of boats, and barges, and ferries criss-crossed the river that split Ilsehaven neatly in two. Bridges would have been more efficient, she supposed, but then the big ships would be unable to pass through the town on their way up or down river. She bet Michael could build a swing bridge that would work, even without computers and machines to help him.

Douglas was arguing with Arlen, and she decided to eavesdrop. She wandered over to listen.

"I want to ask for Henry's protection for them," Douglas was saying. "Rhiannon doesn't have jurisdiction. You must see that."

"It's not my place to say," Arlen said stiffly. "I'm a soldier, your grace. I'm not qualified to say what rights the Reverend Mother—blessings upon her name—has or doesn't have.

Neither do I know her will regarding the queen. I know nothing at all of conspiracies and other worlds, but I do have orders. I *will* discharge them."

"I'm not asking you to ignore your orders, man!" Douglas hissed in frustration. "Just deliver us to Henry *first*, and then to the Reverend Mother."

"That… *might* be acceptable."

"If we're meeting important people," she broke in. "I for one want a bath, and some clean clothes."

Sandy agreed. "A bath? Oh *Lady* yes! I would kill for some shampoo."

Arlen obviously didn't understand the reference, but he nodded and yielded the argument. "My lord has taken rooms within the city. He resides on the far bank at the Dog and Whistle. I'm sure a bath and appropriate clothing can be arranged for all of you."

"Thank you, Captain," Alex said, giving him her best smile.

Arlen inclined his head. "A pleasure to serve," he said, sounding sincere despite the delay he'd agreed to. "My men will take care of your horses. Let us book passage as quickly as may be."

They handed the care of the horses to Arlen's men, and accompanied the captain to one of the ferries. With the liberal application of coin, he persuaded the ferryboat's captain to set off immediately, despite his boat having no other passengers.

The ferryboat was long and narrow with a single mast in the centre. It had more than enough space for paying passengers to stand fore and aft. The central space was for cargo, of which there was a fair amount already piled in evenly spaced rows for balance. Douglas moved to stand at the bow, and she hurried to join him.

Shieri chose a place to lie down atop the crates, taking advantage of the shade provided by the mast and reefed sail.

Michael and Sandy stayed aft with the permission of the ferryboat's captain, and watched as he gave orders to his crew to make sail. Arlen went to join them leaving Tomas standing alone by the port rail watching Alex and Douglas talking. He sighed and shoved his hands deep into his pockets.

Tomas turned abruptly away and found himself pinned by the knowing eyes of the cat. "What the hell are you looking at?"

Shieri stared at him with her too intelligent eyes for a moment longer, but then dismissed him and went to sleep.

Tomas shivered despite the heat.

* * *

14 ~ Dog and Whistle

The Dog and Whistle wasn't the sort of place most would expect a noble to frequent, much less a powerful one like his Grace Henry Moore, and yet it fitted him so well. It was a straightforward inn, providing good food and service for the right price; no frills and nothing hidden, just like the man.

Douglas respected Henry, but more than that, he genuinely liked him as a man. He didn't have many true friends; it was always hard for others to get close to men with the power of life and death over them. Of all those who knew him, he counted only ten of them as true friends, and that included Alex. He didn't count his younger brother, Edmund, among the ten.

Sad really.

Henry Moore was fast becoming number eleven.

"Of course I will, laddy," Henry said, and poured himself another glass of wine. He raised the bottle, offering a refill, but Douglas declined with a shake of the head, before seating himself once more.

They were talking in Henry's room, not downstairs in the common room, for privacy. With the coronation approaching, and so many witches close by watching things like spiders waiting for an unwary fly to enter their webs—including Rhiannon, the spider queen herself—he had felt the need for secrecy more and more. In one way, taking Henry into his confidence was a huge risk. No one was closer to the Reverend Mother's councils than the Dukes of Moore; their alliance was centuries old, strengthened with adamantine chains of old oaths, spells, familial ties, and simple friendship. The Reverend Mother and the Dukes of Moore spoke to outsiders with one voice.

Always.

Putting Alex and her friends into Henry's hands then, would seem foolish in the extreme if not for one truth. Henry Moore was a genuinely gallant man, a man of his word, and one who would die before he dishonoured the name of his forefathers. In that, he reminded him of Edmund. His brother could be frightening in his devotion to a task he'd promised to undertake.

Henry would protect Alex and get her home as he'd said, and should it prove beyond him, he could call upon his alliance with Rhiannon and the Daughters of the Mother— something no other could do. He couldn't conceive of that alliance failing to succeed.

"Do you need a witness for the oath? It will take but a moment to have someone up here."

His face reddened; his embarrassment acute. "Not necessary at all, Henry. Your word is more than sufficient for me, as always. I was lost in thought. It's entirely my error and fault that Alex and her friends are involved in this business. I promised them my help in returning home, and I've not made good on that promise. The truth is, I have no idea how to send them back. Giving them your protection and help in my stead means a great deal to me. I'll not forget."

"I understand, lad. Now tell me more of this problem you say we all have."

Douglas spun his story, beginning with Theon's death

and ending at Ilsehaven. He went into greater detail when describing the happenings in the warehouse back on Alex's world, so that Henry might understand the danger. He left nothing out. Not even his failure to kill Karel, something he bitterly regretted.

"And you say these hand cannons work over distance, like bows?"

He nodded. "They work like siege cannons, but in miniature. Tiny things, but utterly lethal. Tomas has one with him, and could demonstrate for you. They're very quick to learn. You could kill an armoured man with his *gun* after practising just a few times."

"Hmmm, perhaps I'll ask him to show me, but not here in town. We need to keep this as quiet as may be for now. Have you any idea how many of these things Wallace might have?"

"No. None of the shipment I saw got through the gate before it closed."

"That was well done."

"I was aiming for Karel and missed," he admitted. "I hit the talisman he was using and broke it. The backlash from the spell knocked him insensible. The thing is, there are different kinds of *guns*—bigger ones called *rifles*. They have a greater range. We have nothing that could match them one for one."

"And you think the shipment contained the larger kind?"

"I fear so," he agreed. "What if that shipment wasn't the first? It certainly wasn't Karel's first trip to Alex's world. We could be facing an army of peasants armed with these things."

Henry waved that away. "Doubtful. I might not like Wallace very much, but he's not a complete idiot. He won't arm his peasants with weapons they might turn against him."

"He could still equip his trusted men with them."

"Yes, a concern I'll admit. Do you know how they work?"

"Not really. I do know they use a form of black powder."

Henry's eyebrows shot up. "How very interesting. I still have a couple of my grandfather's siege bombards at home, but they're useless—black powder is too dangerous to keep—filthy stuff kills our own men even when we're careful. Even a simple spell stone too near can set the stuff off. Catapults may be slower, but they get the job done. You can imagine what would happen if I kept black powder anywhere in Dun'Moore!"

Douglas laughed. Daughters of the Mother, and therefore magic, were abundant in Dun'Moore. "I know black powder is dangerous. Everyone does. I don't think the powder in Tomas' gun is the same. It hasn't exploded."

"Odd."

"He wears it on a belt around his waist like a sword. He keeps the bullets—they have the powder in them—there too."

Henry winced at the thought. "Well, I'm happy for his good fortune, of course, but his good luck should not extend to Wallace."

"I don't think it's luck," he said doubtfully. "If I thought Tomas was in danger, I would make him throw it in the river. No, they just don't explode as easily."

"That is troubling."

Guns and their possible uses had been on his mind since the day Alex had shown him hers, so he knew what was going through Henry's mind now. An army equipped with reliable black powder weapons, worse than that, weapons of Alex's world with their superior rate of fire and accuracy, could decimate any army sent against it. Wallace could easily retake the Vale of Dreams, and march on Dun'Isten itself. Wallace and Isten were always feuding over control of the Vale, but with such an advantage, he might well lay siege to Isten itself and end the ages old feud forever. Why stop there though? He could march on Hardenburg, or anywhere he chose.

"The queen must be informed," Henry said. "Preferably before the coronation."

"She won't postpone it, not at this late date."

Isabeau couldn't possibly do that, not with every noble and his household already on the road to see the prince crowned.

"True, but perhaps her last act as regent will be to summon Wallace for an accounting. We need to get you to Hardenburg, and quickly too."

"I do need passage downriver."

"Do you need funds?"

"I can call upon my factors—"

"That will take time," Henry said rising to his feet. He opened the iron bound trunk at the bottom of his bed and removed a bulging purse. He weighed it thoughtfully in one hand, shrugged, and added a second similar purse. "Here, take these. There should be plenty for your needs."

He stood to take them. "I could buy my own ship with these."

"I wouldn't advise it, laddy. I'm sure you don't sail as well as you wield a sword."

"You're right about that. Henry..." he looked down, hesitating. "I want to thank you—"

Henry waved that away. "It's nothing. I have more than enough gold, but a man can never have too many friends."

"Thank you for saying that, but I didn't mean the gold. Alex has come to mean a great deal to me."

"I gathered that when you asked for my help, laddy. Don't worry. Shall we visit the lady together to make your goodbyes?"

"We said everything needful on the ferry, and before that on the road."

"If you don't mind my saying, that sounds a little final. No one knows what the future may bring."

What possible future could there be? She was a bonded Daughter of the Mother; he an itinerant lord who hadn't seen home in over a year, and wouldn't be welcomed when he did go back. Even Edmund called him Red Hand, believing him responsible for Theon's death. Some days, he half believed it himself. How could he ask her to give up her entire world to stay with him? She had a life to return to, one that didn't include him.

"Will you tell her for me that I've gone ahead?"

Henry nodded and clasped his hand. "I'll do that, if you're sure?"

"I'm sure."

* * *

15 ~ Amelia

"I still think dunking yourselves in water that way was unhealthy."

"Being clean is a lot healthier than the opposite. You should try it sometime."

The cat rolled onto her back and yawned. **"I do not think I will. I am very clean."**

"It's amazing how a bath and clean clothes can make you feel so much better about things," Sandy said, sitting in front of the mirror to brush her hair . "What do you think?"

"You look like a queen, but I look like a reject from Oliver Twist."

Sandy blew a raspberry. "No you don't. We both look fabulous, and you know it. I can't wait to see Michael's face. I bet Douglas will love your dress."

Her face fell at the reminder. "He left."

"What do you mean he left, how do you know?"

She wiggled her fingers in a vaguely magical gesture. "You know, I just know. He told me he would when Captain Arlen found us. I tried to talk him around on the ferry, but he's worried about the coronation. He's going to ask his friend to take us to Hardenburg, and go on ahead."

"The rat!" Sandy hissed angrily. "He can't just dump us on some stranger and leave!"

"We'll be okay."

"That's not the point! He's supposed to be our friend, dammit. Friends don't just leave each other like this. They're supposed to stick around and help each other. He's acting no better than Lloyd and Alison!"

"Calm down. He *is* our friend, but he has other responsibilities too."

"I can't believe you're defending him," Sandy said tossing the hairbrush onto the vanity with a clatter. "He's leaving you, just like that. Don't you care?"

"All right, yes I care!" she snarled. Shieri rolled back to her feet, ready to pounce as her chosen's frustration and anger flooded into her head through the bond. "You're damn right I care, and I don't like it. Satisfied? I think it sucks what he's doing. I think he's going to get himself hurt or killed, and knows it. That's why he's leaving us here where it's safe! What do you want me to do? I tried talking to him. I tried to reason with him... *fuck!*" she spun away from her friend, and buried her face in her hands. "There's nothing I can do except follow him," she mumbled into her palms.

"I'm sorry. I'm sorry I pushed you. Can you call off your pet... *please*," Sandy said, sounding scared.

Alex reached out to Shieri through the bond and flinched at the rage simmering inside the cat, waiting for release. She had done this with her thoughtless rant.

"She's our friend, Shieri. Calm down now, it's over. Sandy likes you, remember?"

Shieri looked up at her and their eyes connected briefly. The cat shook herself and paced around in a circle, before slumping back to the floor as if nothing had happened.

"She wouldn't hurt you," she soothed. "She was just upset with us arguing. And she's not a pet of any kind."

"Okay," Sandy nodded still watching the cat warily.

"Whatever you say. Yeah."

"Really. It's okay. She and I have a link. It's stronger than others I've experienced before. She would no more harm you than I would."

Sandy snorted. "What about that time at the park? You pushed me into the pond!"

"You deserved that one, and you weren't hurt, just pissed."

"Too right I was pissed. My shoes were ruined! And that other time when…" Sandy sighed. "What are we going to do? Without Doug, I mean."

"Same as before I guess. We head for the Guild at Hardenburg. He's arranged for us to travel with his friend. I suppose we have to go along with that and see what happens. What else can we do?"

Thwack!

She opened the door to find Captain Arlen accompanied by Tomas and Michael. Also with them was Douglas' friend whom they had met briefly earlier, Henry Moore. She invited them to enter, but Henry shook his head and said it was time to go aboard the ship that would carry them downstream.

"Douglas has gone ahead, Lady," Henry said. "He felt it wiser—"

"I felt him leave, and I know his reasons for going. I don't agree with them. I want to follow as quickly as I can."

"As *we* can," Sandy added.

Michael frowned.

Henry inclined his head. "I assumed as much. Arlen commands the Reverend Mother's escort. He has a duty to perform for her. Your wishes and his orders coincide. I'll accompany you, if you will permit?"

She nodded. "Of course, that's very kind of you."

"Not at all," Henry said and stepped aside to allow her to exit and precede him.

They left the inn as a group, while behind them a couple

of Arlen's men loaded a cart with the baggage that Douglas had procured for them. There wasn't much in the trunks, and they weren't heavy, but they *were* bulky. They had a riding dress each, as well as another set of clothes for day-to-day wear, and a few toiletries. He'd supplied hairbrushes too, and a small bottle of perfume, but by far the nicest gift he'd bought them was as a pair of whalebone combs for their hair. Sandy's hair wasn't long enough yet, but Alex had found them useful already. She was already wearing hers. The second trunk held clothes and necessities for the men.

Tomas walked beside Arlen, carrying his sheathed sword in his left hand, probably so he could drop the thing and draw his gun quickly. Michael accompanied Sandy, but he was wearing his sword properly, and walked with one hand on the hilt to keep it from tripping him, just as Douglas had taught him. Both men wore dark green jackets over white puff-sleeved shirts, and they had their tan coloured trousers tucked into new calf-length boots—Douglas' colours.

The colours of Dun'Morgan blended so well on the fen, but they stood out here, surrounded as they were by Henry's uniformed men all wearing Dun'Moore red. Wearing Doug's colours was a bold statement that she knew Tomas resented; he wasn't Doug's man and didn't like the implication, but his sheriff's uniform was beyond repair. The journey through the wood hadn't been kind to it. She could read the discontent in him so easily; it was hard not to try pacifying him. She kept her silence, knowing that if she said anything about it, he would realise what had happened and try to shut her out. That would be tiring for both of them, and pointless. He never had been able to maintain his stupid wall against her.

"Here we are," Henry said, indicating the biggest ship at the docks. "Rhiannon and I will be travelling together on the *Amelia*. She's already aboard. Between you and me, she's no great sailor and wanted to accustom herself to the ship before we set sail."

"Not what I expected," Michael said in a musing tone.

"How's that?" Tomas asked as Arlen's men unloaded the cart nearby. "You expected a cruise liner?"

Michael snorted. "Would have been nice, but no, this makes as much sense as failing watches, working guns, and talking cats."

Amelia didn't make any kind of sense to Alex, but then she didn't have Michael's background. The ship, or maybe it should be called a boat here on a river? Whatever. The ship was long, wide, and reared high out of the water with tall masts that towered into the sky. The masts gave it a top-heavy look. There were four, and she hoped the hull went deep into the water, because the sails could make her roll if not. The river must be deep for such a huge ship to travel safely. Even with every scrap of canvas rigged, *Amelia* must be very slow. Was that was why she had such tall masts?

Amelia's hull was a very dark green, while her upper works were white. There were rows of windows in the sides with wooden shutters or covers standing open; no glass in them that she could see. The forward and aft decks were wide with open hatches leading to the cargo spaces. A gangplank led up to the forward deck where most of the crew were lounging along the rail, watching the last few items entering the cargo hold.

She had never feared water travel before this, but she sympathised with Rhiannon's feelings now if *Amelia* was any example. She really did not like the ship, and Shieri agreed. The cat was sending unease through their bond, or maybe she was reflecting her unease in a kind of feedback loop. She shielded her emotions from the cat, and it seemed to help a little.

Arlen's men carried the luggage aboard, and Henry turned to her. "Shall we?"

She nodded and led the way up the ramp. She stepped on deck and looked around with interest. Sailors were leaning on the rail or talking with their comrades, a few were coiling rope and moving with purpose, but most were simply waiting for the order to get underway. Things changed quickly when Shieri joined her. Everyone paused and all eyes turned to stare.

Another flaming witch, that's all we need...

Nice looking one this time, not like that hag the other day... never seen a cat like that... wonder what her name is.

Lady bless! Is that a Battle Cat? Can't be...

How many of the bitches are we going to carry? Captain is out of his mind... bad luck they is...

Ripples in the web informed her that a woman with power was approaching at her back, a witch then, but not a strong one so it couldn't be Rhiannon. She drew upon her bond with Shieri to wall away the thoughts of the crew, and turned in time to startle the newcomer. The surprise quickly faded on the woman's face, replaced with awe when she saw Shieri. She dragged her eyes away from the cat preening under the added attention, and noticed Henry Moore watching. She performed a quick curtsy to him, which Henry acknowledged with a smile and small bow of his head.

"The Reverend Mother asked me to welcome you aboard, your grace."

"That was kind of her," Henry said, and introduced everyone. "Lady Alex, Lady Sandy, Tomas, and Sandy's husband, Michael. This is Elizabet, the Reverend Mother's favourite niece."

The girl blushed prettily. "Pleased to meet you. I'm to bring you to the Reverend Mother."

Alex smiled, she liked the girl. She was about sixteen, and her wavy red hair framed her freckled face making her look even younger. Her pale blue dress and sturdy shoes spoke of a no nonsense attitude where appearance was concerned. The three rings she wore were gaudy things, and seemed out of place. The girl hid her hands behind her back, when she noticed her interest. There was something odd about the rings, and Elizabet's action in hiding them, but she didn't have time to wheedle the story out of the girl with Rhiannon waiting.

"It's nice to meet you, Elizabet. Do you prefer Liz?"

"Oh, I don't mind," Elizabet said cheerfully. "My brother calls me Liz, but Aunt Rhi… I mean the Reverend Mother, blessings upon her, always calls me Elizabet."

"Liz it is then. The fanged glutton here is my chosen, Shieri."

Shieri yawned widely.

Liz gulped at the sight of the cat's huge fangs. "Hello. The Reverend Mother is looking forward to meeting you all. Please follow me."

"I'll come along as well," Henry said. "Rhiannon and I have something we need to discuss, and I believe Arlen has his report to make."

Arlen nodded, his impatience to conclude his business with Rhiannon making the gesture seem abrupt.

"This way," Liz said.

The ship had seemed enormous standing on the dock, but it felt much smaller walking through its dim interior spaces. The only light sources were small swivel-mounted oil lamps on the walls, designed to move with the motion of the ship and not spill. Liz led the way along the passageway heading aft down the centreline of the ship.

Magic was thick in the air, and the web hummed with so many powerful life threads in such a confined space. All of them were witches. Many of the cabin doors were propped open, and she glanced inside as she walked by. Some of the women smiled at her as she appeared, but others frowned when they caught sight of Shieri at her side. She nodded politely to those that smiled, and ignored the hostile eyes of the others.

A wooden door barred further progress at the end of the passageway. Liz paused to take a breath before raising a hand to knock. Alex noticed the girl had removed her rings, and wondered why.

"Come," a voice said from within the cabin and Liz opened the door.

Inside, three seated women confronted them. The cabin was spacious and well furnished. It made sense that Rhiannon rated a larger cabin. Henry closed the door behind him being the last to enter, but he didn't make the introductions. Liz approached one of the women, the oldest one, and curtsied before turning back to Alex.

"Lady Alex, may I present Reverend Mother Rhiannon?"

She noted the differences between the three women. Two were her age or close to it, slim and wearing expensive dresses. They had their hands clasped loosely in their laps, as they watched Shieri prowl the cabin investigating new scents. Both women had dark hair; one wore hers up, the other down and flowing loose over her shoulders in waves. The woman Liz had curtsied to was older than her companions, and had some grey in her hair. She wore a dark gown and had a shawl loosely draped over her shoulders.

In front of the windows spanning the width of the cabin, a heavy wood frame stood with three owls perched upon it. It wasn't hard to guess that they were chosen. She didn't need their size or the obvious intelligence in their eyes to realise it. Shieri's interest in them was a big clue. The cat had paused before them, cocking her head and staring up at their perch. Probably saying hey. She smiled. She nodded politely to them before turning back to the women.

Liz seemed nervous for some reason, and her eyes kept straying around the room. Alex reached for the web through Shieri and had her answer. All three women were witches as expected, but the woman on the right was the strongest and centre of this web. She was Rhiannon, not the one Liz had introduced.

She pivoted smoothly. "Why the theatrics?"

The other two witches gasped. "Have some respect, child!" they said together.

"I'm really not in the mood for games, and I'm not a child. If you want respect, show some in return."

Rhiannon's face reddened, but before she could say anything, Henry's laugh filled the cabin. She fixed her scowl upon him. "Something amuses you, your Grace?"

Henry grinned at the sour tone. "Many things amuse me. I'm a very jolly fellow as you know."

Rhiannon turned back to Alex. "Your coming has been eagerly anticipated. Please introduce your companions."

She was sure that Rhiannon already knew all their names, but dutifully introduced Shieri and her other friends. Shieri disdained to acknowledge Rhiannon, but the woman didn't seem to notice the snub.

"You're all most welcome here. Captain Arlen, where is his Grace Duke Morgan?"

Arlen stepped forward and came to attention, clicking his heels together and bowing his head briefly. "He has gone ahead to Hardenburg, Mother. I was unable to persuade him of the importance of your summons."

"I see. I'll hear your full report later, but for now, tell me of him. Did he reveal anything of his plans?"

"Only that his need to reach the queen was urgent. He did try to explain, but I must confess his talk of other worlds and the outlandish threats they pose seemed… well, forgive my bluntness, but he seemed overwrought; paranoid even."

Rhiannon nodded thoughtfully.

Henry spoke up. "Douglas asked me to aide Alex and her friends in returning home. I swore to him that I would do all in my power to help. He also discussed his fears regarding Wallace's plans and the coronation. Meaning no disrespect to the good captain, but I found Douglas to be lucid and to the point. He was anxious to reach the queen, and concerned over what he'd learned on his journey, but paranoid? Not a bit of it."

"Thank you, Henry," Rhiannon said. "He's out of reach now, and we cannot help him. *Amelia* will be getting underway shortly. Elizabet, please show our new friends where they might rest. Henry, please stay, we have more to discuss."

Alex would have liked to be present for their discussion. She had a feeling it would be interesting, but there wasn't a polite way to insist. She followed her friends out, hoping that whatever Rhiannon and Henry chose to do, it wouldn't delay her reunion with Douglas.

* * *

16 ~ Tomas

Amelia was huge as river boats went, Tomas supposed, but of course, the old Mississippi paddle boats hadn't been exactly small, and they'd been much faster. *Amelia* would have made the journey in a third the time if sails hadn't powered her. He supposed her size evened things out, and made her profitable to her owners. She was still damn slow, and despite her size, her decks weren't open enough for proper sword drill. There was literally miles of rope in her rigging, four tall masts, hatch covers, coils of rope, the stairways leading down with their hinged covers open now the weather was fine. All of it made for a crowded main deck. The forward and aft decks had less to trip over, but they were small areas, if more open. *Amelia* took a large crew to handle, and they never seemed to rest. The decks were never completely free of people or clutter.

Michael practised with him each morning before the deck became too busy, trying to polish what Douglas had taught them. Neither of them enjoyed it much, but Michael at least was single-minded about it. Sandy was his motivation. He wanted the skills necessary to protect his wife if the time came. Tomas on the other hand, had nothing but a determination to beat Douglas at something on his mind, as he parried Michael and retreated. If struck by them, their wooden practise swords would leave a nasty bruise and an ache, nothing more. He had quite a few bruises already.

Michael grunted and lunged, but Tomas smacked the blade aside, the wood making a resounding crack. "You know," Michael panted. "You're getting pretty good at this."

"It's all I can do to keep you off me. I don't think—" he parried and lunged without a pause, causing Michael to jump backwards. "—I will scare anyone."

"I don't know about that. This is play compared with the real thing. I think you'll surprise yourself."

"Maybe," he said.

He would rather surprise an attacker with his gun. The problem was, he had very little ammunition for it. When the time came, he would need to decide whether to use it or save it for a more dire need later. Of course, dying because he didn't use it made the decision even more interesting, didn't it?

He threw himself forward in a flashy looking roll across the deck, and slashed. "Got you!"

"Ah!" Michael gasped, and clutching his thigh, he hobbled around the deck cursing. "Lady dammit, Tom! That hurts like a bastard!"

His grin wilted. He *had* struck a little hard. "I'm sorry. I didn't mean to hit you that hard. Are you okay?"

Michael grimaced still rubbing his thigh. He stamped his foot and winced. "Dead leg is all. Nothing broken."

"If one of my men had performed such a foolhardy action, I would have him strung up by his thumbs and given five lashes," Captain Arlen said, his voice thick with disapproval.

Tomas shrugged uncomfortably, feeling guilty. "It worked, didn't it?"

"Here against an untutored opponent, and perhaps in a street brawl against a drunken one, it might work, but certainly only once. Only a fool throws away balance in a fight. Leave your feet, or lose sight of the enemy at your peril."

"You sound as if you've had some experience of that?" Michael said, still rubbing his leg trying to restore feeling.

"You might say. Real battle has little in common with practise bouts like this, or duels. Duellists like to think the circle is the epitome of sword mastery. Not so, the battlefield is. I would back any man of mine against a duellist there."

Tomas reclaimed their sheathed swords from the deck where they'd stowed them. He handed Michael's to him. "It's just training, and what you're used to. The duellist would win one on one in the circle."

"Perhaps, but you're not practising for a duel, are you?"

"No, Captain," Michael said. "No duels for us. I want to be prepared to protect my wife and friends if I need to."

"Then you should stop playing, and get serious about your training. I can help you with that. If you think you can keep up with my men."

Tomas smiled at the obvious baiting, but he could already see Michael was willing. Maybe it would be better to practise with others. He already knew most of Michael's moves, and besides, he would rather bruise a stranger.

"I'm in, but can we start tomorrow?" he said as his numerous aches made themselves known.

Arlen nodded. "And you, Michael?"

"I can start right now, the leg is fine."

"Be here in an hour and you can join the men."

"I'll be here." Michael took his leave of them, still rubbing his leg and limping a little.

"Thank you," Tomas said quietly, watching his friend disappear into the passageway that led to the cabins. "He worries about his wife... *a lot.*"

"Being married does that to a man."

"You know that first hand?"

Arlen nodded. "In my case it's a little different. Aimil doesn't travel with me. She lives in Dehra with our daughters, but I still worry. It's the lot of a man to do that, even when we know there's nothing to fear."

Tomas turned and started toward the bow. It was his habit to spend time there, looking ahead to see what he could of their route. Funny really, because back home he wasn't one for looking ahead. He often looked back however, back to his past mistakes more often than not. Back to a stupid boy, and a decision he'd made, that still haunted him to this day. A decision that broke a woman's heart, and ruined his life.

Arlen joined him. "You're unmarried? Is there no one back home?"

"No one," he agreed but then frowned. "I have friends back there of course, but no wife. No family left except my brother, and we haven't seen each other in years."

"A quarrel between you?"

"No, nothing like that. We just drifted apart. Paul went to live in New York—one of my land's biggest cities. He was offered a good job, and he took it. Last I heard, he was making plenty of money and looking to become a partner in the firm. He's a lawyer, a good one too."

"A lawyer is an advocate? One who represents someone in the courts?"

He nodded.

"I don't begin to understand all I've heard, or all I've been told about you and your friends, or how it's even possible for you to be from another world, but I understand duty. I understand your wish to protect Lady Alex. Protecting Daughters of the Mother is Dun'Moore's first duty."

Tomas studied the other ships of the convoy. There were six tall ships sailing with them. None matched the size of *Amelia,* but they were a grand sight nonetheless. All of them carried Rhiannon's witches—Daughters of the Mother—and more of Henry Moore's troops to protect them. It still seemed strange that powerful witches needed men to do that. Alex could certainly handle herself, and she'd made it plain that she didn't want him doing it for her. Not that he would listen, especially now that Doug had bugged out. He couldn't believe his luck there.

"Protecting witches with swords still seems strange."

Arlen cocked his head. "Witches of your world do not require such protection?"

He leaned back against the rail. "Things are different there. We have nothing like Rhiannon or the sisters. Alex is... *special*. A special case you might say. Until Alex, I didn't believe in magic, and even then I tried to deny it. Those who call themselves witches back home have little power, and most people don't believe in magic at all. Skeldon's skills were weak there."

"I'd heard something of the sort. Anonymity protects them then."

"Sort of." He turned to face forward again. The river was empty of other boats or ships ahead, but although it was wide, the river didn't follow a straight course. He couldn't see around the bend they were approaching. "It's not as bad as it used to be, but anyone calling themselves a witch is thought of as strange; harmless, but strange. To be honest, we just laugh and ignore them. I've known that Alex was the real deal for years though. I don't laugh."

Laughing was not something he wanted to do when he thought of Alex. Crying maybe, screaming? No, laughter wasn't something that came to mind, that was for sure.

"Very wise," Arlen said seriously. "Laughing at a woman is never a good idea. Laughing at a Daughter of the Mother would be infinitely worse. They can be very prickly, especially where their dignity is concerned."

"With how things are here, I'm not sure why you think bodyguards are even needed."

"I can see why you might think that way, considering what

you have told me, but no matter how powerful you think magic is, spells take time to cast and require preparation. My men and I fight to give the sisters the time they need."

"But men like Karel don't need as much preparation or time? The Guild doesn't have armies to protect it, or does it? Are men more powerful?"

Arlen winced and looked over his shoulder, probably expecting to find one of the witches glaring at him. "The Guild doesn't do things in the same way, you're right about that. It has no military, except for mercenary guards they hire to protect their halls.

"The sisters are strong when they work together. They support and protect each other, but they're weaker than wizards when alone. You're right about that, not that they would ever admit it. And Tomas? Don't ever suggest they're weaker where they might overhear, you'll not like what happens. So yes, the sisters can cast spells alone or in small groups—covens—you have them on your world?"

He nodded.

"A coven of thirteen sisters is best, with the strength of their spells falling sharply as more are added or removed from the group. No one really knows why that is, but wizards can't form working covens at all. They must work alone."

"I bet that annoys the hell out of the Guild."

Arlen grinned. "The Guild hates it of course, but the Goddess made the world to her plan, and the Guild must live with that, as we all must. Besides, as any of the sisters will tell you, the Goddess and her consort want balance in all things. Men may be stronger individually, but that's balanced by women being stronger than them—far stronger—when they work together. You know that Karel was a rune master, and a powerful rune speaker?"

"I know he got his butt kicked out of the Guild, and they stripped him of titles."

"That's true, but he still has the knowledge. Rune speakers

are the strongest kind of wizard. The sisters have their own ranks, and the strongest among them are web mistresses. You can always tell when a sister will become one, because the Goddess sends a chosen to bond with her."

He grimaced at the reminder. "Alex and Shieri are bonded like that."

Arlen nodded. "They are."

"But Alex isn't a sister like the others, not really."

"She has the strength but not the knowledge, that's true, but she'll learn. The Goddess wouldn't have sent the cat to her if there was any doubt at all. Knowledge can be taught, but the potential is in born—a gift of the Goddess."

He didn't like what he was hearing, but he'd already guessed that Alex wouldn't want to leave when the time came. Firstly, there was her infatuation with Skeldon; it hadn't diminished no matter how hard he'd wished for it. Added to that, there was her bond with Shieri to consider. There would be no budging her now. The bond wouldn't allow them to be separated, he was sure of that, and how likely was it that she could take the cat home with her anyway? Magic was less there and it was a magical creature. It was certainly no ordinary cat, and not just because of its huge size. Alex said it talked to her. The bond might break if they entered a gate, or it might not, and it was obvious the cat was human smart. What would happen to Alex if Shieri turned into a dumb beast? Would it injure her mentally? She would certainly be hurt emotionally by the loss of a friend that way.

He scowled. Shieri might be fine, and the bond untouched. There wasn't any way to know, but he did know Alex. She wouldn't risk it even if she wanted to go back, and he was sure she didn't. Damn Skeldon, damn him for taking her from him like this. She was doubly out of reach now.

He sighed. "I've changed my mind, Captain. I'll join your men today if you don't mind?"

"I've no objections. We have a little time to wait yet... ah, here we go," he said turning to watch thirteen sisters arriving on deck. "As soon as they're finished, I'll get the men up here for some sword drill."

Tomas nodded, turning to watch the witches work their magic. It was a spell of fair weather and wind; they cast it every morning around this time. The same would be happening on all the ships in the convoy.

* * *

17 ~ Rings

Alex looked up with a smile when Michael knocked and opened the door to put his head inside the cabin. "Everyone decent?"

"Sure, come in Michael," she said. "You finished playing?"

Michael limped inside and closed the door. There was very little room in the cabin. Liz and Sandy were sitting on Sandy's bed and Alex had the only chair set before the vanity and mirror. Shieri had found a spot to recline on the floor after Sandy had shoved the cat off her bed. She couldn't abide cat hair on her blankets.

She felt a little sorry for Sandy having to bunk with her, when her husband was just two doors down, but although she'd been intimate with Tomas years ago, they no longer were and she wouldn't encourage him by sharing a cabin with him.

Michael sat on her bed and rubbed his leg. "I wouldn't call it playing. It might save my life one day, if Tomas doesn't kill us both first."

Sandy moved closer to him. "What did he do now?"

Michael hugged her and kissed her cheek. Liz's face

reddened and she looked away. "He didn't do it on purpose."

"He never does."

"No seriously. He's just better than me is all. He tried a fancy move, and whacked me a good one on the thigh. It's just bruised, nothing broken."

"Lucky for him. He should be more careful. Douglas was quick enough to dodge when he did stupid stuff. You're not."

"I'm getting better, but you're right. Douglas was a good teacher. That's why I'm going back up in about an hour to train with Arlen's men."

"Probably safer," Alex said.

Sandy sniffed.

Liz twisted one of her rings around and around. "Captain Arlen's men won the games this year. First prize was the right to escort the Reverend Mother to the coronation. You won't find a better teacher outside Dun'Moore's borders."

Michael smiled at Liz. "That's good to hear, Lady Elizabet."

Liz blushed hotly. "Elizabet or Liz, Michael, we're friends."

"Liz then. So, what have you three been doing?"

"Oh this and that," Alex said. "Liz has been telling us about Dehra. Did you know the city is ancient?"

Michael shook his head.

"The motherhouse there is *thousands* of years old. It sounds like a wonderful place."

Liz nodded eagerly. "The oldest part of the motherhouse is easily three thousand years old. Its always been there they say, but every few hundred years or so, we expand it by adding new sections or rebuilding older parts. Dehra, the city I mean, grew around the motherhouse much faster."

"So there are two castles in Dehra?" Michael asked. "I would like to visit."

"Oh no, the motherhouse isn't a castle. Its walls don't have battlements or towers. Its..., its just not is all. And besides, the Duke's castle is much bigger really."

"I'm sure it's very fine regardless."

Alex tried to imagine it. Maybe it was like the palaces in Europe that she'd read about in magazines, or one of those old monasteries. "So it's just a big house in the city?" she said. It sounded less grand put that way. "It has walls around it, and gardens?"

Liz nodded. "A very big house. The biggest you can imagine!"

Well that was something. She had a good imagination. A house like that could be bigger than the White House, bigger than Buckingham Palace in London, bigger than... well just very big!

Michael's eyes gleamed; he loved architecture. "Is Dehra like Hardenburg?"

Liz shook her head. "Hardenburg is bigger and more spread out, but Dehra is greater than any other city in Inari."

"I can't wait to visit them. Is it anything like Ilsehaven?"

"They're nothing alike. Dehra is a proper city; Ilsehaven is just a trade town."

She smiled a little at Liz's unconscious condescension. She obviously thought the differences were obvious.

They chatted about generalities for a while. About places they had visited, and what they had done there. Liz asked a lot of questions about America and Earth. How was it different? How did they live without magic? It was all very confusing for the girl. Only one moon! She was utterly shocked by that.

Alex answered most of her questions, with Sandy adding things here and there. Liz was shy with Michael, and blushed whenever he spoke. He had a teasing way about him. Not flirting on purpose, just being himself and making her laugh, but it was obvious the girl had lived a sheltered life. Living with the witches in Dehra must have limited her social life, not that Alex really knew what was considered normal in Inari.

The hour fled, and Michael left for his sword practise.

Alex watched as Liz unconsciously twisted one of her rings around and around. She did that a lot. "Liz?"

"Hmmm?"

"Tell me about your rings? It's obvious they're important to you."

Liz flushed. "I'm not supposed to wear them yet. They belonged to my mother, but my test was postponed because of the coronation."

"You have to be tested to wear your own mother's rings?"

Liz blinked uncertainly, but then she glanced at Alex's bare fingers. "Your people don't wear them?"

"We wear them, but I think they mean something different to you. We wear them because they're pretty, or because two people want to show a symbol of their marriage."

"The sisters wear rings to proclaim rank and ability." Liz held up her left hand. Pointing to her pinkie finger first, and then moving finger by finger to her thumb, she said, "Earth, Air, Fire, Water, and Spirit."

"The elements," Sandy said. "You wear a ring to honour them?"

"To show *mastery* of them. We're tested when our teachers think we're proficient in the use of each, and if we pass, we can choose a ring to wear on the correct finger."

"Are the rings magic?" she said, intrigued by the idea.

"They can be. Mine are, but only because my mother had them made with spell stones. The ruby is a firestone. She used it for lighting candles and things. She always said that she preferred saving her own magic for important work.

The sapphire is an airstone. It cools things. The emerald is an earthstone for healing. Rings can be plain metal, or have spell stones, but it's the finger you wear them on that matters."

Alex nodded. "What about your other hand?"

Liz named the fingers of her right hand, pinkie first. "Charm Crafting, Ritual Magic, Focus, Web Magic, and Web Mistress."

"What is focus and web mistress?"

"A focus combines magic for rituals. In a coven, she takes power from the other sisters, and passes it to the coven leader to use. It makes her spells and charms stronger. The focus is usually the coven leader as well, but she doesn't have to be. Web mistress is the highest rank in the sisterhood. Aunt Rhi is a web mistress. She can use line magic for her spells, which makes them super strong, and she can farsee great distances. Combined with spirit magic, she can web walk—that's travelling in spirit form."

"I can do that," Alex said. "The far-seeing thing I mean. I've done it a lot. Douglas and I did the spirit travelling together once. I've never tried it alone."

"That means you should wear rings on both thumbs, and another on your right forefinger for web magic, though far-seeing is only one part of it. You might not pass testing if that's all you can do. Can you use the web in your spells?"

She shrugged. "I don't craft spells. You probably know more than me about magic. I'm self-taught. I can hear thoughts and feel emotion; I can farsee if I try. I can make people do stuff, but I don't like doing that. It feels wrong. I can see what has happened in the past sometimes when I touch things, especially people, and I see ghosts a lot. If I touch a dead body, I can usually see how they died."

Liz paled, ghost white. "You must be very strong in spirit magic. Ghosts and seeing through the mists of time are spirit powers. They're rare. Spirit might be your element—your strongest power I mean. It connects with so many other things, like far-seeing and web walking. Compulsion is a spirit power too, and battle magic." She nodded at Shieri. "And your chosen is a battle cat. That makes so much sense!"

"I'm glad you think so. It makes none to me."

"It would if you'd had training. You're supposed to wear five rings before doing any kind of battle magic."

"No ring for that?"

Liz shook her head. "Battle magic is just elemental charms and spells used in battle. We don't train to fight. We could if we had to, but we have Dun'Moore's soldiers for that."

That made sense.

She could easily imagine spells meant to light a campfire setting fire to a person. The thought made her shudder in revulsion. Probably the other elements could kill as well. Air used to suffocate or freeze someone, fire to burn, water to drown, earth to... suffocate again maybe or crush? Spirit... she didn't want to think about ripping someone's life energy or their soul out, but deep down she knew that's what Karel had meant to do to her. He called it draining. Draining a witch's magic would be the same as draining her life away.

"Well," she said. "I don't have any rings or training, so I guess you outrank me."

Liz laughed, but she was taken with the idea. "We need to start your lessons. I bet I could have you wearing your first ring before we reach Hardenburg."

"I wouldn't want to get you in trouble."

Liz waved that away. "We're allowed to practise with each other. Formal lessons won't resume until we reach the Stonybrook chapterhouse, but there's nothing to stop us practising on the way. I have testing when we get there, and some of the others do as well."

"I wouldn't want to use up your practise time."

"Don't worry about that. I'll get more practise teaching you, than I would alone."

Excitement began to churn in her belly, and Sandy looked eager to learn as well. This was going to be fun!

* * *

Part IV

18 ~ Hardenburg

Lloyd slowly drew the rune on his slate, keeping his mind focused on its shape, how his chalk laid down the graceful curves and sweeps, how the perfectly even pressure he applied with his chalk kept the lines balanced. They must be neither too thick nor too thin upon the slate, so that magic could flow evenly through the rune, and around the continuous line. A line too thin could cause the magic to overwhelm the rune and break it. A line too thick could do the same, but in a more dangerous way—the greater the magic, the bigger the detonation should something go wrong. An unbalanced rune, one containing uneven lines, or one imperfectly shaped, was just as bad—it would have unintended results when activated.

As he worked, he was careful not to think the rune's name or consider its properties. It was a fundamental truth of rune craft, that concentrating too much upon its purpose would fill its structure with magic and activate it. That could be very dangerous. An unfinished rune filled with magic, would be like pulling the trigger on a gas pump without fitting it into the tank of his car, and then striking a match to it for good measure! He grimaced as his concentration wavered, but his hand kept moving at the carefully controlled pace he had learned was necessary for this rune, and its lines were not compromised. Karel, scum sucking evil bastard that he was, had demonstrated the danger by allowing him to err on purpose early in their association. The pain was a salutary lesson, and although he hated him, he had to admit that Karel was very talented. He would have made an unsurpassed teacher, if he hadn't been such a self-centred bastard. As it was, the oath forced him to teach his craft, but it didn't force him to be a considerate teacher.

He finished the rune, making sure the chalk finished exactly on a line. There must be no break in the rune's borders for it to function correctly. He put aside his chalk and massaged his cramping fingers. He would have preferred pen and paper, but they were very expensive in this culture, and only used by the rich or by professional scriveners. Rune masters too of course, but then, they never made mistakes. Commoners and apprentices used chalk and slate, or a messenger hired to deliver a memorised letter. The messenger guild was the closest thing to UPS that Inari had; the oath all messengers swore kept them honest.

The ache in his fingers slowly receded, and he scrutinised his work. It looked good in the meagre light of his single lamp. He used a silk fan to waft air over the slate to remove chalk dust—he didn't dare touch the slate with his fingers. Any smudges of the lines would ruin the rune. He took the slate to his window to be sure it was perfect. It was late afternoon in Hardenburg; the cloudy sky lit his room poorly, but if his rune worked, cloudy skies and poor lamps wouldn't matter.

The rune represented his first small practical use of what he'd learned. Other runes in his small repertoire had their uses; one in particular was very good with locks. He grinned, remembering how he had practised that one. Alison would have loved it; she would have laughed... His mood darkened, and his thoughts turned grim. Her death at Karel's hands still haunted him. It was that memory that drove him on beyond pain and tiredness. He had to learn all he could as quickly as he could, so that he could join the Guild where he'd be safe.

The Guild would be his haven. A place full of people like him who wanted to learn the ways of magic in peace. Full of people who did not hurt others for gain, but instead worked for the betterment of the Guild and those it served. The Guild: shining beacon of justice and light, champion of freedom and balance... yadda yadda yadda.

He snorted. The Guild must have very talented publicists, because, although it was powerful and its members feared by most, it was also respected as being impartial and fair. It was neutral in all disputes, serving everyone equally—those who could pay for its services anyway—and was incorruptible. Everyone believed it, or said they did. He wasn't so sanguine. Power corrupts was an axiom he believed absolutely. Karel was proof that not all Guild members were trustworthy, but perhaps the Guild as an organisation was—Karel had been kicked out after all. Whatever the case, he planned to make it his home.

The rune looked perfect, but the only way to be certain was to test it. Karel never allowed him to use magic unsupervised, but he'd left earlier with Mardus in tow, and he wouldn't be back for hours. Besides, he never visited this room. He was willing to risk Karel's displeasure when the pay off would be another step toward freedom and independence.

He placed the slate gently upon his table and rubbed his hands together nervously. The innocent drawing sat there inert, waiting for him to focus and name it. He took a deep steadying breath and traced the lines of the rune with his eyes—the smooth curves and stark angles intersecting just so, the perfection of geometry...

"Leuksa!" he snapped.

Power filled him and rushed into the rune, filling the lines he had drawn in an instant. The rune glowed like moonlight and rose burning above the slate. Chalk lines blackened and disappeared leaving the glowing rune hovering in the air. He watched entranced, and delight filled him. It was perfect. The rune slowly increased in size, filling the room with soft radiant light. As it grew, it became diffuse, fading away like early morning mist at sunrise. The rune finally vanished, leaving a blank slate upon the table, and a room well lit from no discernible source.

He looked around in satisfaction, and extinguished the unneeded lamp. He should be able to work well into the night from now on, doubling his time to practise and learn. The room would remain well lit forever. He frowned when he realised he didn't know how to turn the rune off, or even if it could be turned off. He didn't particularly care what happened after he left, but what about when he needed to sleep? He shrugged. He could wear a mask or something. He didn't sleep much anyway, not with Karel nearby, and Alison's death waiting in his nightmares.

Feeling sombre now, he poured himself a glass of wine, and went back to the window to watch people passing by.

Hardenburg had exceeded his wildest expectations when he first arrived. It was a big city and heavily fortified behind huge walls. There were parks as big as wild woods, while other parks had been cultivated into gardens with places to sit and talk with friends. The palace was a wonder, just as Michael thought it would be. The towers were so tall, it would take him hours to climb to the top. The palace had been a fortress once, but it no longer served that function. It had been rebuilt as a testament to power, rather than as a practical dwelling for royals. It looked more like a fantasy castle in Disneyland now, complete with guardsmen in shiny breastplates and royal blue uniforms.

The streets of Hardenburg were cobbled and narrow, lit at night by lamps spelled alight by Guild rune speakers.

The Guildhall itself was something he'd been eager to see. Finished in white stone with many golden domes on its roof shining in the sunlight, it was an imposing sight, and beautiful. Tall columns flanked the grand entrance, reached by climbing dozens of wide steps. A magnificent plaza fronted the building, with statues and fountains for people to admire. It was another impressive testament to the Guild's wealth. He was sure the effect it had upon visitors was intentional.

Hardenburg was the centre of Inari's power and culture. Ostentatious buildings and clever fountains powered by magic, vied with huge statues of kings, queens, and long dead heroes looming over the rooftops to awe visitors from far-flung countries. The city was a powerful statement.

'Gaze upon what we have wrought. Be amazed.'

Hardenburg couldn't match the scale of cities back home, but even so, it housed close to a million people. Before his arrival, he'd imagined a medieval town in Europe stinking to high heaven with human waste in the streets. The reality was far different. Magic was everywhere in the city; it was used for even the most mundane things, like keeping the streets clean. It was a relief considering Europe's history of plague, but plague was something Inari need never fear. He hadn't seen a single rat or garbage strewn street.

Magic was part of everyday life. Most carried at least one rune stone to make life easier, and many carried a selection of them to use. The Guild was the primary source of those stones, and that gave it economic power unsurpassed in Inari. There were people who could use magic without needing stones of course, but even Douglas, who had a small talent in magic, carried three or four for convenience. He had met people who wore their rune stones as jewellery even, and used them as a kind of status symbol. Kendrick, a friend he'd met in the local tavern, wore a rune stone pendant on a long gold chain around his neck. It was the stone that first drew his attention and made him introduce himself. The pendant turned out to be a kind of ward stone—it glowed in the presence of harmful magic. Thoughts of Kendrick made him aware of the time. He was supposed to meet him in the Broken Arrow for a meal soon. He busied himself with a quick wash and change of clothes.

An obscure cousin to Duke Wallace had provided the house, and it came supplied with everything he needed. Food, clothing, even money. He had a small purse of coin to entertain himself with in the local eateries and taverns. He felt no gratitude or loyalty for the kindness shown him. Karel was a wanted man; he couldn't take up residence just anywhere, especially not in Hardenburg itself without risk. Using the house was practicality not kindness. It was a good place to hide. Not that Karel saw things that way; he was far too arrogant to consider it hiding. He had his own agenda, and only used the house because it served his purposes. With magic to disguise him, he spent a good deal of his time out and about doing the Goddess alone knew what.

He finished his preparations and paused by the window again, frowning down at the pedestrians in the street he saw passing the iron gate. There were guards there, all armed with modern guns from back home. He'd been shocked to see them at first, but not anymore. Karel had planned far ahead and had access to whatever he needed. His criminal status didn't seem to affect him adversely at all! His magical disguise meant he could do whatever he wished unimpeded, even here in the heart of the kingdom. That disguise was the only reason the prisoner at the end of the hall was still alive. It was an uncomfortable thought. He should do something for him, Fergus was right about that at least, but he didn't know what he could do. If he tried to free the man, they would both have to run far and fast.

He wasn't ready to take that step.

He sighed. He was a coward and knew it. Karel scared the spit out of him. It was all right for Fergus to cajole him and urge action, he was just the damn gardener! It wouldn't be him risking death or worse to save a stranger. If Fergus was so concerned about it, why hadn't he done something? He had magic of his own; why wait until making the attempt turned it into a suicide mission?

He shook his head gently, remembering how easily Karel had killed Alison; he could kill the prisoner just as easily, and probably would when he had no further need of him. The realisation made him feel worse. He snarled. Fergus had no right to make him feel guilty! No damn right at all! He'd made his decision. He would join the Guild. That was the safe thing to do, the sensible thing. The masters there could free the prisoner, and take care of Karel at the same time.

He checked his appearance in the mirror, and then headed downstairs. Before he reached the front door, a liveried servant appeared as if by magic with a cloak, and helped him don it.

Lloyd nodded his thanks.

"Will you be needing the coach, sir?"

"No thanks, I'll walk."

"Very well, sir. Have a good evening."

He left the house and headed toward the main gate. The guards there nodded to him and opened it, but they didn't speak. He smiled his thanks. He turned right upon leaving the grounds, and followed the cobbled lane toward the tavern. It was only a short distance, roughly a ten-minute walk. Just as he was about to enter the tavern, the city's bells began tolling six. He paused as hundreds of them chimed the hour. Hardenburg was famed for its clocks that kept perfect time. There was an example of every type of clock imaginable displayed somewhere in Hardenburg.

He stepped into the tavern.

* * *

19 ~ Broken Arrow

Although there were many taverns in Hardenburg, the Broken Arrow was still a very popular place to visit. Unlike some taverns that catered to a particular group of customers—and were almost an extension of their guilds as a result—the Broken Arrow's patrons varied widely. They sought business deals between guilds, and not just good food. All were welcomed, and the owner did very well for himself.

Lloyd paused just inside the tavern, letting his eyes adjust to the room's gloom. The lamps upon the walls provided an intimate level of light, but he suspected any offer to improve it would be rebuffed; everyone liked it just the way it was. As usual, the common room was busy with people eating, drinking, and talking. The din of multiple conversations blended together with the clinking sounds of knives and forks upon plates. Waitresses wove between the tables carrying trays of food and drink. Most drank wine with their food, but ales and beers were available if requested. The common room was one big open area, but it was filled, perhaps even overfilled, with round tables each with two or three comfortable chairs. There must have been close to hundred people already seated, with more entering all the time.

He scanned faces, but he couldn't see Kendrick until his friend stood and waved to attract attention. He had claimed a table in the far corner. Lloyd raised a hand to show that he'd seen him, and headed in that direction, but he felt a little uncertain when he realised his friend wasn't alone. His companion was an older man, and like Kendrick, he wore the rich blue robes decorated with silver thread of the Guild.

"I know how interested you are in the Guild, so I asked Bevyn to join us. I hope you don't mind," Kendrick said.

Bevyn stood briefly and shook his hand. "Bevyn Perahta at your service."

"Lloyd Hawkridge, a pleasure to meet you," Lloyd said, releasing the man's hand and taking his seat. "Have you known Kendrick long?"

"I knew his father, rest his soul. Wine?"

"Please," he said, and held out his glass.

Kendrick gestured and a waitress arrived to take their orders.

Lloyd chose a light soup as a starter, and the spicy chicken for a main course. It came with plenty of vegetables, and the sauce was particularly fiery, just how he liked it. The waitress recommended a white wine to accompany it, and he agreed. He'd tried it before, and it was good. Bevyn and Kendrick chose to follow his lead with the soup, but preferred a less spicy dish for their main course. They chose the fish.

"While we wait, tell me how you met Kendrick," Bevyn said and sipped his wine.

Lloyd raised his glass to give himself time to think. There was no secret about how they'd met, but he had to decide how much to reveal of his own background. Did he dare tell them how he'd arrived in Inari, or should he make up a story; would he be believed if he told the truth? His lack of knowledge about Inari would surely trip him up if he tried to lie. The truth then, but an edited truth.

"We met right here at the Broken Arrow. I didn't know

my way around the city; I still don't really. I found this place by accident, and came in for a meal. I noticed Kendrick's pendant, and asked him about it."

Bevyn nodded. "It's striking I admit, but a bit overblown."

"I like it this way," Kendrick said indignantly. "It adds distinction."

Bevyn snorted.

"I'm glad he chose it. If not for that, I wouldn't have spoken with him. We might never have become friends."

"Kendrick told me of your interest in the Guild. Might you entertain the notion of a sponsor?"

His hopes leapt. Could Bevyn really be hinting at the possibility of sponsoring him? One of the things he'd learned from Karel, was the Guild's organisation and its induction policies. Anyone could approach the Guild, but that didn't guarantee a happy outcome. A successful applicant might be offered membership based upon a test, but then he would have to spend years working his way up the ranks. That seemed fair to him. An apprenticeship was what he'd been expecting, but there was a way to speed the process—sponsorship. Sponsors took charge of their apprentice's training personally, and they often took time out to tutor them. In a way, Karel had been his sponsor until now, one he dare not claim openly.

Sponsorship was an honour that few enjoyed, and that realisation made him take a mental step back. Why would Bevyn bring it up with someone he'd only just met? Surely if he was serious about teaching, he would already have an apprentice.

"A sponsor would be a dream come true," he said carefully. "But I haven't approached the Guild for the test yet."

"Why hesitate? It's obvious to me that you'll pass it. In your case, the test is a formality."

Kendrick grinned and clasped his shoulder. "That's good news, eh Lloyd?"

"Yes, very good," he said, but he was puzzled. "Why is it a formality?"

"I can tell that you recently crafted a rune. The test takes far less effort and skill than the merest rune does to create. So you'll pass. The question is whether or not you deserve sponsorship. You do realise the honour I do you by suggesting this?"

"Absolutely. There can't be very many chosen each year."

"Ah, then you really don't know. I'd wondered."

"Wondered what?"

"If you were playing my nephew for a fool to reach me."

Kendrick spluttered his apologies.

"Your nephew?" he said looking to Kendrick and back to Bevyn in puzzlement. "Kendrick's father was...?"

Bevyn nodded. "My brother."

"But Perahta... Kendrick?" Lloyd looked to his friend for an explanation.

"My father had a falling out with the family."

Bevyn snorted.

Kendrick's face reddened. "My father changed his name to Patriz when he severed his ties to my grandfather. I still use it to honour him, but there's no breach any longer."

Bevyn was watching Lloyd's face carefully. Whatever he saw there must have reassured him because he smiled. "You have no idea who I am, do you?"

He shook his head warily.

"It seems Lloyd is indeed your true friend."

"I told you he was!" Kendrick turned toward him. "Truly! I told him this was all unnecessary."

"It's fine. Whatever this is about, I am your friend."

The food's arrival stymied conversation and they ate their meals thinking private thoughts. Afterwards, they took their time over more wine, and Bevyn finally revealed the secret.

"You're quite right that very few are chosen for sponsorship," Bevyn began as he absently rotated his tall-stemmed wine glass between his fingers. "Only a few handfuls a year are picked. Always the best and brightest. If you were to join them, you might suffer some resentment at first. To be blunt, you're older than they are, and have less knowledge than even a first year apprentice."

Lloyd nodded.

"And then of course there's my position to consider. Being sponsored by me isn't necessarily as beneficial to you as you might assume. You'll be under greater scrutiny as my... I won't say enemies, we're all Guild after all. Let's call them rivals. My rivals may wish to use you as a way to harm my reputation."

He understood that Bevyn felt his position within the Guild was an important one, but he still didn't know what that position was. "Who are you?"

"I'm the Guild's Master Archivist," Bevyn said pretentiously, but then he frowned as he realised something. "You don't know what that means, I can tell. How can you not?"

That question was getting too close to things he didn't want to answer. He couldn't tell them about Karel. He wouldn't dare even if he trusted them not to tell others.

"I told you that I'm new to Hardenburg. I know very little about the Guild. You're only the second rune speaker I've spoken with."

Bevyn frowned harder. "The Guild is everywhere in Inari, or its members are. Your accent is strange, but you don't come from the empire."

"I'm from much further away than Sawai."

"Indeed?"

Did he take the chance and tell them how he'd arrived? This might be his only chance to enter the Guild. Bevyn was suspicious. If an archivist was a high position, and by the way he'd announced it, it was probably very high, Bevyn could block his entry entirely. He took a deep breath and sent a prayer winging its way to the Lady.

Please Lady, hear my plea. Help me convince them I'm a friend.

Feeling better and a little more confident, he began his tale with the bombshell. "I'm from another world. I swear on my life and power, that this world is not the world of my birth. Lady strike me down this instant if I lie."

Bevyn's eyes widened as magic swirled and the Goddess witnessed the oath. "Flames man! You can't, you mustn't..."

Lloyd smiled as the oath took him, and left him unscathed. Of course it had. He had spoken the unvarnished truth, but to Bevyn and Kendrick he had just committed suicide before witnesses. They watched, expecting him to expire right before their eyes. When he took up his wine again and drank, their dismay turned to shock as the truth dawned.

Conversation around the room had lapsed as everyone turned to find the source of the magic. Oaths weren't unusual, but neither were they common. Business partners often asked the Lady to bear witness to things. Not often in a tavern, true, but then the Broken Arrow wasn't a common tavern. Slowly conversation picked up again as the patrons lost interest.

"By the Lady," Bevyn whispered. "How is it possible?"

"That's part of what I'm hoping the Guild will help me with." He was determined to help Alex and the others find what they needed to get home. He didn't plan upon leaving with them, but he did feel an obligation to them. He frowned; he didn't like to lie to his new friends, but he couldn't tell them the whole of the story. "There are some things I don't wish to discuss, not yet. I hope you'll understand my position on this. Suffice it to say, I don't know how to return to my world. I need your help with that."

Bevyn nodded, his eyes betraying his excitement. "I'll sponsor you, and together we'll find the answers you seek."

Kendrick clapped him on the shoulder.

"Congratulations!"

"Thanks." He clasped Bevyn's hand. "Thank you. This means a great deal to me. Can I ask another favour of you, of both of you?"

Kendrick nodded at once, but Bevyn was cagier as befit his greater experience. "Ask, and I may grant it."

"I want to be Lloyd Hawkridge the Guild apprentice, not Lloyd Hawkridge the freak. Will you keep my origins a secret?"

Kendrick nodded. "I will, you have my word."

Bevyn was slower to agree. He frowned in thought and then nodded at some conclusion he'd reached. "There are those in the Guild who demand my loyalty, and should they ask directly, I would feel constrained to answer, but I'll not tell anyone without asking your permission first. Good enough?"

"More than good enough. Thank you."

Bevyn nodded. "Well! Let us drink to my new apprentice."

Lloyd refilled their glasses and drank the toast, already planning a way to extricate himself from Karel's clutches without confronting him directly.

* * *

.

20 ~ The Guild

Lloyd considered it unwise in the extreme to confront Karel at any time. Doing so to release him from their mentor and apprentice relationship, seemed like a bad idea. So he cheated.

He wrote a letter and packed his things.

He considered the clothes and other items supplied to him, as his by right. He'd earned them by putting up with Karel and his companions for so long. He briefly considered visiting Fergus one final time to say goodbye, but upon greater reflection, he decided against it. He wasn't entirely sure what a self-proclaimed green man stood for, and Fergus thought that anyone with ambitions of giving up their independence to join the Guild were idiots; he'd made that plain enough. He was sure Fergus' offer of teaching was well meant, but he'd refused the offer. He wanted to be part of something bigger. He wanted to wear Guild colours, and become part of its community.

He left the house by coach and didn't look back. The letter he'd left behind would release Karel from the bargain they'd made regarding teaching, but not his oath. Only the Lady could do that, and she would not. He should be safe, but he wanted to be installed at the Guild before Karel read it. Why take chances?

The coach trip was short and quite pleasant. Here he was, a modern man, a product of a modern age, travelling by coach in a world of magic. It boggled the mind. His preconceptions of what it must have been like living in a time when machines didn't hold sway, had been shattered by his arrival in Hardenburg. It was a civilised city; as modern in its way as any city on Earth, but powered by magic and spells, not electricity and machines. It was well managed and clean. Cleaner than many cities on Earth even today. The Guild had a lot to do with that, but not everything. The palace bureaucrats did their work well. The patrol was trusted and honest, and crime was low within the city. Not nonexistent, nothing was perfect, but low. The Guild's spells saw to it that street lighting worked, and the sewers remained clear. A lowly use for magic one might think, but an important one for the population's health. There was still room for magic in fun things. Festivals always had sky fire displays—magic used like fireworks back home. The clocks, bells, and fountains also came to mind.

Lady, he loved it here. It was where he belonged.

The black lacquered coach pulled up outside the Guildhall, and he climbed out. The driver busied himself with untying the luggage secured on the back. Kendrick hurried down the steps from the grand forum, followed by two apprentices. All three were wearing the silver trimmed blue robes that he yearned to earn and wear.

The driver approached him, and he handed a fistful of coin over. A hefty tip, but why not? It was only money, and meant nothing to him. The driver's eyes widened in appreciation. He tipped his hat, and climbed back onto his coach. A light tap with the long whip he held, and the horses started away.

"You didn't have to trouble yourself," he said, when his

friend reached him. "I'm sure I could've found my way to the right place."

Kendrick shook his hand. "No doubt you would eventually, but this is quicker. We have to meet Bevyn after I get you settled. He wants you on the roster, and through testing this morning. Just a formality. His sponsorship jumps you to the head of the line."

Lloyd could almost see the apprentice's ears pricking up at mention of sponsorship, and knew the news would fly through the hall. Kendrick waved a hand at the bags, and the apprentices bent to their task.

"You did that on purpose. Why?" he said, as they followed the apprentices.

Kendrick kept his voice low. "Bevyn's orders. The new intake is like chum in the water around here. If you'd come into testing like any other petitioner, you would've been snapped up before you could blink."

"Bevyn's rivals?"

"Precisely."

"Why would I be snapped up?"

"How many petitioners in a year do you think wander through the doors already able to craft runes? I'll tell you. None. You're a born rune crafter."

"Thanks for the vote of confidence—"

"No, you misunderstand me. I'm not complimenting you. All of us learn how to use magic and craft runes, but some are born with a genuine gift for it. Bevyn says you're one of them."

He didn't protest. He would love for Bevyn's opinion to be true, but feared that what he'd sensed was only Karel's ruthless form of teaching. His ability hadn't simply burgeoned on its own from a natural gift. It had been pulled into the light by an evil man shackled to the task by an oath.

"Well, I'm glad I have friends to protect me then."

Kendrick smiled. "We'll do that, and teach you how to

do it yourself."

The Guildhall was a huge place, second only in size and splendour to the palace itself. The entrance opened into the grand forum, an open hall with granite tiled floors, and huge columns marching into the distance, supporting a vaulted ceiling of pale stone. It was a very busy place, with robed figures hurrying about, mingling with visitors from far flung cities and countries. Voices blended into a low rumble as people discussed business deals, or asked for advice. There were tables set up in alcoves with lines of people waiting to ask the seated figures for direction to their meetings, or to make deals of one kind or another.

Lloyd's head was on a swivel as he tried to take it all in.

They passed through the grand forum, left the chaos behind, and entered a courtyard under an open sky. The apprentices marched straight across the square, their boots crunching upon the patterned gravel. He noticed an apprentice repairing the designs to one side of the square, and hoped it was a punishment, not a duty he'd be required to perform. He wasn't here for housekeeping chores, but he was willing to do his bit. He would do anything he had to. He wanted to belong.

Hundreds of windows overlooked the square. He wondered if they were all classrooms. Some of them must be, but there were too many. Some had to be apartments for guild members. The Guildhall was actually a group of halls and wings joined together. The impressive facade of the grand forum, seen from the plaza with its wide steps and imposing columns, was the face of the Guild that outsiders saw when they visited to negotiate their deals, but this area was for insiders. It made him feel good, as if already an insider.

The apprentices led the way inside and up four flights of stairs to an apartment. Kendrick told them to leave the bags in the bedroom, and then dismissed them.

Lloyd wandered around, investigating the suite of rooms

he'd been given. There were three. The sitting room was the largest, but still small compared with his old room. He didn't care. It was big enough for entertaining a couple of friends in the evenings. The furnishings were plain, though in good repair. A fireplace had all the makings, but it was unlit. The lamps on the mantle, on the table, and on the walls were also unlit making the rooms gloomy. The seats were dark brown overstuffed leather monsters, but they looked comfortable.

He crossed the room and opened the door on that side. It led to a bathroom. He was pleased to see interior plumbing again. He'd been surprised to see that sort of thing when they first took up residence at Wallace's house, but Hardenburg really was a modern city in a lot of ways. Magically heated water for baths, wasn't a surprise anymore. No toilets though, but there would be a chamber pot under the bed. He went into the bedroom, and found his friend already unpacking for him. It embarrassed him. Kendrick wasn't his servant.

"I'll do that," he said. "Leave it."

"It's fine," Kendrick said, shutting the drawer. "We'll get it done now, and you'll have the rest of the day free."

He moved to help. It didn't take long to hang his shirts in the little wardrobe, or put away his trousers and under things in the other drawers. The empty bags went into the bottom of the wardrobe. He hoped he wouldn't need them again for a long time. He planned to make Hardenburg his home. The Guild had chapterhouses in most cities, just as the witches did. Balancing the scale, he suspected they would say. Wherever the Guild went, there too went the witches. Watching, waiting... judging. He supposed he might need to visit some of them one day, but in his heart this was home.

"Ready?" Kendrick asked.

"For testing?"

"Bevyn first, but yes, that too."

"I can't wait."

* * *

21 ~ Testing

Kendrick led Lloyd along the corridors, chatting away. They encountered plenty of people, and Kendrick greeted some by name. He introduced him as Bevyn's new apprentice, and at first he thought his friend was just doing so off hand, but it happened too often. More, Kendrick didn't vary the script, as if he'd memorised it. In a quiet moment between encounters, he asked him about it.

"Bevyn told me to make sure you're known as his from the first."

"Why, do you know?"

"The news of your sponsorship will be all over the Guild before the end of the day. That should stop any attempt to lure you away from Bevyn, but more importantly, it should stop them enquiring into your background. No benefit for them, do you see?"

He nodded. It impressed him that Bevyn had taken steps so quickly to protect his secret. Why would anyone take the time to investigate him, once it was widely known that he was already Bevyn's apprentice?

Kendrick knocked on a door, and they entered together without waiting. The room wasn't an apartment this time. It was furnished as a comfortable study. Bevyn was already present with two other men. He didn't recognise either of Bevyn's friends, but Kendrick introduced them as Guildmaster Warren Halvard, and Master of Novices Hubert Atella. He shook their hands, and took a seat when invited.

Bevyn began the meeting. "As I explained to you in the Broken Arrow, there are those within the Guild who have first call upon my loyalty. As we agreed, I'm asking for your permission to divulge our secret regarding your origins. Do I have it?"

He'd expected something of the sort. At least it was happening here in controlled surroundings unlike last time, and if his secret had to be shared, he preferred it be done all at once. He gave his permission with a nod.

"Thank you," Bevyn said solemnly, but then he grinned. He turned back to the others. "I asked for this meeting to introduce Lloyd as my soon to be apprentice, but also to divulge something astounding that he told me under oath. Lloyd is from another world, and he needs our help to return home."

The two men looked at Bevyn in total disbelief.

He smiled and compounded things. "I can see you don't believe him, so why don't I swear again so we can move on? I swear this world is not the world of my birth. May the Goddess strike me down this instant if I lie."

As before, magic swirled and bound him to the oath. It dissipated leaving him unharmed. Bevyn's friends looked on in horror, just as Bevyn had done last time, and he laughed. He couldn't help himself. He raised a hand and apologised.

"I'm not laughing at you, but at the situation... your faces," he said and snorted. "Sorry again. You look as shocked as Bevyn and Kendrick did when I told them. Horrified, absolutely horrified." He calmed himself and nodded. "Horrified," he said dourly. "I don't actually want to go home, but I do need to learn how it can be done. I came here with others, but we were separated. I like it here in the

Guild, and want to stay, but the others will need a way to return home. I want to help them."

The Guildmaster pulled himself together first. "Then you chose your sponsor well."

"Not really. I didn't know that Bevyn was the Guild's Master Archivist before Kendrick introduced us. It was blind luck."

"Or the hand of the Goddess. I'm the Guildmaster, but even I don't know everything there is to know about the treasures held in the vaults. The items that I *am* aware of are dangerous enough. Bevyn is far more knowledgeable than I. I do know of one or two artefacts that were purported to open gates. One was lost years ago. The other is locked away, and for a very good reason." He glanced uneasily at Bevyn, and he nodded. "The one I'm thinking of requires a full coven of thirteen witches to activate. The Guild is the repository for all artefacts dating back to the War of Power, no matter their use or origin, but this one cannot be used by men."

"You know of no others?" Lloyd said, concerned now.

"I didn't say that. There are many things held here that have unknown uses. One of Bevyn's duties is to oversee research into them. The work is time consuming, and extremely dangerous. There were weapons used to destroy entire armies toward the end of the war. Some of those may be stored here."

He was really looking forward to joining Bevyn and his people in the archives. Researching the uses of magic, and the tools made with it? Fascinating! He would be in paradise, but the time consuming part troubled him. Douglas and the others were on their way to the city by an indirect route, but they would arrive eventually, and he wanted to have something ready to placate them.

"The item I seek, if found… would you agree to its use to return my friends home? As I said, I like it here and want to stay, but I owe them a way home."

The Guildmaster nodded. "If found and a way to use it safely becomes known, then I would be willing to have it used on their behalf. It would be used by me or people I designate, and not taken out of the hall."

"That goes without saying," he agreed.

"No. I'm saying it here and now. Before any use, there will be oaths heard and sworn. The lost talisman was stolen precisely because too much trust was extended to one unworthy of it. That will not happen again."

He knew where the lost talisman was. It lay discarded and broken at Dun'Morogh, broken by a bullet fired at Karel by Douglas Skeldon. He wouldn't divulge that. Mentioning Karel's name would cast doubt upon his own trustworthiness.

"Agreed."

"Let us move on to your testing and induction into the Guild. Testing and the oversight of novices is Hubert's area."

Hubert nodded. "Testing isn't normally handled directly by me or my office, but in anticipation of this meeting, I brought the necessary items with me." He produced a black velvet bag from beneath his robes. "Let's use the desk."

Lloyd stood and joined Hubert as he removed a selection of rune stones and gems from the bag. He smoothed the empty bag out upon the desk, and then laid the gems on top in a neat row before circling them with the runes. Lloyd could feel the magic in the gems and wanted to touch them. He wanted to stroke them like pets.

There were five gems, all beautiful in colour and form, but he couldn't take his eyes off the ruby. It seemed to glow; it attracted him more than the others. The opal did as well, but not as much.

Hubert's voice was low as he crooned hypnotically. "Feel them without touching. Know them for what they are. Tell me their uses."

"The ruby is fire, and it wants me to pick it up," he said.

"It glows. I can feel its warmth in my head."

"Excellent. Your primary element is fire. Tell me, if the ruby were not present, which stone would call strongest?"

"Opal."

Hubert's eyebrows climbed. "Really, how interesting. Can you tell me what it does?"

"I think it might be used to see things far away."

"Think?"

"Is. I meant is used to see far distances."

"You don't sound sure."

"I'm certain, but the ruby is distracting. It wants me to touch it." He reached to pick up the ruby, but Hubert intercepted his hand.

"Not yet."

He nodded reluctantly. He needed to pick up that stone. It was his, somehow, though he'd never set eyes on it before. It was his.

"After the opal, which of the three remaining stones call most strongly?"

"They feel about the same. None of them make me want to stroke them. The blue one, is it sapphire? It's water and I think it might purify and cool. The green one is earth. It feels very weak, almost not there at all. Is it a healing charm?"

"Yes. Earth is often our weakest element as fire is often the strongest. The opposite is true of witches. And finally?"

"I don't recognise the stone."

"Agate."

The agate was potato shaped and polished. He could see layers of alternating colours. White through various shades of orange. It was pretty, but its magic was weak, at least to him.

"It must be air, but that's just a deduction based upon the others. I don't know what it does, but a guess would be something to do with weather."

"Very good," Hubert said and gathered up all the stones

except the opal and ruby. "Take the strongest stone in your right hand."

He didn't need to be told twice. His hand snatched the ruby, and he sighed with relief as his yearning was satisfied. He held it in his hand and stroked it with his thumb. He starred at it, and the glow brightened enough to throw shadows on the wall.

"Excellent," Hubert said. "Kendrick, the candle?"

"Right here."

"I want you to light the candle, Lloyd."

"I don't have any matches. I know there's a rune, but I haven't practised enough with it yet."

"You don't need a rune or matches. Just make fire."

He began to raise the stone, he knew it held fire. Knew it.

"No. Not the stone. Use your magic, the magic within you. Light the candle."

He frowned at the candle in its holder. Kendrick had placed it on the desk before him. The stone blazed in his fist, and the candle just took light. Amazed, he looked down at the now dead ruby, and then at his audience. They smiled.

"You have a strong affinity with fire," the Guildmaster said as Hubert took the ruby from him. He didn't protest. It was nothing to him now. "The stones are activated by the powers of those being tested. The rune circle is the important thing, not the spell stones. That always surprises people afterwards. I don't know why really, when you consider what the Guild is best known for."

Runes. The Guild was best known for its rune speakers, and the magic of rune craft. He nodded to show that he understood.

"The circle takes power from you, and imbues the stones with it. The amount is in exact proportion to your abilities, so that the ruby in your case became the strongest, and the agate the weakest. When you lit the candle, your desire to light it allowed the power in the ruby out and into the wick. It's a simple way to bypass your lack of skill and training to prove your aptitude."

"And if I had chosen the opal?"

"We would supply a bowl of water and you would have scried for us. The image would have appeared within the water. Although your strengths in fire and spirit mean you would do better using a brazier once fully trained, water is safer for a beginner."

"Amazing," he said. "Did I pass the test?"

"You did, but Bevyn already knew you would. You have crafted basic runes already, yes?"

"A couple."

"That would be enough to pass, but the test is our traditional requirement for entrance. Sponsorship is already deemed special treatment without waving the test as well."

Hubert put away the gems and runes, and made the velvet bag disappear beneath his robes. Kendrick extinguished the candle, and retrieved a new robe. He handed it to Bevyn.

"Welcome to the Guild," Bevyn said, and gave the robe to Lloyd. "I can hardly wait to get started on your training."

He shook Bevyn's hand and took the robe. "Thanks. I feel the same way." He pulled his robe on, leaving the cowl down, and Kendrick helped tidy it. Guild robes had deep cowls, similar to a monk's hood. They were worn down when inside and smoothed over the shoulders. "Thanks."

"Bevyn is responsible for your welfare and training," the Guildmaster said, "but I think you'll understand when I say that I'll be watching you closely. Others will watch for their own reasons. As Bevyn's apprentice, you have a unique position, and it comes with responsibilities. Anything you do, good or bad, will reflect upon him."

"I understand."

"Excellent. Hubert and I have other business to discuss. I'll leave you in Bevyn's capable hands."

Lloyd followed his friends out of the Guildmaster's study and into his new life.

* * *

22 ~ Sell Sword

Douglas entered the city using the disguise Henry's gold had paid for, and took rooms at one of the less reputable inns on the waterfront. It seemed the sensible thing to do, not knowing whether Karel and his owner was in the city.

Henry's kindness in supplying him with funds had allowed him to travel rapidly on fast ships to reach the city well before coronation day. There had been more than enough gold left over to buy a few necessities, such as clothes and armour to outfit him as a mercenary, and a full set of kit that any caravan guard would own. His duffel bulged upon his shoulder as he entered The Swan. Anyone witnessing his arrival would assume two things. One, he was either a mercenary or a sailor; maybe both—ships needed guards too after all. And two, he was looking for lodgings and work.

The final part of his disguise was a spell to disguise his features. It was a mere party trick, not a true seeming. Such illusions were far beyond his abilities, as was the cheap festival mask he was using. The spell used for parties and festivals blurred facial features, but it couldn't do more than that. His hair colour was lighter, his skin much darker as if he'd been working upon open decks in the sun, his eyes appeared closer together, and his nose thinner but more hooked. It would work for casual observers, but party tricks had limits. Anyone who really looked, really *concentrated* upon his features, would pierce the illusion and recognise it for the spell it was. As soon as that happened, it would break for that person, and it wouldn't work again. That wouldn't happen with a proper seeming, but such things were expensive, made by the Guild's best artificers. His party trick would do fine, until he felt ready to approach the palace.

He swung his duffel off his shoulder to land upon the floor between his feet, as the innkeeper approached. The wispy-haired sweaty-faced man took him in with a glance and calculated his worth in coin. Douglas didn't quite snort at the mercenary gleam in the pudgy man's eyes, having expected no less from the owner of such a place. Henry's remaining gold was packed away in his duffel, wrapped in a spare shirt, but he had a small purse of silvers and coppers at his belt; the innkeeper had noticed it, and was very happy to greet him like an old friend.

"Rooms, food, baths? Yes, yes. I can supply all that and more to a fine fellow such as yourself!"

"All three, and I'll need the room for about ten days."

"Ten!"

"I just finished up my contract," he said, and jingled his purse. "I'll be looking for a new one, but no hurry. The coronation should provide a distraction, eh?"

The innkeeper laughed. "And more! There's to be a festival and sky fire. Rumours say the Guild has been working on something special. A display the likes we've never seen, they say."

"I don't doubt it. The room?"

"Well, ten days now... a silver a day seem fair?"

He blinked in surprise. It was fair, too fair. "What's wrong with it?" he asked warily.

The innkeeper grinned. "Nothing is wrong with it! But

ten days is ten silver. A gold. Food and baths, that's another gold, all in advance and no refunds if you decide to leave early."

"Oh, that's what's wrong with it," he said sourly, to stay in character. He had more than enough coin to cover the cost, but the average caravan guard would at the very least grumble about it. "The food comes from the palace kitchens, does it?"

"No, but it does come with small beer, and for free! If you want wine or other spirits, you'll pay as you go."

A gold for food and baths was daylight robbery, but he could easily afford it, and the coronation meant that the inn wouldn't lack for trade. He could easily find himself on the street if he tried to bargain. Wine and other drink being extra was standard. Everyone had preferences, but even small beer wasn't too bad when all he'd had aboard ship was watered rum. He counted two golds worth of silver and copper into the innkeeper's eager hand, leaving his purse much deflated, and then the innkeeper led him through the common room toward the stairs.

The pudgy man puffed and hoisted his bulk slowly up the short flight of stairs, as if scaling mountains, and then led the way along the corridor to a room. Douglas stepped inside and dropped his duffel on a chair by the window. He twitched the curtain aside and peered outside. He had a good view of the street. He turned back and checked the bed. The springs were firm. It would be comfortable he was sure. He nodded to the innkeeper and took the iron key offered to him.

"A bath?"

"At the end of the hall. I'll send up hot water and towels."

He nodded.

The innkeeper left, and he closed his door. He would bathe before going down for a meal.

After a bath and change of clothes, Douglas locked his room, and went back to the common room. He left his duffel on the bed not fearing theft. There was nothing in it of value. Henry's gold was under the bed, hidden in the corner of the room with a *see-me-not* spell laid upon it. He had plenty of money with him, having filled his purse with coin before hiding the rest.

The common room was busier than before, but a serving girl showed him to an empty table. The innkeeper must have reserved it for him, as it was the only one free. When offered a selection of food, he chose a tasty sounding beef stew that came with heaps of vegetables, fresh bread with butter, and a pitcher of cider. He preferred cider to small beer or ale. Wine would be better still, but he needed to keep his wits about him, and he hadn't drunk anything stronger than watered rum since before his brief exile to Alex's world.

He frowned as thoughts of Alex and his feelings for her intruded. What by the Lady was he going to do about her? He shook his head as possibilities and impossibilities vied for his attention.

The food was as good as he could have hoped, but it didn't wipe the frown from his face. The serving girl must have noticed him frowning, because she came by to ask if he needed more food or drink. He shook his head, and she left to attend another customer. He watched her hips swaying as she walked away, and noticed the other men taking an interest, but unlike them, he had no thoughts of bedding the girl. In her place, he imagined Alex.

He shook his head again. He reached for the bread, and a knife to spread the butter thickly upon it.

He had no right to think of Alex that way, none at all, and doubly so now that she'd been chosen by the Goddess. A bonded Daughter of the Mother never took a husband. He supposed they must take lovers occasionally, they were only human after all, but the thought was an uncomfortable one to contemplate. Chosen were special. All the sisters were for their intimate relationship with the Goddess, but those who had bonded were more special because of their rarity. The Goddess herself singled them out. It didn't happen by chance. Shieri had been sent to join Alex, and that meant the Goddess had a plan for her. A destiny could be a hard thing to live with. He hoped it would be a good one, something she would embrace. Whether hard or easy, she would have no choice but to fulfil the Goddess' will.

He ate his fill, and sat back at his ease to watch the goings on. Customers arrived, others departed. The innkeeper and his serving girls, bustled about greeting them and taking their coppers. The inn was doing a roaring trade. He noticed a lot of sell swords amongst the customers. There were always caravan guards and mercenaries visiting the capital. It was a major port, and all trading cities were a hub for hiring armed men for protection. He did note a lot of swarthy-faced men amongst them. There was no reason Sawainese mercenaries shouldn't visit Hardenburg. Plenty did hire out upon ships crossing the eastern ocean to brave the pirate-infested waters found on the far coast, but the numbers surprised him a little. He would have expected such numbers closer to the Vale of Dreams, not here.

He sipped his tankard of cider, trying to plan his next move. He wanted to visit the palace and lay all his troubles at the queen's feet. Let her deal with Wallace and his treachery. Let her call him for an accounting while he watched the man squirm! He would be very interested to hear Wallace's excuse for the army encamped on Dun'Harden's border. There couldn't possibly be any good reason for it. Calling up his clan's forces that way, smacked of rebellion. What else could it mean? Nothing he could think of.

He finished his tankard and refilled it from the pitcher with another frown blossoming upon his face. He seemed to be frowning in puzzlement a lot lately, and he was tired of it. He wanted to know what was going on without doubts intruding, he just wanted to know for a change. He always came back to that in the end. What was Wallace playing at? He couldn't possibly have any real expectation of overthrowing the queen. None would support him. All the clans would rise up against him! And yet, Wallace had raised his forces regardless, and his vassals apparently supported him in that. It was beyond expectation that they all would, yet they had. He didn't understand it. If he'd tried something so stupid, half his vassals would have refused outright, while the other half demanded he face them in the challenge circle!

Whatever Wallace's excuse was, the queen was the one to deal with it. For now at least. Prince Erland would take the throne soon. The coronation had been set for a few weeks hence, and then they would have a proper King again, one descended of the unbroken Inarian royal line. Queen Isabeau had performed well as regent, but she was descended of Sawai. It shouldn't matter that her brother was the Emperor, but it did to all too many people. He wasn't one of those paranoid fools, and considered her bloodline an asset to Inari, not a thing to fear, but he was in the minority. Many believed the queen favoured her brother unduly over Inari's traditional allies, but whatever the truth of the matter, Inari and Sawai had enjoyed a peaceful decade of trade under her rulership. That was all anyone could want from a ruler surely? Peace and prosperity; wasn't that what everyone wanted?

He finished his cider, and was thinking about returning to his room, when his plan abruptly changed. A man entered the inn and stopped just inside, obviously waiting for his eyes to adjust before advancing further. It was Mardus! He jumped to his feet, his chair scraping across the floor with his movement. Mardus turned at the sudden sound, and his eyes widened in surprise. He bolted out the door.

"Stop him someone!" Douglas yelled, but no one did of course. The customers just stared at him in befuddlement.

"Here now!" the innkeeper yelled. "What's amiss?"

Douglas didn't have time to explain, and he didn't stop his charge for the door. He made it outside, blinking dazzled eyes, in time to see Mardus dodging between pedestrians. He gave chase. He could have cheered when Mardus rammed another man, and both men went down in a tangle of limbs. He gained some ground then, but Mardus was up and running all too quickly. They dodged in front of a coach and horses, making the beasts shy and causing the driver to lash out with his whip. He ducked away from the wicked tip as it cracked close to his face. The sound was remarkably similar to that made by Alex's gun.

Mardus ducked into an alley.

Douglas was nearly within reach of him as they burst out of the far end, and onto another busy street. He threw himself forward in a desperate lunge, and caught a fistful of Mardus' coat. Staggering and gasping for breath, they fell almost under another coach's wheels. Mardus cursed and rolled desperately aside, avoiding death or injury by the narrowest of margins.

They grappled, each trying for a better hold on the other, but finally Mardus squirmed free and was away again. Douglas cursed and gave chase. The man was faster than a fox with hounds on his scent!

Another alley, another street. He'd lost his bearings long since. Finally, Mardus made a mistake and chose a blind alley where he turned at bay. Douglas stopped just inside the entrance, drew sword, and advanced warily. Mardus reached for his belt knife; for some reason he wasn't wearing his sword. His eyes widened as a thought struck him. Instead of pulling his knife, his hand went behind his back, and reappeared holding a gun!

Douglas froze, shock draining the colour from his face.

Mardus laughed, gasping for breath, but his aim was steady. "I forgot," he gasped. "I forgot I had the stupid thing." He laughed again, but swallowed back his hilarity. "I could kill you now. Drop the sword and maybe I won't."

And maybe he would too.

Douglas hesitated and a shot rang out. Yes, indeed it did sound like a whip cracking upon the air. He let his sword drop, wincing at the clang it made upon the cobbles. He silently apologised to the blade, and to Michael's father for any injury done to it.

"Very wise, m'lord. Karel ordered me to bring you to him, should I ever get the chance. I don't think he believed that would happen, but I'm not taking the chance of crossing him. That's both good and bad for you. You get to live a while longer, but I don't think he'll make your remaining time pleasant."

"No doubt," Douglas said in disgust. "I have gold back at the inn. It's yours if you let me go."

Mardus' eyes brightened with interest. "Is that so? Well then, after I deliver you to him, I'll be sure to pay your room at The Swan a visit. Step away from the sword."

He didn't see that he had any choice; he backed up and let Mardus retrieve the blade.

"Nice, but not much use against one of these." Mardus said, brandishing the gun. "There are going to be a lot of changes around here very soon. Karel has big plans, the biggest!"

"Do tell."

"Ah... ah... ah! Nice try. I've heard that story, the one where the evil henchman—that would be me—reveals all his master's secrets." Mardus grinned. "It never works out well for him, does it? Turn around and walk ahead of me. Turn left at the end, and don't try to run. I don't mind shooting you in the back. Front, back... it's all the same to me. This thing makes the challenge circle and chivalry obsolete. A brave new world is coming!"

Douglas turned and began walking, thinking furiously.

The gun did change everything. Mardus was right about that. Running from a bowman was chancy, and most wouldn't risk it. He might have tried it, considering where they were. Mardus might not have been willing to aim a bow at a man's retreating back in public, but the gun was so easy to conceal. No one would know what it was, or what the noise of a shot meant. It really did sound like a whip upon the air. Most wouldn't pay it any attention, and Mardus could easily hide it. If he ran, he would be dead in moments, and to no good purpose.

He turned left as ordered, listening to Mardus' steps close behind him. Maybe he could spin about and knock the gun out of line... risky, but possible. His eyes darted about desperately. He could shout for help. Even if none came to his aid, it would attract attention, and Mardus would be under scrutiny. He drew breath to do just that, and felt the gun poke him in the back.

"Don't!" Mardus snarled. "I swear you're dead the moment you give voice to a shout out here. I swear it!"

Magic swirled about them, binding Mardus to the oath.

Douglas released his breath, and cursed. Mardus laughed and prodded him forward again. He continued his plodding walk. It didn't matter that the Goddess had witnessed the oath. He would have believed the man regardless, but now that he was bound, there was no question of the outcome. Mardus had to make good on the threat no matter what, or be proven an oath breaker. Cursed by the Goddess, oath breakers didn't live long.

Mardus marched him through the city and finally to a gate set in a high wall. Douglas recognised the area. It was a district of the city where many nobles maintained a house for their comfort while visiting the capital. He didn't know who this one belonged to, but Wallace seemed a good bet. The iron gate swung wide as they neared, and they entered the grounds.

The guard on the gate didn't look him in the eye, but busied himself locking up behind them. He was swarthy faced, and he held himself stiffly erect. Douglas was willing to wager there was military service in his background. A mercenary or caravan guard probably. He hadn't been born in Inari, not with that skin tone or eye colour. He was a pure blood son of Sawai, descended of the nomadic tribes on the other side of the mountains, or Douglas had never met one. He wore a curving dagger at his belt in an ornate sheath, and carried a wide bladed sword on one hip, but it was the holstered gun on the opposite hip that made Douglas stare. It took a prod in the back to get him moving again.

His thoughts raced. How many of Alex's cursed guns were loose upon the world? He knew he'd been right to fear them. What if the bigger ones were here too? What then? Rifles were infinitely more dangerous than the small ones, but all of them were a disaster waiting to happen. He had to escape and warn the queen! He had to!

They entered the house, and he was unsurprised to find more men of Sawai in guard positions. They all had a gun in addition to their accustomed swords and daggers. His heart sank at the sight. Wallace had sold out to the empire. Why? Why would any nobleman sell his honour to Sawai? It didn't make any sense, but it didn't have to. Wallace was a traitor, and this proved it beyond doubt. He had to find a way to escape before Karel succeeded in his plans. Considering the timing, it must have something to do with Erland's coronation.

"In there," Mardus said, indicating a guarded door.

Douglas hesitated, expecting the guard to open it for him, but when the man made no move, he worked the handle himself. He pushed inside with Mardus close on his heels, and found Wallace sitting behind a desk. He was reading a huge leather bound tome, lying flat upon the desk, and he looked with annoyance writ upon his face at the interruption. His expression turned to one of delight when he recognised who had come calling.

"Welcome, your Grace! What a delightful surprise," Wallace said, rising and coming out from behind the desk. "My dear Mardus, you have earned yourself a bonus this day!"

Mardus grinned.

* * *

23 ~ Prisoners

Douglas slammed his fist against the door in frustration, and cursed himself for a fool a moment later, shaking his hand free of pain all the while. The spell on the door would do him no permanent harm, but it hurt enough to dissuade further adventures. Besides, what did he think would happen? Did he expect Wallace and Mardus to turn around, and come right back to let him out? He kicked the door ignoring the flash of azure light as the ward reacted again. He kicked it again, out of pure frustration.

Laughter at his back had him spinning to look. In the darkness, he could just make out a figure reclining in a chair with legs outstretched, crossed at the ankles. A picture of a man at his ease.

"You!" he snarled, and charged the man only to take a boot in the belly. He staggered back, and prepared to charge again.

"Me?" Wallace said with an insolent grin. "Are you sure?"

That brought him up short. He frowned at the still locked door, and then at Wallace. The truth was he wasn't, sure that is.

"Fool."

"I'm going to kill you," Douglas said, deadly calm. In his head, he saw himself on a desolate and muddy road, screaming his throat raw, cradling his brother's body. "You're dead." He nodded slowly to himself. Would he ever stop screaming for Theon? "Dead."

"Fool," Wallace sneered again. "Who do you think you're talking to?"

"My brother's murderer."

"I didn't kill Theon. Karel did. Surely, you've realised that by now? I've been his captive for months."

"You're lying."

"Why would I bother?"

He frowned. "Why hold you and not simply kill you?"

"I'm no rune speaker, but even I know that blood magic requires the blood of the living to work."

Douglas nodded. That was known.

"Then there's your answer. The doppelganger spell wouldn't work if I were dead."

"That was Karel just now then."

Wallace nodded.

"Do you know his plans?"

"Regicide."

"The queen?"

"Erland."

"Erland!" he gasped. "But why?"

"You don't know anything do you?" Wallace said, regarding him with pitying eyes. "Did your brother teach you nothing before he died? Left you to take over in ignorance did he? Erland is a true son of his father, that's why. King Boyden was no friend to Sawai, despite marrying Isabeau at the end of his life. He only did so to protect Erland until he could ascend the throne. All knew it back then, but when Isabeau fell pregnant so quickly, and Princess Caitlin was born, it became convenient to forget the reasons for the marriage."

"She's been a good regent," Douglas protested, but his mood was darkening. Boyden had died of the wasting sickness. He'd known long before his demise that he was dying. His marriage to Isabeau was, as Wallace said, a political one. "She's kept the peace."

"She has, and you won't hear me criticise her, not for doing what she was forced to do. Her brother gave her no choice. She wasn't free back then, and she isn't now, don't think otherwise."

"Are you saying she's part of this? That she knows about Karel, about guns, about the Sawai mercenaries infesting the capital. She knows her son is to be assassinated?"

"Not her son. Erland."

"But—"

"*Oh all right!* Stepson then," Wallace said testily. "She may hold affection for Erland. I have no insights into her feelings for the boy, but mark my words, she does love her daughter."

"I don't doubt it."

"Nor should you. Sawai was granted favoured trading status when Boyden married Isabeau, and she has maintained that status as Erland's regent since, but that time is ending. If you were her brother, would you not want to extend things? Why not another ten years or longer? Why not forever?"

Douglas frowned. "If Erland dies..."

"Exactly. Isabeau becomes regent for her daughter. In ten years, Caitlin ascends the throne and marries. Isabeau will teach her daughter to favour Sawai, and the emperor will no doubt choose whom Caitlin is to marry. In ten years we could very well have a Sawainese king on the throne of Inari."

He recoiled at the thought. He spun on his heel, thinking furiously, but then he stopped. What was he doing? Since when had he ever believed a thing Wallace said? He came to Hardenburg knowing beyond question, that the man had turned traitor. He had witnessed his army and vassals on the border by the Goddess! He spun angrily back to confront Wallace.

"Nice try, but I've seen your forces gathered on Dun'Harden's border ready to attack."

Wallace snorted. "We assembled to defend the border against Isten, not attack Harden. Isten and Sawai are in league with each other. Didn't you wonder why my vassals were so willing to follow me? Didn't you consider their reasoning at all?"

"Of course I did!" he snapped, but he hadn't been able to discern their motivations, no matter how hard he'd tried. It had confused him, because he knew his own clan would have refused to obey him. "Convenient to blame Isten, when all know of the bad blood between you," he said, but even he didn't believe what he was saying, as the magnitude of his error sank in. Karel had played him for a fool; how he must be laughing.

"Convenient? I suppose, but true nonetheless."

"So you say."

"Very well. Why then, if I raised my forces to attack Dun'Harden, have I not done so? Its been months. Surely by this time, my evil plan would have come to fruition."

Douglas flushed at the sarcasm. "You're a prisoner. You've been out of contact—"

"You're not such a fool!" Wallace snapped, his eyes flashing. "Stop acting like it. My vassals don't need me to hold their hands, just as yours don't need you. They are their own men. Besides, my brothers are in command while I'm absent."

He located a spindle-backed chair and moved it closer. He sat with his elbows on knees, and his face in his hands, trying to think it through. He was responsible for high and low justice in Dun'Morgan. His father and tutors had trained his mind to evaluate what he heard, and separate truth from fiction. He would apply his lessons here, and ignore the source of the information for the moment.

"Tell me about Isten," he began. "Why would Conner be party to regicide?"

"My fault probably. Our feud has become a bitter thing. These last few years we've raided and counter raided each other constantly. He would slight me, I would respond, he would raid one of my villages, I would raid one of his. Each escalation predictable and within reason. My father and his were no different, and our grandfathers too. Traditionally, we would both step back before raising our vassals, and keep it between our own houses."

Douglas heard the defensiveness creeping into Wallace's words clearly. "But something changed. What did you do?"

"You don't know what it's like living so near the Vale. Uncanny damn place. All kinds of strange things wander out of it, but it's the tinkers and traders that cause us the most grief. They're always trying to smuggle things in through the Vale, and out to Sawai through it. Isten and I, when not feuding between ourselves, spend most of our time trying to stop them."

"And?"

"And Isten started turning a blind eye. He tried to keep the bribes quiet, but it didn't take long for the rumours to leak out. I saw my opportunity to hurt him, and took what I knew to the queen. She sided with me and imposed a levy on Isten trade. It was a good judgement—Conner had been avoiding tax, and he hadn't been paying his dues to the crown. The queen was right to impose the levy, but I think that was the moment of decision for him. He allied himself with the empire. My guess is that the emperor promised him my head, probably in exchange for his support of Isabeau as regent for her daughter."

"We can't let that happen."

"How do you propose we stop it? We're prisoners in case you hadn't noticed."

"You haven't tried to escape?"

Wallace shrugged. "I've tried, but I'm no rune speaker. Karel warded the windows and door. A servant brings food to me in here, but there are always two guards with him. They all carry the hand cannons you saw."

"Guns. They're called guns or pistols."

Wallace glared. "What difference does that make?"

"None at all, I was just saying."

"The servants take the chamber pot out each morning, and supply wash water and towels, but I haven't shaved in weeks. I tried to use the razor they supplied on one of the guards. They took it off me. When I tried the same thing with a butter knife, they took that too. I have to eat with my fingers like a damn peasant now. I suppose I'm lucky they bother to feed me at all, but as I said, they need a live donor for the blood magic Karel uses."

He nodded uneasily, remembering the vial of blood Karel had taken from him before locking him in here. He rubbed his arm where the bandage remained hidden beneath his shirt. He needed to get that blood back. Doppelganger spells were far from the only spells that used blood. Although Karel could commit any sort of crime while wearing his visage, such illusions were benign. They did the blood donor no actual harm. Other spells weren't so friendly. With his blood to use, Karel could hex him from a great distance. He had to get that blood back, and see it destroyed.

"There are two of us now. We can overpower the guards."

"We can try," Wallace said, but he didn't sound very enthusiastic. "We have to try, I suppose."

"We have to do more than try. Erland's life depends upon us escaping this trap. Any ideas?"

"Dawn is the best time. Karel always leaves the house early. We don't have any chance of escape with him still here."

"Two guards you said?"

"One servant and two guards. There might be two of each now that you're here."

"Or even more."

"Or more," Wallace agreed grimly. "We'll just have to see."

They had no choice. They just had to hope that with Karel gone, an opportunity to escape would arise.

Douglas stood and went to investigate the rest of the suite. There was a single bedchamber containing a canopy bed and various bits of furniture. None of it interested him. He re-entered the sitting room and frowned at Wallace. He hadn't moved. He was still slumped in his chair, legs crossed at the ankles and straight out before him. If he slid any lower in his seat, he would be lying down.

He turned away and opened the last door only to discover an empty room. It was the wardrobe. The shelves and empty rack for clothes mocked him with their uselessness. He slapped the door closed impatiently, and Wallace snorted without looking up.

He flushed at the contempt he imagined decorated Wallace's face. What had he expected to find? A weapon's rack with swords and armour ready to don? He wandered back into the bedchamber to rest. There was little else to do. He lay upon the bed and thought about Alex. Where was she now and doing what? He imagined her safe beside Henry, aboard a ship.

He glanced at the windows. The weather was fine and looked set to remain so. The Guild would be pleased about that. They didn't like performing sky fire displays in the rain, but they didn't like using weather magic to avoid it either. It was expensive for them, because small interventions like preventing rain over the city could cause flooding somewhere else. To prevent that, the Guild would have to monitor and tinker with air currents and other arcane things, until nature returned to balance.

A lot of things could be unbalanced by small events that later took huge efforts and time to correct. Wallace's eagerness to seek the queen's aid, had led to Conner's decision to ally with Sawai, which in turn had led to a plot to assassinate Erland. That alliance had led to Theon's death in a roundabout way, which in turn had led to his brief exile on Alex's world, and finally to his captivity here. All of it was due to one man's vindictiveness.

Wallace's hatred of all things Isten might yet bring down the entire kingdom, or at the very least, lead it into a protracted war with Sawai. All of King Boyden's careful political plotting and manoeuvring, could be undone with the single pull of a trigger.

By the Lady, he had to get out of here and stop it!

He sighed and turned on his side. He wasn't tired and it was too early to sleep, but he wished for it. It would speed the time. He wanted the day to flee and the night along with it, so that he might try to escape come the morn. Wallace was right; they needed Karel out of the house before they tried. The morning couldn't come fast enough.

He closed his eyes hoping for sleep, but instead of dreams, he found Alex waiting for him, looking as she had back at the Dog and Whistle. She wore the clothes he'd bought for her, and her hair was unbound. Tumbled upon her shoulders that way, and from a distance, it made her look younger than her years. Alex was no untried girl though. She was a woman grown, and one of the Goddess' chosen—a bonded Daughter of the Mother.

He groaned as he tried not to think about that. It made her utterly unattainable. No man had a right to think of her the way he was thinking right now. He had no right! No right to imagine her wearing the outlandish and extremely tight fitting jeans she'd worn the night they'd met, or remember the tiny miniskirt she'd been wearing when Karel dragged her through the rune gate, or the pale perfection of her bare legs.

Lady help him, she was too damn beautiful to force out of his thoughts! What was he going to do? Chosen never married, and besides, he had responsibilities here. He couldn't follow her home. This was his world, not the other, and he wouldn't abandon his children to Edmund's care, no matter how much they loved their uncle. *He* was their father, not Edmund. He rolled onto his other side, wishing for something that could never be. Alex was not his, and could never be his.

He forced her out of his head by thinking about Anna, his lost love, his beloved wife. He concentrated upon her, wishing himself home so that he could stare at her portrait. He did that a lot when alone in their room. He'd kept everything the way she liked it. Her jewellery box on the dresser, her perfumes and powders, her brushes and combs—everything positioned neatly.

On those harrowing days when he felt her loss most keenly, he would touch them, and feel her spirit draw closer to comfort him. She lingered in that room. It wasn't his imagination that let him hear her voice the most clearly there of all places in Skeldon Castle. Her scent, her spirit, her memory and kindness, permeated that room. That was the reason he kept it locked, and didn't allow even the servants to enter. He was certain Anna resided there, watching him, waiting for him to join her.

He groaned and mumbled as sleep took him. In his dreams, Anna smiled, and opened her arms wide to greet him. He laughed joyfully and went to join her.

* * *

24 ~ Escape

The door opened and Douglas tensed, ready for Wallace to move, but he didn't, and no one entered the room. From his hiding place beside the door, he couldn't see what the problem was. Wallace flicked a look toward him, and shook his head minutely, before backing up with his hands raised and out to his sides.

A man wearing the livery of a servant entered, followed by a serving girl. Both carried trays laden with food. A third man entered with a bowl of steaming water and towels hung over one arm. None of them spoke, but went about their duties as if providing for prisoners was nothing out of the ordinary. They had been doing it long enough to become accustomed to it. When they turned to leave, they darted a look at him as if they'd known all along he was there.

He sighed and stepped out from his hiding place to see what had cowed Wallace. He looked around the open door as the servants trooped out, and found four guards with guns drawn and aimed. The man in charge nodded to him without speaking, and pulled the door closed. The lock clicked. He sighed in disappointment, and turned to find that Wallace was already investigating the food. He left his reluctant companion to it, and chose to wash hands and face. Let Wallace use his dirty wash water after he was done.

After washing, he quickly dried himself and took the second tray onto his lap. The food was tasty. Thick meaty sausages, roasted potatoes cooked until crisp at the edges, fried eggs, and a cup of strong tea. The sausages were venison and rabbit, and he devoured it all as if starving. He hadn't eaten anything since his meal at The Swan yesterday. He frowned as he ate, wondering whether Mardus had visited the inn in search of the gold he'd left there. Would the innkeeper prevent him? It didn't matter. He didn't care about the gold or anything he'd left behind, but it would be nice to think well of the innkeeper. If the pudgy man could inconvenience Mardus somehow, perhaps by setting the guard onto him, he would call the gold well spent and let the innkeeper keep it.

Wallace finished first. "That answers one question."

He nodded.

"We'll need a new plan."

Obvious, but true enough. He tried to think of one, but in the end it came down to the guards being ready for tricks. They wouldn't fall for obvious things like staging a fight. He frowned. He didn't think they would. He needed to be subtle. Not one of his strong points.

"We could stage a fight and when they come in to break it up—" Wallace began. Subtle wasn't his strong point either, apparently.

"They'll be ready for something like that."

"If you have a better notion, I'm willing to hear it."

He sipped his tea. "Magic, it will have to be."

"And you have an accomplished rune speaker in your pocket, do you?"

"I know a few tricks."

"We need more than tricks!"

"You had better hope not. Nothing I can do will break

a ward that Karel set. We need something subtle, something simple that the guards won't expect. Where we went wrong last time was having me hide. When they didn't see two of us, they must have guessed what we were trying to do."

Wallace nodded reluctantly. "And your solution?"

"Give them what they expect to see, or rather, we appear to give them what they expect while hiding the reality."

"You can craft such a seeming?"

"I think so. It depends a lot on them seeing what they expect. I can't craft real Guild quality illusions, but maybe I can make them see two captive men in a dimly lit room where they know two men reside."

"So they see the illusion. What is the reality?"

He shrugged. "Me sneaking out the door using a *you-see-me-not* spell."

Wallace shook his head in disbelief. "They'll not fall for that."

"They might."

"They won't, man! Be serious a moment. Would you fall for it?"

"No, but *they* might. They've been trusting Karel's ward to deal with magic issues. You better hope they do fall for it, because I don't have anything else. You?"

Wallace scowled. "You know I haven't."

"Well then, we'll try it. When would be the best time?"

"We've already missed our best chance. The next is when they bring food at noon, or tomorrow morning at breakfast."

"Tonight?"

"No. Karel will be back by then."

He nodded at that. He wouldn't risk magic with Karel on the premises. "The noon meal then, but we'll need to darken the room. That might make them wary, but hopefully not enough that they'll notice me slipping out."

Wallace looked doubtful, and truth to tell, he wasn't

confident either, but they had to try it. He didn't have another plan. They entered the bedchamber together to arrange things. They rolled up spare blankets and stuffed them into the bed to create the shape of someone asleep. Wallace pulled the heavy drapes across the windows to cut the light. Side by side, they studied the scene

"This will never work," Wallace said in disgust. "We need something for a head at least."

Douglas fiddled with the pillows, thumping a depression into one and fussing with its position. He stepped back, trying to imagine his head on that pillow sleeping upon his side—he always did. His eyes would be closed; his slow and even breathing would be shallow. He pictured himself deeply asleep and dreaming pleasant dreams of home and Anna, just as he had last night. He conjured the image, and held it firmly in the forefront of his thoughts. He willed it strongly to be perfect in its details. He saw it clearly in his head, and made it so real, that even he would believe it.

> "In my mind a memory,
> Magic and will align,
> Dream become reality,
> Light and shadow combine."

The air shimmered, and a sleeping figure wavered into being. He swayed, feeling suddenly light-headed from the effort. He was a weak wizard as such things were judged, and spells of this sort without preparation were hard for him at the best of times. Without his *taufr* or any other tools, he was surprised he'd been able to do it at all. Desperation did indeed lend strength in magic. Determination and will were key in spell craft, and there was nothing like desperate need to spur on such things.

"By the Lady, man. You did it!" Wallace said in delight. He thumped Douglas enthusiastically on one shoulder. "We have a chance at last. This could work if they don't try to wake him... *it* I mean."

He nodded. The seeming did look damn good from a distance. Even up close, it looked just like him, but if anyone tried to touch the sleeping Lord Skeldon, the illusion would break. They had to hope that simple courtesy would make the guards look, but not touch. It was all they could hope for.

They left the bedchamber and darkened the sitting room with the drapes across windows again. The room was larger than the bedchamber, and shadows suddenly cloaked the walls and furniture, creating secrets where there'd been none earlier. The middle of the room was dim, but not too dark to make out the armchair that Wallace habitually used to watch the door. That was good. They didn't want to make the guards so wary that they wouldn't allow the servants to enter.

> *"Dragon's breath, chameleon sight,*
> *I command the shrouded sea,*
> *I blend the mist; I mix the light,*
> *To bend all around me."*

He didn't quite wince at the bastardised version of the cantrip he'd learned as a boy. Cobbled together it might be, but he'd only changed a single word and it *did* still rhyme, as it had to do or fail; more importantly, he willed it so. He insisted the change work, and by the lack of focus in Wallace's eyes, it had.

He moved to stand beside the door out of the way. No one should bump into him standing there, and two steps would see him out the door as quick as thought. Wallace's eyes followed the sound of his steps as he moved, and he reminded himself to step quietly come the time.

Wallace sat in the armchair to wait and watch the door.

When the servants returned with fresh trays of food

at noon, a darkened room greeted them, and the guards understandably prevented them from entering. Instead, they sent two of their number forward, guns in hand, to scout the room. Douglas watched them from his hiding place near the door, invisible under his spell and hardly daring to breath. An older man led the search. Sawai didn't use the same titles for its officers and rankers, but it did use similar positions. This man would be the sergeant of the guard, what the empire called a patrol leader.

The sergeant aimed his gun at Wallace, and searched the shadows with his eyes. "Where is he?" he growled.

"He's taking a nap. It's his turn."

"Turn?"

Wallace shrugged. "I got the bed last night."

A lie, but the guards wouldn't know. Wallace had shared the bed with him last night, but the guards hadn't checked on them until this morning, long after they had risen for the day.

"Check," the sergeant said to his companion.

The guard opened the door to the bedchamber and peered into the unlit room. A few moments later, he closed the door very quietly and nodded to his sergeant. Both men holstered their guns and waved the servants in. Douglas sagged, his knees gone suddenly weak. Freedom was within his grasp. By the Lady, it was going to work. Blessed be!

The two young women placed their burdens upon the table, grabbed the breakfast trays, and quickly made their escape from the room. Douglas followed them closely out the door. The guards outside the room stepped aside to allow the servants to pass, and he along with them. He was out!

He was careful to follow the servants closely, but not so close that he risked a collision with them. He kept his movements economical and quiet, and didn't allow himself to hurry. He wanted to sprint out of the house and get to Erland, but one misstep would be the end of his hopes. He forced himself to stay with the girls as they chatted inanely.

Apparently, Wallace was ever so handsome. He rolled his eyes. Lord Wallace made for such a tragic figure, blah, blah. No mention of the handsome and tragic Lord Skeldon he noticed. Well, good looks wasn't something attributed to him by anyone he cared about, unless it happened to be Alex. Most recalled darker things when thinking of him, not his looks. Naming him Red Hand wasn't a compliment.

He followed the girls all the way to the kitchens, and only left them once assured he was away from any guards. All of them seemed to be upstairs or guarding the entrance hall. That made perfect sense to him, and he was grateful for the respite it allowed him. He needed to plan his next move and get outside. That first of all, but it was far from all he needed. He couldn't use the main gate; he needed to scale the wall, but he wasn't sure if he could do that easily or not. When he arrived, he'd been too busy not getting shot to notice the wall. Did it have good finger holds on the inside, or was it smooth? It would be smoothly plastered on the outside to prevent thieves scaling it, and he didn't need to look to know that, but on the inside? It was an aesthetic choice, not one based upon security. He wouldn't find ropes and grapnel lying about for the taking. He better hope it was scalable, or he would be stuck.

He ducked into the pantry the first chance he had, and used it to watch the goings on. The staff were busy and unaware of him. They had a lot of mouths to feed, and that took preparation. Manor houses like this one were never still. There was always something that needed doing. His own house in the capital was smaller than this, but even so, he knew Bryan—its overseer—would be busily keeping things just so. He prided himself on always being ready to serve his lord, and he imparted that sense of duty to those under his authority. He wondered who the overseer here was, and looked for him or her, but the bustle gave him no clues.

He watched for an opportunity, and the moment it arrived, he took it. The cook ordered one of her girls to take the peelings and other food waste outside. There would be a compost heap in the gardens somewhere waiting for it. The grounds-keeper would have insisted upon support from the kitchen, just as the cook would have insisted the garden supply her with a few hard to obtain herbs. The young woman headed for the exit carrying a bucket in each hand. Douglas tagged along, and slipped outside right behind her.

He peeled away from the path she followed as soon as he could, and ducked behind a tree to get his bearings. He was outside but not free. He decided upon a direction based upon his scant knowledge of the house, and headed away from where he hoped the front entrance lay. If unlucky, he would find himself meeting the guards stationed there, but he had a good sense of direction. He soon found himself alone in a quiet part of the garden at the back of the house, well removed from any observers.

The wall was smoothly plastered and sheer.

He cursed his luck and followed the barrier hoping for something like a sally port. Although more suited to a castle, such things weren't unheard of in places like this. Nobles were all paranoid, and a secret way out wasn't beyond expectation. A hidden gate, barred on the inside of course, would be just the thing. His own house in Hardenburg had one; this place probably did too. He should have asked Wallace about it.

"Here now! What are you doing sneaking about?"

He froze, pretending to be a hole in the air.

"I asked you a question."

Cursing under his breath, he turned to find the gardener staring right at him. He was silver haired and bearded, carrying one of the tools of his trade. He held the rake casually in one hand, but Douglas eyed it warily. It could become a quarterstaff in a heartbeat, and the man looked the type who might know how to use one. As if divining the thought, the gardener took the rake up in both hands and held it cross body. A classic defensive posture for any staff wielder.

"I err…"

"You're one of the prisoners," the gardener said and lowered his weapon, eyes darting furiously around. He grabbed Douglas' arm and hurried him away. "Damn fool. You'll get old Fergus killed, see if you don't. This way. Hurry! Do you think you're out for a stroll, my lord? Well you ain't!"

"I don't, I mean… what?" He felt off balance. Fergus shouldn't have seen through the spell. "You have magic?"

"Figured that out, did you?"

He nodded.

"I'm a green man," Fergus said. "This is my *place.*"

A green man. The term was ancient and meant he was a wizard, but one tied to the land. The way he emphasised *place*, meant his place of power was here in the garden, or maybe he meant Hardenburg. The point though, was that his magic was limited to a location. Green men couldn't leave their place. If they did, their power would fade.

"Where do you take me, and why help?"

"You want to leave don't you?"

"Yes but—"

"Then leave," Fergus said and shoved him through the wall!

Douglas stumbled backwards, waving his arms for balance, and found himself in the street facing a white-plastered wall. He reached out and found it solid. That hadn't been a small use of magic. If Fergus could transpose solid brick into nothing and back again, he was no mere hedge wizard! Magic of that calibre was Guild level.

"You still here?" Fergus said, thrusting his head and shoulders through the wall.

Douglas gasped in surprise.

"I thought you had places to be, my lord?"

"I do, but—"

"Best be off then, don't you think? If you see Lloyd, tell him I still think he's making a poor choice."

"But—"

Fergus withdrew and the wall solidified.

Douglas looked hurriedly around, and walked away, thinking furiously. It didn't have any relevance to his mission at the palace as far as he could see, but a green man taking the time to befriend Lloyd was intriguing. He would pass on the message given the chance... after he beat Lloyd bloody for betraying Alex first. He wouldn't kill him now though. Probably. Fergus seemed to hold Lloyd in some esteem. The affection in his voice had been unmistakable. How Lloyd had befriended a green man so quickly would be a tale worth hearing. Perhaps they would all live long enough to hear it.

He headed directly for the palace, intending to spill his guts to the first person he saw with the authority to get him an audience with the prince. Erland was his first choice, because despite his wish to trust in the regent, Wallace had managed to seed doubts in his mind regarding her. He didn't believe Isabeau would sanction harm to Erland; truly, he didn't, but he couldn't risk it. He had no right to risk it. He would lay out all he knew, all that Wallace suspected, and let the prince decide whether to tell his mother. Erland would be king within the month. All would abide by his decisions this close to the coronation, or risk his displeasure when he ascended the throne.

It was a long walk, and his feet were aching by the time the palace came into sight. It had taken more than an hour, and it worried him. What was happening back at the house? Hopefully nothing. With luck, the guards would stay out of the room, and wouldn't learn of his escape until tonight.

Luck.

He wasn't comfortable trusting in it. His luck had been bad all year, beginning with Theon's death, and ending with his capture yesterday by Mardus; luck or no, there was nothing he could do to affect matters back at the house. Enlisting Erland's aid to rescue Wallace was all he had.

He reached Crown Plaza, and breathed a sigh of relief. With growing confidence, he braved the busy space, ignoring the beauty surrounding him. He'd loved this place as a boy. The magical fountains had always fascinated him, and the towering statues awed him. His father had spun tall tales about them, spinning stories of how the men and women became heroes, and how the Guild had immortalised them in stone. His father would point to each statue, and ask him to name them and their deeds. A test of his knowledge and attention.

He smiled as he remembered that.

"Stop there my lord, or you're a dead man," Karel said from behind him.

He stopped, and his smile drained away. He was less than an arrow's flight from the palace. He could shout, and be heard by the palace guards stationed at the gate. He could. He could shout. They would come... he took another step.

"Last warning. You'll die, and I'll walk casually away. No one will notice what happened for quite a while. The rune I have in mind is an interesting way to kill," Karel said cheerfully, as if discussing the weather. "Petrification. Being turned to stone hurts a great deal, but I'll wrap you in silence as I cast it. No one will hear your screams."

Douglas didn't doubt Karel would enjoy using such an evil spell. "I'll kill you one day. Do your worst and be damned!"

Karel laughed. "I've a feeling the Goddess chose my destiny long ago. Your threats mean nothing to me. Turn and head back the way you came."

He wanted to scream in frustration, but he obeyed, thinking furiously of ways to get the drop on Karel. Where life remained, there was hope. He would find a way to escape again, and make him pay. He would do it or die in the attempt.

* * *

25 ~ Trials

The door opened and Liz slipped out of the cabin. Alex's heart sank. The girl looked pale and shocked. She must have failed her testing. The Reverend Mother had surprised everyone when she announced the trials. The plan had been to wait until they reached the chapterhouse at Stonybrook.

Rhiannon ruled her people like a queen, and didn't need to explain herself to anyone. She certainly hadn't explained the decision to the novices. Alex didn't really consider herself a novice—she was much older than the other students—but Rhiannon and the other witches *did* consider her that way. They had made it quite clear that she was under their authority, Sandy too, and that both of them *would* submit to training and testing. She hadn't objected to that. She wanted to learn, and Shieri was insistent about it as well. The cat was very vain, like all cats; she wanted *her* chosen properly ringed and respected by the sisters.

"Are you okay?" she asked, and Liz nodded shakily. "Which one did you fail?"

"I didn't." Liz raised her left hand. She was wearing all three of her mother's rings.

"Lady bless, congratulations!" She hugged the girl. "But

why do you look so shocked?"

"Aunt Rhi says she wants me to test for water and spirit come the full moon! That's... that's..."

"A lot of work."

"I'll never be ready in time!" Liz wailed.

Alex laughed, and received an indignant glare. "Look at your rings, and tell me you can't do it. You didn't think you could pass those three this morning. Of course you can do it!"

Liz admired her rings and smiled. "You're right."

"Of course I am."

The cabin door opened and Miriam peered out. "Next candidate."

"I guess that's me."

"Good luck," Liz whispered. "I know you can do it."

It was good that someone did.

Alex took a deep breath, and went to join Miriam as she stepped back into Rhiannon's cabin. Shieri paced her, and together they entered the Reverend Mother's presence. She didn't try to curtsy; it made her feel stupid. She offered a bob of the head as her show of respect, and wasn't reprimanded for it.

Miriam took her seat on Rhiannon's right, playing the part of the Maiden. Sister Ehlana, the third judge, was the oldest of the three. She was the Hag's avatar. Rhiannon of course was the Mother, sitting upon the throne in the centre. They weren't really thrones, but the notion appealed. The three certainly sat upon them as if they were.

Alex offered her little bow to their chosen where they watched the room from their perch. The three owls stared at her intently, but they didn't acknowledge her. Shieri sat, and leaned gently against her right leg in a show of support.

"You are well, child?" Rhiannon asked.

Child? She suppressed her snort of laughter. Rhiannon was a match for her in age, but she was playing her part as everyone expected of her. She always called the sisters, child, even those old enough to be her grandmother. It was part of being the Reverend Mother.

"Yes, thank you, Mother," she responded dutifully. Liz had taught her what to expect and say.

"Your studies have progressed? You have been prepared for this trial?"

"Elizabet has taught me well, Mother."

"We shall see. Name the disciplines you wish to demonstrate for us."

"Fire, spirit, and web mistress, Mother."

Ehlana and Miriam both drew shocked breaths, but Rhiannon's reaction was more controlled. Her eyes widened a little, but that was all.

"Ambitious of you," Rhiannon said. "Are you certain, child? There's no shame in withdrawing."

To Alex, the web mistress trial—considered the highest rank by the sisters—was the least worrying. She came to Inari already well practised at using that particular talent. She was more than proficient; too much so in some ways. She hadn't been able to turn her magic off before bonding with Shieri.

"I'm sure, Mother."

"Very well. You may begin."

She approached the table standing to one side of the cabin, and surveyed all the paraphernalia laid out for her use. The candles, bowls of water and incense, the athame... everything she might want or need were all there, spread upon the white linen tablecloth. She chose the nearest candle, a white one, and placed it in the empty holder. The holder was silver, shiny and pretty, but simple in form—its only decoration some engraving encircling the spherical base. Roses and vines, she thought it was meant to represent.

She concentrated upon the candle, and tried to remember that if she failed, it wouldn't be the end of the world. So what if she didn't win her stupid rings? She didn't need them to feel good about herself, and besides, there was plenty of time. It wasn't as if there was much else to do but practise while aboard ship. Liz would probably be the most upset if she failed. As her teacher and still a student herself, she had more to lose. She was determined to do her best and not to let the girl down.

She reached for her magic through her bond with Shieri, and concentrated upon the charm's words. The cat looked up at her, feeling magic flow between them, but she didn't comment. She wouldn't risk the distraction.

"Is something wrong?" Rhiannon whispered. "She doesn't seem ready."

"I don't know, Mother," Ehlana said. "I must say that I'm not comfortable with giving anyone a special dispensation this way. It sets a bad precedent. She's hardly had time to learn how to be a novice, and already we propose to raise her to the sisterhood."

"True, but she came to us late. She's hardly a child. Why, she must be nearly thirty if she's a day. Waiting the customary year seems cruel for someone of her advanced years."

Bitch!

So okay, it *was* true that she was older than the other students, but she was hardly old. Rhiannon was about the same age as she was. She forced her thoughts back to the trials. She had to concentrate! She wouldn't let these sour old women question Liz's teaching. She focused her intent upon lighting the candle, and chanted the words in a carefully modulated tempo.

> *"Salamander's blood and parchment burn*
> *Bring the thing for which I yearn*
> *O sacred, powerful, element fire*
> *I beg thee now, grant my desire"*

The candle's wick took light, and she sighed in relief,

making the flame flicker and dance. She grinned at Shieri, sensing the cat's love and approval through the bond. She returned the feeling. After all her worry, lighting the candle had been no harder than it had been in her cabin. Liz would be proud.

"What say you? Does she satisfy the requirement?"

"Yes, Mother," Miriam said grudgingly. "She has mastered fire."

Rhiannon nodded. "Proceed with the next trial."

Spirit. There were various things she could do with spirit, but compelling the Reverend Mother to cluck like a chicken or bark like a dog, though funny as heck to contemplate, wouldn't get her a pass mark. She was pretty sure it would get her something she wouldn't like. Something painful probably.

She chose the obvious test of scrying.

If her element had been fire, she would have used a flame or hot coals. There was a brazier on the table for that. Had her element been water, a water-filled bowl would have done. Liz's element was earth, and she used crystals. She had a bona fide crystal ball and everything! It had made her laugh the first time Liz had shown her the thing, but once she demonstrated its use, she hadn't laughed. Watching Tomas at his sword practice within the crystal's depths had cured her of any hilarity. Crystals were powerful tools in skilled hands.

Scrying with air or spirit used mirrors. Although spirit was considered elemental magic, it wasn't truly one of the elements at all. It was Aether—the source of life—and different from the elements in that she could use anything she wanted to scry with it. She had practised with Liz's crystal ball, and with mirrors, and even bowls of water. She could use anything really, but she preferred a mirror. Liz thought that air would be her second strongest talent because of that preference, but Alex wasn't so sure. She'd found air hard to work with, and had decided against testing for it or earth today. Earth was often a woman's strongest talent, and used for healing, but she was different. She was so bad at it, that she couldn't heal a paper cut! It was her weakest element.

She made a space on the table, and propped the mirror against the largest bowl of water so that the judges could see it. It was a rectangular mirror with a gilded wooden frame, about twelve inches wide and double that high. It was certainly big enough to give a good show to Rhiannon, but what should she show her? She would like to find Douglas, but she didn't want to risk failure. He had magic and could use it to block her. He'd done it back home to stop Karel finding them. She frowned for a moment in thought, and then decided to play it safe. She would try for Tomas.

She focused upon the mirror with an image of Tomas firmly in mind. Concentration with any magic was important, but especially so with scrying. If she'd been using her web magic to find Tomas, she would've seen him in her mind's eye. Quickly too, because although she hadn't known the name of it before coming to Inari, she'd used web magic often at home. Making an image appear in a mirror was an extra step, sort of tacked on to what she normally did. Despite Liz's lessons, she still didn't really understand why scrying was considered a spirit talent, and not simply web magic. They both used spirit.

With the image of Tomas firmly fixed in her mind, she pulled magic through her bond with Shieri, and sank it into the mirror's surface. The glass shimmered and swam as if turned to water.

"Mirror mirror reveal to me,
what I wish with honesty.
Search within and you will see,
upon my mind a memory."

The mirror responded perfectly. One moment the surface

of the glass shimmered with ripples like the water of a pond responding to a breeze, the next, a picture had replaced it. It was as clear as the best modern television could produce back home—clearer even. She had touched the surface of an active scrying mirror before, so she knew that no matter how much it looked like a portal, it wasn't actually a window into another place. The glass was still there, and would be icy cold to the touch, but it was only a picture. Scrying captured reality like a video camera, and played it on the surface of the mirror.

She watched Tomas practising his sword drill, while Captain Arlen gave a critique on posture and stance. The voices of the other men nearby came through quite clearly. She pulled her attention away from the mirror, careful not to release the magic flowing into it from her bond with Shieri, and found Rhiannon's eyes. The woman studied the image thoughtfully. Ehlana and Miriam seemed more interested in Shieri where she sat watching them in return.

"They use their magic to test me, to see if we are tired or struggling to keep the mirror awake," Shieri said with disdain heavy in her emotions and voice. **"As if a mere trick like this could tire me. Am I not Shieriraneth? Am I not Chosen? Am I not the largest, the fastest, the strongest and most beautiful of my generation?"**

Alex barely held back a snort. *"Are you not the vainest cat in existence?"*

"Your scrying is very clear," Rhiannon said, sounding as if she begrudged the praise. "But then it should be. You didn't range very far afield."

"I only know a few places, Mother. I can show you the Dog and Whistle at Ilsehaven if you like."

"That won't be necessary." Rhiannon turned to the other judges. "Well?"

"They're barely paying attention to it, yet the mirror has maintained a strong image," Ehlana commented. She sounded impressed this time.

Alex wondered why. Was scrying meant to be harder than fire magic? It wasn't, not to her, but then her element was spirit. She suddenly wondered what Ehlana's element was. Probably earth; that was common.

Miriam nodded. "If her chosen relaxed any further, she would fall asleep."

Shieri sent her amusement through the bond. **"If they don't get on with it, I will."**

"Don't you dare."

"Then we all agree?"

Miriam and Ehlana nodded.

"You have passed the second trial, Child," Rhiannon announced.

"Thank you, Mother. May I release the mirror?"

"You may."

She released her hold on her magic, and the mirror became just a shiny surface again. Moments later, the glass fogged with moisture from the air, and frost suddenly coated it. That always happened. It would clear in a minute or two.

"Do you still wish to try for your third ring?" Rhiannon said. "There is no shame in withdrawing."

"So you said earlier, Mother, but I want to continue."

"That is unfortunate. Normally you would use the web to travel to one of our chapterhouses, but you do not know any of them."

"And Ilsehaven?"

"Far too easy for this test."

Shieri growled. **"They try to cheat us of a third ring."**

"They wouldn't do that."

"They would. They will. Unless you think of something, we will fail the third test. I do not fail. Do something!"

"I have web walked back home many times, Mother. I mean, I didn't know it was called that, but I've always been able to do it."

Rhiannon frowned. "Always? What does that mean?"

"I was nine when I started having nightmares, visions, and seeing ghosts."

Ehlana shifted at hearing that, and darted a startled look at Miriam. She didn't notice. Her expression held fascination.

"Nine," Rhiannon breathed. "And you were alone? No sisters to support and teach you?"

"Things are different on my world. Magic is less and not understood. Most don't believe in it at all. It's trickery there, just entertainment."

"But you survived, prospered even."

"In a way. I figured out how to keep from hearing people's thoughts. I built a wall around mine, or I imagined a rock and concentrated upon it."

"A man's technique," Miriam muttered scornfully.

"It worked," she said. "Sort of."

"But not well."

"No, not well."

"There are two reasons for that," Rhiannon said. "Elizabet tells me your earth powers are very weak. Barely there even. Whether you knew it or not, you were using earth to shield yourself. The other reason is that brute force is a man's method. They put up barriers against the web, rather than calming and guiding it. Men always prefer force, and I include the ungifted in that, not just the Guild. You have noticed that the web of all life is calm around you and your sisters?"

"Yes, Mother."

"But it was not always so. Correct?"

"I was overwhelmed when I arrived here. Lord Skeldon made a ward stone pendent for me. It cut me off from the web so that I could ride."

Ehlana hissed angrily. "Only criminals are cut off from

their magic so cruelly."

"He did put one on Karel as well. It wasn't pleasant, but it was necessary. Before he made it, the web kept distracting me. I spent an entire day web walking, and didn't realise what had happened until we stopped to make camp."

Rhiannon's look sharpened. "You walked the web while riding? No preparation, and for the entire day?"

"Yes, Mother. Walking the web is easy for me. Anything that uses spirit is. I spend more of my time and effort trying not to do it accidentally, than I ever need when doing it on purpose. I never need charms or rituals."

Rhiannon nodded thoughtfully. "Those of us called by the Goddess are blessed with chosen to help us when we venture into the world alone. That is why you no longer needed the ward stone after your bonding. Those not so blessed have their sisters living with them. Together we calm and guide the web; we do not wall ourselves away from it as men do. There's no need."

That made sense. Douglas had mentioned that the sisters used different methods for doing things, and had shrugged the matter away as completely normal. To him, woman's secrets were not for men, and he accepted that as a fundamental truth. He wasn't even curious about the possible differences.

Rhiannon discussed the next trial with the others, trying to find a solution to her lack of training and knowledge of the sisterhood. Normally, she would use the web to visit a sister in a far distant chapterhouse, learn something from her, and return. That was out of the question for her. She didn't know anyone not already on *Amelia*... well there was Douglas, but he would be no help here.

Finally, Rhiannon turned her attention back to Alex. "In the throne room within the palace at Hardenburg, there is an item. It is located beside the throne on a pedestal. What is it? Journey there using the web, and learn the answer."

That sounded simple enough, though she'd never seen the city or the palace. She was sure such a place would be obvious. A palace was a palace right? How hard could it be?

She nodded. "Yes, Mother."

* * *

26 ~ The Web

Alex closed her eyes and reached out to the web, letting herself become one with it. It welcomed her joyously, filling her to bursting with love and power. Shieri truly was a gift of the Goddess. She would never have dared surrender to the web like this if not for her bond with the cat. The web took her up and out of her body, allowing her to become part of it. It wasn't spirit walking. She knew the difference after doing that with Douglas, but it was similar. She was truly a part of the web, not using it to power a spell. Shieri was with her as she sped away from *Amelia*. The ghostly form of the great cat kept pace with her. In her mind, Shieri looked even more formidable than she did in life. She wondered what she looked like to her chosen.

She didn't know the way to Hardenburg, but the web did. The land was the web, and the web was the land. Nothing alive was separate from it. To it, the city was a blight upon the land, but not in a malevolent way. It felt the same to it as a mountain would. A nearly barren place, but one with many people living there. It took only a few minutes to find the city, and it was huge! Michael would be so pleased when he saw it.

With the ghost of Shieri by her side, she explored the great capital of Inari. She passed through open plazas with their fountains and statues, admired the clocks and bell towers, and noted the busy inns. She imagined that Douglas was staying in one of them. He probably was, but there were too many of them and not enough time to search for him. Besides, she couldn't talk with him; he wouldn't be able to see her.

She sped through the streets, ignoring the huge mansion houses, and entered a new district. The web wanted her to see something. A park. It wanted her to greet the ancient trees growing there. There were a lot of parks in Hardenburg, each one an oasis amid so much stone. She submitted to the web's insistence, and spent some time in a grove. It was a wellspring of power, strongly connected to the web. She knew that if the city had not been there, a stone circle would have marked and honoured it. She wondered if Rhiannon knew about it. She must. The Guild might not be aware, but no witch with the ability to web walk could have missed it.

Regretfully she left the grove behind, and began searching for the palace. There were many grand buildings, some with plazas and huge statues towering high into the air. Men and women with wise faces or stern expressions, looked down upon the people walking far below, or gazed into the distance over the rooftops and out to sea. Many of the buildings were grand enough to be palaces, but there were two huge structures that she felt most drawn to. One was the Guildhall and one the palace. She was certain. It became obvious which was which as she neared one of them. It was the Guildhall, definitely. The men she saw there were wearing robes similar to the one Karel had worn. Besides, the place hummed with power.

Magic.

She quickly withdrew and entered the other building.

It had been a fortress once, but over time, successive

monarchs had added rooms and wings, slowly converting it over the centuries into the palace it now was. She soon realised that it wasn't just a residence for royalty; it must be the centre of government too. That quickly became obvious as she moved through offices and halls filled with bureaucrats sitting at rows of desks.

She shuddered at the thought of working in such a place, mired within a pile of stone for hours on end, never seeing the sun, writing lists and accounts and Lady knows what upon parchment with quill pens. No computers here, but the lack didn't stop the gargantuan machine that was bureaucracy and government from grinding on, producing laws and reports forever.

She found the throne room after speeding through the palace corridors and halls. There had been no clues for her to follow, and the web had been no help. To it, the palace was just a small hollow mountain. It didn't know or care what a throne might be. She had resorted to dashing about aimlessly, hoping to get lucky. She had sped through room after room looking for something grand enough to be a throne, and finally found it.

The golden chair was on a dais as she had expected, at the far end of a large guarded hall. Stone columns marched through the room supporting the vaulted ceiling, and a guard wearing royal blue uniform and shiny breastplate stood close to each one. The columns pointed the way by framing the dais and throne at the head of the hall.

She willed herself forward and she was there. Shieri circled the throne and the pedestal beside it. The throne was a massive chair, tall-backed as expected, but there the resemblance to Rhiannon's chair ended. It was intricately carved, and gilded. The only concession to comfort was the blue velvet cushion and padded backrest. She doubted its maker had designed it for sitting in comfort. It was a status symbol, as was the dais.

She turned her attention to the short pedestal on the left as she faced the throne. It was a low marble column with a crystal ball the size of a basketball mounted upon it. She frowned at the thing. She could go back now and report, but the globe intrigued her. Was it for scrying? The web tried to help by touching it, and it blazed with light. She jumped in shock, and found herself back at the entrance. Shieri looked up at her, startled, but the cat's surprise was nothing compared to the mayhem she'd caused in the room. The guards were all running toward the throne, shouting about an intruder.

She wasn't interested in their antics. The marble floor had turned into a beautiful three-dimensional map of Inari, complete with mountains rearing up and the ocean. She stepped onto the map and wandered around checking out the cities and towns looking for Dun'Morgan, Doug's home. She found it, but before she could really study it, the map disappeared. She scowled at the guard who had touched the globe and deactivated it.

As quick as thought itself, she left the palace and raced back to her body.

She opened her eyes back in Rhiannon's cabin. She didn't know how long she'd been gone, but it couldn't have been more than a minute or two. Time was always strange when she did this kind of thing; the web had no concept of it passing. That was one reason it was so dangerous. Her bond with Shieri made it safer, but nothing could make it completely safe.

"You are well, child?" Rhiannon said, studying her expression. "You were gone only a few minutes."

She glanced at the clock on the cabinet, but she hadn't checked the time before leaving so couldn't really judge. A minute in Inari wasn't much shorter than a minute back home, but it was different. Othala used a twenty-four hour day, which Michael found significant for some reason. The clock's face was divided into twelve hours just like at home, but Michael had to reset his watch every day around noon because the days were shorter.

"I can never tell how long I've been gone."

"That is normal," Ehlana said. "A web mistress always asks a friend to watch over her for exactly that reason."

"To wake her?"

"To *shield* her, child. Interrupting her magic would end the walk."

She didn't like the sound of that. Wouldn't that have stranded her in Hardenburg? She thought about it, but realised that of course it wouldn't. She hadn't really left *Amelia* after all, and all living things were connected to the web. Interrupting her magic would simply make her lose control of the walk, and the web would snap her back into her body.

"So," Rhiannon said when there were no more comments or questions. "Did you succeed? I will hear your report now."

"There is a crystal globe mounted upon a low marble pedestal next to the throne. It's about this big around." She held her hands apart to indicate the size. "I thought it was just a really big crystal ball for scrying, but when I touched it, a map appeared upon the floor."

"You touched it? That's—" Miriam began.

"Impossible," all three women said together.

"Well, I didn't touch it, that's true. The web did. I think it was trying to be helpful," she admitted, and fidgeted at the looks they were giving her. "*I didn't do it on purpose!* And I think the guards *way* over reacted."

"The guards?" Rhiannon said faintly.

"The web touched the globe and it lit up. The map appeared and the guards all ran to investigate. They thought there was an intruder messing with their stuff I guess. I didn't break anything." She shifted guiltily and couldn't meet their eyes. "*Really*, it's fine! They just turned it off, and I came back here."

They were staring at her.

"It's *fine*, honest!"

Rhiannon pursed her lips and nodded slowly. "Very well. The globe as you guessed is used for scrying. It's very old, a relic from before the War of Power. The Guild created it for the monarchy—well, men I suppose I should say. The Guild was founded in its present form after the war. It was just one of many before that. It allows the queen to scry the kingdom and have her courtiers see it in the form of a map, or her generals in time of war."

"Cool," she said but Rhiannon looked confused. She had said the word in English. "I mean I like the idea. It isn't really like a map then."

"No, it's *exactly* like that."

"No, I mean what it shows is real time. If the queen used it right now, she would see *Amelia* approaching the city. Am I right?"

"Yes. It creates a map of the kingdom seen as if by a bird on the wing."

"I understand."

Rhiannon looked to Ehlana and Miriam enquiringly, and they both nodded. "You have passed your third trial, child."

"Thank you, Mother."

"You may choose three rings and display them from this moment forward. Miriam, the rings if you would?"

Miriam fetched a richly lacquered thin wooden case. She stopped before Alex, and lifted the hinged lid to show her the treasure it contained. There were dozens of rings spread out on the green velvet interior of the case. Silver rings, gold rings, rings with gemstones, and rings without stones of any kind. She didn't know if any of them were spell stones, but she thought not. They felt empty. The wide silver bands attracted her eye and she chose a matched pair. They would look good on her thumbs she decided. They didn't have stones, but they did have nice geometric engraving. She tried them on and they fit.

She needed a ring for the middle finger of her left hand. She frowned at the selection and a ruby ring attracted her. It was red anyway. She assumed the gem was a real ruby. The band was thin this time, but silver again. There were some nice gold ones, but her eyes kept going back to the silver ones and the ruby in particular. She gave in to whim and chose it. She could have a fire charm laid on it like Liz's fire ring, or she could do it herself one day after she'd learned charm magic. She tried it on, knowing she would need to have it resized, but...

"No way! It fits perfectly!"

Miriam closed the case. "Of course it does."

"But—"

"The case helps you choose," Rhiannon said and shrugged as if it wasn't remarkable. "You choose the type and style, the case gives you the right size. It's spirit magic. A simple compulsion."

She nodded but it made her feel icky. She didn't like compulsion magic used on her. Two-faced maybe, definitely two-faced considering how easily she used it on people sometimes.

"In a few days we make port at Hardenburg," Rhiannon said all business again now. "You will accompany me as part of my retinue when I visit the palace and pay my respects to the queen."

"Yes, Mother," she dutifully said, though she did wonder why she was being given such an honour. "May I go?"

Rhiannon nodded.

She gave the three her politest nod, collected Shieri, and got the heck out of there before she did something to ruin Rhiannon's good mood.

* * *

Part V

27 ~ Chapterhouse

Rather than dock at Hardenburg in the night and risk his ship, *Amelia's* captain elected to wait for dawn. He dropped anchor in the harbour, and because etiquette dictated that the Reverend Mother be first to land, the other ships followed his example.

At tide turn the next day, *Amelia* led the way into port and docked. Alex had been ready for hours by then. She hadn't been able to sleep, knowing they'd finally reached their ultimate destination. From the moment they'd arrived through the gate, Douglas had insisted upon reaching Hardenburg. His stories and descriptions hadn't done the city justice. Her previous visit in spirit had given her an appreciation of what she would see, but arriving in person and seeing those huge statues towering over the roofs was different in person.

Sandy drew Michael's attention and pointed to the palace towers. They were obvious and very tall. No one would ever want to spend the time to climb them, but if they did, they would have a marvellous view for miles around.

"What do you think?" Alex said.

Shieri had her chin on the rail, watching the coaches

and horses assembling on the docks. **"Some of them look tasty."**

Alex laughed.

"What does she say?" Sandy asked her.

"Shieri thinks the horses look tasty."

"Hah! I don't think Rhiannon would like walking to the chapterhouse. Better not eat the transportation, Shieri."

"I am not hungry."

"She's not hungry," she repeated for Sandy's benefit. "But I bet if she were, she wouldn't care about making the Reverend Mother hoof it."

Sandy smiled.

"You've been quiet," Alex said, turning to Tomas. He was standing off to one side, with one hand casually on the grip of his gun. He wasn't holding it with the intent to draw or anything. It was just habit. He had his sheathed sword in his left hand as usual. "What's up?"

He shrugged. "Just wondering where we'll be tomorrow, or next week, or next year. We're no closer to getting home than we were our first day here."

"We've ridden or sailed hundreds of miles, maybe thousands since then," she protested.

"Sure, but none of it means anything if we don't find what we need here."

That was true. Getting to the city was arguably the easy part of Tomas' quest. His quest, not hers. She had no interest in leaving. Her personal quest, if she could be said to have a quest, was running down a certain Lord Skeldon and making him admit his feelings for her. She knew he had them. Her magic made it pretty much impossible to hide such things, but making him admit them to himself was another matter; making him act upon them was something else again. She wouldn't settle for anything less. Screw the sisterhood's no marriage rules. She wasn't really one of them anyway.

"Yes you are."

"Tell them that, and besides, I don't care."

"I do, and She does. We are Her Chosen."

"I don't know the Lady's will, Shieri, but I know mine."

"There is no rule to stop you taking a mate."

"But everyone says the sisters don't marry," she protested.

"That might be so, but there is no rule against it. The Goddess loves life and the balance. She would not make such a foolish rule. You should ask Rhiannon if you doubt me."

"It's not that I doubt you, but none of the sisters are married."

"You have met them all?"

"Well... no but—" she broke off, frowning in thought. *"I can't ask Rhiannon."*

"I do not see why you cannot, but you could ask Elizabet instead."

Alex nodded. She would rather do that. She wouldn't obey such a rule if there was one, but she'd at least like to know what the rules were before she broke them.

She turned in time to see Rhiannon come up on deck with Ehlana and Miriam in tow. At their backs, a stream of baggage-laden sailors poured out from below decks, followed by more of the sisters and all of their baggage, carried this time by Arlen's men. She craned her neck to watch as three owls circled the ship a few times before winging away toward the chapterhouse. She assumed that was their destination. They were fast flyers, and they quickly vanished from sight.

Things got a little crazy for the next few minutes as everyone debarked from the ship, and found places in the coaches waiting to receive them. Arlen's men mounted their horses, and readied themselves to escort the sisters. The captain split his force in two, and sandwiched the coaches between each half. Tomas and Michael mounted horses, and became part of the escort accompanying Henry at the head of the column. Alex joined Sandy and Elizabet in Rhiannon's coach; it was the largest, and Shieri needed the extra space. Miriam sniffed snootily, but she did make room for the cat so that she wasn't lying upon their feet.

"Owls are so much more convenient," Ehlana muttered.

"Hmmm," Rhiannon agreed.

"Hey!" Alex protested, feeling a spike of hurt emanate from her chosen. "Shieri is the best chosen anyone could want. She's the fiercest and most loyal cat ever!"

"And the biggest," Miriam said with a chuckle as she tugged her skirts from beneath the supine cat.

"And the most beautiful," she agreed remembering her first days with the cat. She grinned. "She told me so."

Shieri growled, but she was amused now.

Miriam laughed. "Cats think a lot of themselves, don't they?"

The coach pulled away.

"How many chosen are battle cats?" Sandy asked.

"They're rare," Rhiannon said. "I believe we have three, including Shieri."

That surprised Alex until she remembered the crowd's awe when they arrived at Ilsehaven "Does the Goddess usually choose owls?"

"Owls *are* more common," Elizabet said. "But other birds are chosen too. We have wolves, cats of every sort, owls, hawks, falcons."

"All predators," Alex pointed out. "Carnivores."

"Always," Rhiannon agreed.

"Shieri said something about that. She thinks horses are too stupid to be chosen."

"I'm sure the Goddess could choose a horse if She wills, but She hasn't yet."

"I don't think She ever will," Miriam said. "A horse following a sister around the chapterhouse would be a little awkward, and what about accommodations?"

"And stairs," Elizabet added.

Alex smiled, trying to imagine a giant horse following the girl around. All chosen were super-sized. Smokey and Nuisance, her horses back home, had needed a lot of care and exercise. She doubted Elizabet would appreciate the need to muck out her room for example, even if it was on the ground floor of the motherhouse in Dehra.

"If She chooses you, and you bond with a horse, you'll love each other. Believe me," Alex said. The cat looked up at her and their gazes connected. Love flowed between them. "I promise you. You won't care about stairs."

The journey to the chapterhouse was a surprise. No one had mentioned it, but the chapterhouse was miles down the high road leading from the capital. She spent the time gazing out the window at the sights like a tourist as they threaded their way along cobbled streets. The people of Hardenburg fascinated her more than the buildings. They were quaint and all, but she wasn't Michael with his passion for all things architectural.

Arlen, preceded by a pair of banner men displaying the banners of Dun'Moore and the sisterhood, escorted the convoy of coaches to the city gates and through them into the countryside beyond. The land near the city consisted of fields of wheat and corn to feed the people.

She stared out of the window, taking everything in. The breeze blowing from the coast played with the long stalks, and turned the fields into a beautiful golden sea. She watched with delight as waves of grain sped ahead of the coach urged on by the wind.

"There's one for the scrapbook," Sandy whispered.

Alex nodded. A camera wouldn't work here, but Sandy was right. She would never forget this.

The people of Stonybrook Village were out in their hundreds, hoping to catch a glimpse of the Reverend Mother on her way to the chapterhouse. She leaned forward to show herself at the coach's windows, and gave the people a little wave. Alex thought the queenly act was a bit over the top, but the people loved it. They cheered when they saw her, and she smiled at them benignly.

"We're nearly there," Elizabet said. "Stonybrook serves the chapterhouse."

"Serves?" she said. "How do you mean?"

"You know, with food and the goods it needs. Servants too. Any chapterhouse needs a town or village like this one to supply it."

"Only about half the people living in any chapterhouse are sisters," Miriam explained. "The rest are servants, guards, cooks, gardeners... oh, all sorts of people. Their families and friends live in nearby villages like this."

That made sense. The local farms probably sold their harvests to the villagers as well as the chapterhouse, and relied upon them in their turn. The village needed the farms to supply it with food, the farms needed the village to buy their produce, and sell them manufactured goods she bet, and the chapterhouse relied upon both of them for all its needs including workers. She wondered what the sisters supplied in exchange besides money. Healing maybe. Anything requiring magic was within their area of expertise.

They continued on through the village and didn't stop, though she was sure the folk would have been delighted to fete the Reverend Mother. Arlen forged on, determined to discharge his duty and install the sisters safely in the chapterhouse.

"Are we going back to visit your queen today?" Sandy said.

Rhiannon shook her head. "I'll send a herald to announce our arrival, and request an audience for tomorrow. That's soon enough."

"Do you think Douglas will be there?" Alex said. "He must have arrived ages ago."

"A week or two, certainly," Rhiannon said. "Amelia is a slow ship, but not that slow. Lord Skeldon will no doubt be there waiting for us. That's to the good. We can learn what Isabeau has in mind to address his concerns. With the coronation coming, she doesn't have much time left to call Duke Wallace to account."

"You think she will?"

"She should, but if not, Prince Erland will when he ascends the throne. It isn't long to wait, but if the matter can be dealt with before he's crowned, it would be better. Strife with one of his nobles so early in his reign wouldn't be a good omen."

Alex nodded, but she didn't really consider any of that her business. It only interested her in so far as it affected Douglas; his obsession with Wallace needed to end before they could explore a relationship together.

"There it is," Elizabet said, hanging halfway out the window.

"A little decorum if you please," Rhiannon said to her niece, but she was smiling fondly at her back.

Alex joined the girl, ignoring Rhiannon's sigh, and saw her first glimpse of Hardenburg's chapterhouse. It was really the Stonybrook chapterhouse, but Hardenburg was the capital of the entire kingdom. There was prestige in linking them together. It did make her wonder why it wasn't closer to the city, but maybe the chapterhouse came first. The city was on the coast for trade reasons. It was a port city.

The elevation of the highroad gave a wonderful view of things. The early morning sun illuminated the valley as it broke through scudding clouds. It was as if the Lady chose that moment to switch on a huge spotlight, and pin the chapterhouse in place, revealing its buildings and walled grounds cradled by farmlands in all directions. The valley seemed prosperous, and the fields were as bountiful as those they'd seen earlier. The Lady had blessed the land, and the sisters had proven themselves good stewards of her gifts.

The chapterhouse wasn't a single building but many, with high walls surrounding them. She remembered Elizabet describing the motherhouse in Dehra as a big manor house, not a castle. Technically the chapterhouse here wasn't a castle either, but it was as big as one. The walls weren't crenelated, and they didn't have towers or battlements, but they did have a huge portcullis as any respectable castle would have. The walls were light grey in colour, made of dressed stone not brick, ancient and weathered. The buildings were multi-storey with many windows reflecting the sunlight, with dark coloured slate tiles on their roofs.

The column reached the junction connecting the highroad to the chapterhouse, and Captain Arlen escorted the coaches along the adjoining lane toward the entrance. The portcullis was already up allowing him to escort the coaches into the grounds without stopping.

Alex sat back and stroked Shieri thoughtfully. They'd arrived safely, and she could think about the next step. She would accompany Rhiannon to the palace tomorrow, and they would learn that Douglas had things well in hand. As soon as she could, she would corner him, and they would hash things out. She was determined that by the end of the day, they would reach an understanding. Shieri would hold him down if necessary!

* * *

28 ~ Fire

"Now this one," Bevyn said, opening another shallow drawer in the wall of drawers before them. "Is interesting. It's a favourite of mine. Hubert had me study it when I was a novice. It was the first artefact that I deciphered for him. A useful little thing. What do you think of it?"

Lloyd stepped up beside the archivist to study the drawer's contents. There were a number of items laid out neatly within the velvet-lined space, each wildly different to its neighbours. An index card had been pinned neatly next to each one with a code number and description written neatly in black ink. He'd learned what the numbers meant. The first three digits were the aisle number within the huge archive, the next four designated the drawer and its position within the aisle, and the final two were an item's position within the drawer itself. It was a simple but necessary system when many of the items were rune stones, and looked the same as any number of other gems stored here. A sapphire was a sapphire, a ruby a ruby. Without the index, no one would be able to find anything.

Some of the items in the archive were statuettes carved from plain stone; others were made of silver or gold. Some were uncut gems or crystals formed into spheres. Their forms were an aesthetic choice, not one based upon necessity, and didn't affect function as long as the runes used were perfect in theirs. Imperfectly formed runes were extremely unpredictable and dangerous.

"May I?" he asked, and Bevyn nodded. He picked up the statuette and studied it. It was heavier than it looked and seemed to squirm in his hand. Startled, he nearly dropped it. "What the hell?"

Bevyn laughed. "Interesting isn't it?"

"That's one word for it," he muttered, peering at it closely.

The statuette was of a woman wearing a flowing dress, and holding a bowl in both hands above her head. It was made of gold, or a gold coloured metal at least. It could be an alloy he supposed, but he doubted it. It was very heavy for its size, which was about six inches in length. He frowned at it, trying to get a sense of what it did. He turned it over and studied the runes engraved in its base. He had a feeling it would have something to do with air or water. His eyes narrowed as he noticed the woman's dress also had very faint engraving. Now that he'd noticed, he realised the entire thing was covered in intricate runes. How had he missed that?

"Your opinion?" Bevyn said.

"I've no idea how to make it work, but I think it's used to affect the weather."

"Very good! It took me much longer to realise that. What gave you the insight?"

"I don't know. It just felt right."

Bevyn looked disappointed. "I had a feeling you would say that. You're a natural born rune crafter, Lloyd, but that's not always going to be of benefit to you. You'll still need to learn the how and why of things to advance here. You can't simply rely upon intuition."

He replaced the statuette in its drawer and closed it. "I

want to learn. I've always wanted to know the what, the how, and the why of things."

"You've come to the right place then. The Guild is many things to many people, but to those wearing the robes, it's a place of learning first."

He smiled. "That's why I'm here."

Bevyn returned the smile, and with a wave of his hand, indicated a direction. Lloyd joined him as they navigated the stacks.

Goddess he loved it here. The darkly polished wooden stacks rose high into the shadows beneath the arched ceiling, each containing thousands of drawers and shelves with mysterious contents. The wheeled ladders dared him to climb them, and the brass handles of the drawers made his palms itch to use them. He could spend years delving their secrets, and he would, given his way. If he hadn't met Bevyn and secured his sponsorship, and if he hadn't known that the archive was where he wanted to work, he would have described something just like it given a choice.

"You have the look of a man receiving a gift," Bevyn observed.

"I've been looking for this place my entire life without knowing of its existence."

"Ah?"

"Things on my world are very different. Not better," he hastened to add. "But different. There are many distractions there, and many things I suspect you would call wonders, but the more people own, the more they want. They lose touch with what's truly important."

"People are people no matter their origins. The powerful want more power, the wealthy more money, and those without either one will strive all their lives to gain those things."

"True, but chasing them is a fool's game. I've done that most of my life, but was I ever really happy? No. Wandering the stacks with you each day is the closest to happy I've been in a long time."

"I'm glad. With an attitude like that, you'll fit right in with us. As for rank, I hope you understand that you'll be Master Archivist over my dead body."

He grinned. "Not planning to retire to the country then?"

Bevyn snorted. "Whatever for? I can find quicker ways to expire than being bored to death. All of us, the archivists I mean, love this old place. The gaining of knowledge for its own sake is any archivist's passion, and that's the main reason why we're not artisans. They care more for *the what,* and less for the how and why, you see?"

He nodded. That made perfect sense to him. His lessons with the artisans were interesting and necessary. He wanted to learn everything they could teach him, because incompetence in any area would be painful and unacceptable to him. The Guild was his home now, and he wanted to fit in. Putting his skills and knowledge into practice was important, but not more important than the knowledge itself. The artisans would disagree, and that made Bevyn's point more apt. His temperament and talents definitely leaned in the archivist's direction.

"I've had good report of you," Bevyn went on. "You're doing well with your studies so far."

"I'm happy with progress," he admitted, not wanting to boast of his successes.

When he'd first arrived, he'd worried that his age and origins would work against him, but if anything, they'd actually helped him in a strange way. His classmates were universally ten or more years younger than he was, and because of that, they enjoyed showing him how superior their knowledge was. Kendrick thought they were trying to make him give up, but if so, they would fail. When they tried to rub his nose in his ignorance, he pretended not to notice their condescension. He thanked them for showing him the uses of a rune, or the proper way to craft it, or even how to combine an inscribed rune with one created by voice or gesture. They probably thought he was too stupid to know he was being insulted, but far from making him quit, the impromptu lessons had greatly improved his skills. His greatest gain though was his classmate's reluctant, and yes exasperated more often than not, respect for his tenacity. They hadn't yet realised he was playing them. Hopefully, by the time they did, they would no longer care. He'd noticed one or two had already dropped out of the game. They were neutrals now, if not yet friends.

"Your practical skills have advanced beyond even my expectations," Bevyn said. "But your understanding of how and why certain runes and techniques work is still lacking. It's to be expected when most of your time is spent with our artisans."

He frowned, feeling a little defensive. "You arranged my lessons. You chose my tutors."

"I'm not criticising you, I'm making an observation. You've progressed far faster than Hubert or I assumed you would. We had planned to broaden your curriculum as necessary later this year, but I think we'd do you a disservice if we wait. We've decided to bring things forward."

He felt a tingle of excitement at the news. "Are there enough hours in the day?"

Bevyn smiled. "I suspect you'd find time regardless. Would you not?"

He nodded seriously.

"I thought so. When you're not at lessons or with me, I want you down here working alongside your fellow archivists."

Fellow archivists; he liked the sound of that. "I'd like that."

"You'll work with Emrys. He's the most experienced, and

to be blunt, he's getting on in years. I don't want to lose his knowledge. If I make it a favour to me, he'll teach you."

"Two birds, one stone."

"Precisely. He can be a disagreeable curmudgeon, but I've a hunch you two will get along famously."

"Oh?" he said raising an eyebrow.

Bevyn laughed as he thought of something. "I won't spoil the surprise. I'll arrange things with him today. You currently have afternoons free."

"From lessons," he agreed. "But not free as such. I practise my runes, or I visit with you and Kendrick."

"Well, I'll leave Emrys to decide what he'll require, but I would set aside at least a few afternoons a week for him."

He nodded, and took his leave. Bevyn needed to seek out Emrys and Lloyd wanted a meal before going back to his room. He hadn't stopped to eat before visiting the archive.

The dining hall was always a busy place. The huge kitchens kept it supplied with good quality food and drink during daylight hours, with a formal meal at noon. He'd missed that meal hours ago, but there was always something hot and tasty on offer. It encouraged people to use the hall for more than the midday meal. Anyone who wanted to meet friends without going into the city could do that here, and be assured of free food and drink to facilitate things. So when he entered the hall intent upon grabbing a plate of something filling—he was hoping there might be some of the sausages left—and a tankard of cider, he wasn't surprised by the babble of voices that filled the hall. What did surprise him, was the subject. The Reverend Mother and her witches had arrived.

As he filled a plate with thick sausages, fresh buttered bread, steaming potatoes, and green beans, he listened to all the speculation about Rhiannon's arrival. Apparently, Duke Henry Moore, hundreds of his soldiers, and dozens of witches, had escorted her to the capital. He joined a group of students already seated at one of the long tables and listened to them as he ate.

"Her chosen is a battle cat," Jayden said, and an uncomfortable silence descended.

Lloyd paused in surprise, noting uneasy glances being swapped among his companions. He didn't understand the significance, but he couldn't say so without causing questions that he couldn't answer. A native of Inari probably wouldn't need explanations.

"She came through a rune gate," Jayden added, taking great delight in everyone's attention.

Utter silence fell with that announcement accompanied by disbelieving looks. Lloyd choked on his food and coughed, attracting attention he didn't want. He reached for his tankard to clear his throat, and raised a hand in apology. They responded with scornful looks, but then turned their attention back to Jayden.

Lloyd's thoughts raced along paths to the only conclusion he could reach on so little information. The mention of a gate couldn't be coincidence. The only artefact not under the Guild's control was broken, and that meant the portal this woman had arrived through couldn't be other than the same one he'd used. He didn't know who this woman was, or the significance of a battle cat, but it could only be Sandy or Alex. If he had to guess which it was, he would choose Alex. How she had come to travel with the Reverend Mother, and bond with a familiar he didn't know, but that didn't matter. She was here, in the capital right now, and he hadn't made any progress towards finding a way home for her and the others.

He stared at his plate. He'd lost his appetite.

"It's true!"

"Don't talk rot," Trefor said scornfully. "There hasn't been a stable rune gate in centuries. The last one crashed at the end of the War of Power. Have you ever visited the Vale of Dreams? I have. Those things are dangerous!"

"Wait what?" Lloyd said. "Gates can become unstable?"

Trefor nodded. "The Vale of Dreams was caused by one." He shrugged. "There was a battle, and one side or the other tried to use a gate to retreat through. Or maybe they tried to bring reinforcements through. No one knows for sure, but the gate became unstable, or some fool attacked it with magic, and forced it to crash. It devastated the valley killing everyone nearby, and turned it into the uncanny desert it is today."

"Dangerous indeed," he said and Trefor nodded.

"I swear it's true, may my teeth fall out if I lie!" Jayden said, glaring at Trefor for stealing the attention. Magic swirled around him as the Goddess bound him to the oath. "See?"

His audience whispered among themselves.

Trefor snorted. "Stunts won't convince me. So your source told you she came through a gate, did he swear to it?"

Jayden hesitated.

"I thought not."

Lloyd didn't doubt the story. He didn't need oaths or the Goddess to convince him. He believed. He turned back to eating his meal. Although his appetite for food had fled, he needed a good meal in his belly. Rune crafting took energy, and this news made him want to try something. He believed Alex and the others were here, but he wanted to verify it, and besides, he'd planned to practice anyway.

The group broke up when Jayden and Trefor left. They had lessons to attend. The others wandered away leaving him to finish his food, which he did frowning all the while. He finished eating and hurried up to his room. He locked his door against distractions, and fetched his brazier from its cupboard.

His strongest element, like many in the Guild, was fire, and he found scrying using anything but hot coals or naked flames harder. He could do it after a fashion; his teachers had insisted that he learn how to use other things like bowls of water and mirrors, but he hated how powerless he felt doing it that way. Using anything but fire made him feel weak again, as he used to feel back in the states. He shouldn't think of it that way; everyone had strengths and weaknesses. Besides, even his weakest element was infinitely stronger here. It was just that he'd become used to more.

He used a firestone to light his brazier, and positioned it on the table. He stared into the flames and centred his thoughts on the coals. They were only just beginning to glow a dull red, but fire was fire. The temperature was immaterial. He slowed his breathing, and allowed his thoughts to see the shape of a rune, its lines just so, its geometry perfectly aligned with his need to see far and see true. It appeared deep within the coals, waiting for him to fill it with his will and power...

"Far-iku-*sten!*" he snapped, and magic rushed through him into the rune.

The flames turned blue, and an image appeared perfectly formed in their depths. He forced his attention not to waver, kept the magic flowing smoothly into the rune, and studied the image. It was definitely Alex. She was sitting with Sandy and there was a huge cat asleep at her feet. He stared at it in amazement. So that was a battle cat was it? A giant lynx... it opened its eyes, and turned its head to look at him. It yawned and revealed huge fangs. That was no lynx! It was a flaming sabre-toothed tiger or something! Come to think of it, now that he had time to study it, he could see that it did have faint grey stripes. It really could be one of the fabled prehistoric cats for all he knew. Othala after all, wasn't Earth. If dragons could be real here, and he knew that they were—though they weren't the giant sentient lizard-like creatures of Earth mythology—then sabre-tooth tigers could be too.

He listened to Alex's conversation with Sandy for a few minutes, but they were discussing an upcoming trip to the palace, and he didn't care about that. He wondered where Douglas and the other men were keeping themselves. He would have to meet them at some point. He wasn't looking forward to that. Michael would be particularly hard to apologise to, and he had to tell them about Alison.

He let the rune go. The flames turned a natural yellow orange, and he used the brazier's lid to snuff them. He left the brazier on the table to cool, and poured himself a glass of water. He drank away his thirst and frowned thoughtfully. Alex and Sandy weren't in Hardenburg right now; they were a few miles in land at the chapterhouse near Stonybrook. It made sense, he supposed. Where else would a pair of witches stay except with other witches? Besides, there was the Reverend Mother to consider. She was top witch, and had probably ordered everyone to stay with her.

Thrap-thrap!

He turned to answer his door, expecting to greet Kendrick, but the young man waiting outside with a satchel slung across his chest was unknown to him.

"Yes?" he asked.

"Lloyd Hawkridge?"

"I am, yes."

"A message for you, sir," the man said and offered an envelope.

He took it, and fumbled beneath his robe for a coin.

"No need, sir," the young man said, proudly indicating the messenger guild badge pinned to his chest. He nodded politely, and marched away.

Lloyd closed his door frowning at the envelope. Who was sending him messages, and why? He didn't know anyone outside the Guild. He tore the envelope open and read the note. It consisted of a single sentence; a single *calamitous* sentence, and his breath rushed out as if he'd been punched in the gut. His past deeds were coming back to haunt him. The threefold law was about to bite him on the butt.

"Big time," he mumbled bleakly. He needed to find Kendrick.

* * *

29 ~ Apologies

Lloyd stormed into Kendrick's office in a high state of agitation. He'd just come from his room after scrying Wallace's manor house. Douglas was indeed a prisoner, just as the message said.

"Lloyd!" Kendrick said, pleased to see him. "To what do I owe the pleasure? I can't leave just yet—"

"Read this," he said, thrusting the note into his friend's hand.

Kendrick frowned at the message and read aloud. "Red hand has joined your friend at the end of the hall. F." He looked up in puzzlement. "Who is F?"

"Fergus. A recent acquaintance of mine. He's a green man. Do you know the term?"

Kendrick nodded and frowned at the note. He turned it over, but the other side was blank. "I can see you're upset, but I fail to see why. This means something to you?"

Lloyd grimaced. Without some background, the note didn't mean anything. He had to tell him about Karel for the note to make any sense. He hoped Kendrick and he would still be friends afterwards.

"May I sit?"

"Of course!" Kendrick said and flushed. "Forgive my lack of courtesy. Can I get you anything? Wine perhaps?"

He took a seat, but waved away the offer of wine. "This is hard for me. I need to tell you some things that I've kept back from you. I apologise for that, but I feared to reveal it before now because... well, I was worried it would prevent me entering the Guild."

Kendrick frowned and he sat behind his desk again. "Go on," he said warily.

"I swear on my life and powers, that I've done nothing to bring harm to the Guild," he said, and magic swirled. Kendrick's expression smoothed as the Goddess adjudged him truthful. "I never told you how I came to this world. My friends and I came through a rune gate."

"I had assumed so."

"It wasn't voluntary for some of us. One of us, Alex Yorke, was kidnapped. She's a witch, one of three in our group. The rest of us followed to rescue her." He took a deep breath, and prayed that his friend wouldn't freak out. "There were seven of us. You know Lord Skeldon?"

"Douglas Skeldon?"

He nodded.

"We've never met, but he's well known... ah! He must be the Red Hand in your note. How did he become part of your group?"

"He came to my world with a man named Karel."

Kendrick's jaw dropped.

"Say something," he said, uncomfortable under his friend's suddenly wary and assessing eyes.

"I think you'd better explain, or I'll fetch the Guildmaster, and you can explain yourself to him."

He winced. "You heard my oath. I've done nothing to endanger the Guild. As for Douglas, he witnessed Karel sacrificing someone to open a gate to my world, and tried to intervene. It all went wrong, and he ended up stuck on my world with a broken leg. He met Alex there, and she agreed to help him find Karel and get home. She called her friend, Michael is his name, and he brought the rest of us along to help. Karel is wanted for murder there."

"Here too," Kendrick said. "Many times over. He's wanted for a lot of crimes."

"I know. Anyway, we tracked him down, intending to force him to take Doug home through a gate, but it went wrong. We ended up here, with Karel unconscious and the gate talisman lying shattered."

Kendrick sat up straight. "The talisman is destroyed?"

"I saw it. It lies broken at Dun'Morogh."

"That's excellent news!"

He grimaced, failing to see the bright side.

"Sorry, but you must see how dangerous such a thing was in Karel's hands. The world is a much safer place now."

"Obviously I see that, but don't expect me to celebrate its destruction. It was a way home for my friends. They arrived in Hardenburg this morning. They're staying with the witches at Stonybrook."

"And the message?"

He shrugged. "I met Fergus while staying at a house here in the city. He's the gardener. I don't know him that well, but I trust he wouldn't lie. As you guessed, Red Hand is Douglas. The man at the end of the hall is Duke Wallace. They're both prisoners."

Kendrick stared.

"Say something."

"I don't know *what* to say. We should inform Bevyn and the Guildmaster of this."

"I was hoping you could get me an invitation to visit the Stonybrook chapterhouse. I need to tell my friends that I'm safe, and that Douglas is a prisoner."

"I can try, but Bevyn would be far better. The Reverend Mother is in residence. They won't let just anyone visit while she's there, but Bevyn's rank should get us in. The Guildmaster definitely can."

He hesitated, trying to decide what was best. The Guild was neutral in all disputes, but surely this was a special case. What would the Guildmaster say about it? He didn't know, but Kendrick might.

"Assume for a minute that we tell Bevyn and the Guildmaster. What will they do? Would they raid the house to free Douglas?"

Kendrick blinked. "Certainly not!"

"That's what I thought. The Guild's neutrality is something I learned early on."

"That's a given, but that isn't the reason. It's because we don't have any soldiers, and before you point to the guards that we *do* have, remember they're mercenaries. We would have to re-negotiate the terms of their contracts first."

He frowned. "What do you think I should do then?"

"I think you need to ask Bevyn that. Anything you do reflects upon him don't forget."

He nodded. He didn't want to do anything to hurt Bevyn's position or reputation, but what if he decided not to become involved? At the very least, he had to tell Alex about Douglas so that she could do something. Putting all of the responsibility on her didn't sit well with him, but if Bevyn forbade him from getting involved, what else could he do?

"Let's ask him then," he said. "Will you come?"

"Wouldn't miss it for the world!"

Lloyd summoned a smile, and followed his friend out of the room, but he was worried. He could be borrowing trouble and over thinking things, but he was almost certain that Bevyn would want to consult with the Guildmaster.

They found Bevyn in his study working upon a pet project of his. It was an artefact that he'd been studying for years. He welcomed them and offered wine. Kendrick accepted, but Lloyd was feeling increasingly anxious. He politely refused. When invited, he explained why they were visiting, and Bevyn listened intently. That he'd arrived through a rune gate was no revelation. Like Kendrick, Bevyn had always assumed it, but Karel's name and the breaking of the talisman he'd stolen, *did* garner a reaction.

"Excellent!" Bevyn said fiercely. "That's great news! I must inform the Guildmaster."

"I don't understand," he said. "You don't care that Karel is running around doing only the Goddess knows what?"

"Oh I care. I care more than you can know, but the talisman he stole was incredibly dangerous. You may not realise this, but rune gates aren't limited to portals between worlds. Used correctly, a gate could be opened from anywhere into this very room!"

His thoughts flashed to Trefor in the dining hall, and his story about the unstable gate that crashed in the Vale of Dreams. Trefor said the gate was being used to bring in reinforcements at the time. He hadn't considered what that might mean, but of course, it meant that both ends of the gate had terminated on this world. Nowhere had been safe from Karel with that talisman in his possession. His thoughts flashed to all the treasures held below.

"The archive—"

"Exactly," Bevyn interrupted. "It's warded and has many layers of protection, not all of them are to prevent Karel from stealing the things stored there, but many of them are. They were added after the Guildmaster expelled him, but we've never been able to confirm whether they work or not."

He nodded. That made sense. "Because you don't know whether he's already tried and failed to break in, or whether he just hasn't learned how yet. I understand. The other protections you mentioned are for… what?"

"Containment. The runes worked into the walls protect the rest of the Guild from anything that might go wrong down there. Tinkering with things that we don't know the uses of, is a perilous undertaking. We've been careful and lucky so far. The protections have worked on the rare occasion they've been needed."

"Good to know. Anyway, the talisman we used to get here lies broken at Dun'Morogh. I learned today that my friends have finally arrived. They came with the Reverend Mother."

Bevyn's eyes brightened with interest. "I'd like to meet them."

"And they you, I'm sure. That brings me to why Kendrick and I came to see you. I need your advice."

"That sounds serious."

"Very. A messenger came with this," he said and offered the note.

Bevyn frowned and read it. "Red Hand has joined your friend at the end of the hall. F. Hmmm, Red Hand is obviously Lord Skeldon."

He nodded. "F stands for Fergus. He's a green man and the gardener for the house I was staying in before coming to live here at the Guild. The friend he mentions is Duke Wallace, but he isn't a friend. I barely met him. According to Fergus, Douglas and Wallace are both prisoners." Bevyn stared at him, and he looked away. "I couldn't tell you everything. I'm sorry for that, but if I'd mentioned my connection with Karel..." he sighed.

"I understand why you think it was necessary to hide this at the beginning of our association, but you've been here for more than a month. Surely by this time you know that you can trust me? A simple oath would have put my mind at ease."

"I should have told you."

"You should have. You said that you wanted my advice?"

He nodded. "I need to free Douglas, but Kendrick says the Guild can't help directly. No soldiers, he says."

"That's assuming you need soldiers in the first place. Could we not use magic alone?"

"We?"

"You're Guild now, Lloyd. We help one another. Of course it's we."

He smiled. "Thank you. As for using magic, it's possible, but the guards have guns. They're weapons from my world. I guess you could call them hand cannons."

Bevyn's eyebrows disappeared into his hair. "How interesting. I would like to examine one."

"They can kill at great distances, and very quickly. I'm not sure we can get close enough to use our magic, not quickly enough to stop the guards shooting us."

Bevyn frowned. "Dangerous indeed, especially in the wrong hands. They should be locked in the archive."

"That would be best," he agreed. "I think rushing the house with a lot of soldiers is the only way. I'm not sure if their breastplates will stop the bullets—there are different kinds, and some can go through metal—but they'll be safer than we would be."

"Not necessarily," Kendrick said. "There are shield spells we can use if we have time."

"True," Bevyn said thoughtfully. "We could use magic to protect the soldiers as well. Again, we would need preparation time, but we could enhance their armour with runes easily enough. Wards of that kind were used extensively during the War of Power. They're still taught."

"That would be good, but as you said, the Guild doesn't have any soldiers we can use. Am I right that the Reverend Mother does?"

Bevyn hesitated. "Technically no, but she can call upon Dun'Moore with every expectation of receiving aid no questions asked. The Daughters and Dun'Moore are closely allied."

"None closer," Kendrick added.

Bevyn nodded. "For all intents and purposes, they speak with one voice."

"That was my assumption," Lloyd said. "Can you get me an audience?"

"Probably, but not soon. If you're serious about this, I recommend going direct to Henry Moore. He can bring up the matter with Rhiannon, though I don't see how that's really necessary. The Guild can supply any magic required to enhance his men's armour."

"All right. When can we go?"

"Assuming the Guildmaster approves, within the hour I should think," Bevyn said and Lloyd's stomach sank. Bevyn noticed his sour expression. "We cannot proceed without his approval. This isn't a simple matter of visiting your friends who just happen to be staying at Stonybrook. Henry is Duke Moore, a peer of the realm, and Rhiannon is—in her own mind at least—the equal of the Guildmaster."

"I know, but I'd hoped we could do this quietly. The more people who know something out of the ordinary is happening, the more likely it is for something to go wrong. We have Karel to consider. If he hears even a whisper about a rescue attempt, he's more than capable of killing the prisoners for spite."

"Well then, we'll have to take steps to avoid that, won't we?"

He nodded, and wondered how.

Bevyn stood. "Wait here, I won't be long."

Before he could say a word, Bevyn was out the door, intent upon his errand. Lloyd turned to Kendrick, who stood to pour himself more wine. This time he accepted a glass when Kendrick offered.

"What do you suppose he meant?" he said, and sampled his glass. The wine had a fruity aftertaste. He quite liked it.

Kendrick shrugged. "No idea, but I imagine he's gone to ask the Guildmaster for his approval. We need that before we do anything."

Bevyn returned after a quarter of an hour or so, but he

wasn't alone. Lloyd and Kendrick stood to greet Guildmaster Halvard as he entered.

"So," Halvard began. "Bevyn tells me that you're in need of an invitation to the Stonybrook chapterhouse."

He nodded. "I'd like to speak with Duke Moore, yes."

"And your friends of course."

"That would be good. I need to tell them about Douglas."

"Ah yes, Lord Skeldon is a prisoner you say. And Lord Wallace?"

"Him too."

"Really?" Halvard said sceptically. "That's very strange, because I saw Lord Wallace at the palace not long ago. This morning in fact."

He didn't flinch from the Guildmaster's sharp look. "That would have been Karel, not Wallace. He's using the doppelganger spell quite freely."

Bevyn hissed in disgust. "Blood magic."

"Blood magic is why Wallace and Douglas are still alive. It's my understanding that it requires donors to be living."

"Not all blood magic, but the doppelganger spell does. It uses the laws of magical contagion to create the illusion. You see, what happen is—"

"Not now, Bevyn, if you please," the Guildmaster said testily. "There will be time for lessons later. The point is that some blood magic spells require a sacrifice of blood, while others require the sacrifice *and* a viable link to a living donor. If rescuing the wayward lords hadn't been essential before, it is now. I cannot have Karel visiting the palace, interacting with the queen, the prince, and any lord that takes his fancy whenever he feels like it! He's a renegade and my responsibility even now. He must be revealed and brought to justice."

"I agree," Lloyd said.

"It's lucky that I have to pay my respects to Rhiannon at Stonybrook then, isn't it? The word is already spreading through the hall about my official visit."

Lloyd grinned.

"Should I call for your carriage to be brought around, Guildmaster?" Kendrick asked.

"No need. It's already waiting in the plaza for us. Come along. We can't keep Rhiannon waiting."

They trooped out of the room in the Guildmaster's wake.

* * *

30 ~ Stonybrook

Lloyd was impressed. Not only had the Guildmaster finessed them an interview with Duke Henry Moore, he'd made it seem easy and like a preplanned occasion. No one would guess he'd cobbled the entire thing together at short notice, or the reasons behind it. The trip by coach would have been pleasant under other circumstances, but Lloyd couldn't help brooding upon the reasons it was necessary. He was heading toward another turning point in his life. He could feel it looming.

Looking back, he could identify others he'd navigated. There was Michael's invitation to join a circle as his guest, and that had led to a permanent place in Silver Mist, his coven. Alex Yorke's phone call was another. A week earlier and he would have been out of state on a work related trip, and he wouldn't have been available to accompany Michael. Leaping through the rune gate was utter idiocy and another turning point. Why had he done it? He couldn't explain it even now, but he was thankful. He loved it here. It must have been the hand of the Goddess. That was the only explanation he could think of. The urge to take a chance, to throw the dice and leap into the unknown, had come upon him out of nowhere, and he'd heeded it.

His disastrous decision to betray the others and help Karel escape had come last of all. That was the only one he regretted, for it had led directly to Alison's death and his nightmares. The Goddess would judge him for it one day. Perhaps one day soon. He believed in her, and the rede. He couldn't conceive of a fit punishment for his crime, let alone one that would adhere to the principles enshrined in the three-fold law, but he knew the Goddess could and would. He believed in the power of three; by rights, he should pay with his life three times over for Alison, but that was an absurd impossibility. He didn't know what would happen, but something would, and soon. He could feel another change coming, another turning point in his life loomed just ahead.

He'd imagined the chapterhouse would look something like a nunnery. It would have walled grounds to shut out the world's distractions, and its ancient stones would be dingy moss-covered things, screaming their antiquity. The gardens would be tilled by stern-seeming women—the witches whose home it was—growing their own food as they lived their lives in grim solitude.

Stonybrook's reality was very far from his imaginings.

The grounds were indeed walled, but that was the only thing he got right. When the coach drove through the open and welcoming gates, he saw red-coated soldiers drilling upon the grounds. There *were* extensive gardens, but they weren't for growing vegetables. They were beautiful things with many colourful flowerbeds and trees heavy with fruit. The lawns were lushly green and well kept. He wondered how many people it took to maintain; it must require an army of gardeners like Fergus. He wondered if they used magic to keep it so well.

The thought intrigued him.

The coach pulled up outside the main house, and stopped

to let them out. The building was a large stone manor with many leaded windows and a grey tiled roof. He counted four stories in all, and estimated its population must be in the hundreds. He didn't know how many of them would be witches dwelling at Stonybrook full time. Many living here would be servants, and then there were all the visitors. He was sure the Reverend Mother had brought a large retinue of witches with her, plus the Dun'Moore soldiery accompanying their duke as escort. Perhaps the other buildings he'd seen from the heights, were barracks and servant's quarters. Some were, he was sure, others would be stables and stores. The soldiers must need a lot of horses and equipment. Food as well.

The Guildmaster dismounted from the coach followed by Bevyn and Kendrick. Lloyd climbed out last of all. The others all outranked him, and protocol had to be maintained in front of outsiders. The Guildmaster was an important personage; a visit by him was an extraordinary event, not a casual one. Well aware of all the curious eyes turned their way, he straightened to his full height, determined to make a good impression. Wearing his robe and representing the Guild, he would do nothing to embarrass either himself or his companions on a state visit.

A uniformed man greeted them in the foyer of the house, and ushered them into Henry Moore's presence with no wasted motions or time. The Duke was a solid looking man; obviously a soldier. He wasn't wearing a sword or anything like that, but he had that stiff shoulders-back bearing military men often had. His clothes were very fine, as any noble's clothing should be in this culture, but his coat had a military cut. Unlike his men's uniforms, it was black not Dun'Moore red, and sported silvery grey embroidery. He was wearing calf-length boots and tight trousers that displayed muscled thighs. He must spend a lot of time in the saddle. The style of his clothes suggested he preferred wearing uniform, but his tailor had made allowances for the occasion. The black did suit him. It made his ginger hair and full beard stand out. He'd tied his ponytail with a black ribbon at the nape of his neck. He looked every inch the rich nobleman.

"Warren!" Henry said in delight. "To what do I owe this pleasure? You didn't have to come all the way out here. I could have come to you."

The Guildmaster beamed. "Bored already?"

"Well..."

Both men laughed.

Lloyd looked on in bemused silence. He hadn't known the two were friends. He listened as they enquired about acquaintances they both knew and family, but then the Guildmaster came to the reason they were visiting.

"Henry, may I present Novice Lloyd Hawkridge?"

Henry offered his hand. "Of course! Any friend of yours..." he broke off with a frown. "Lloyd Hawkridge?"

He nodded and shook the offered hand. "That's right."

"You wouldn't happen to know Douglas Skeldon by chance?"

He winced as the handshake turned into a knuckle crusher. "I would, and I'd prefer it if you didn't break my hand until after I've explained myself."

"I vouch for him, Henry."

Henry glanced at his friend and released his grip. "For you, Warren, only for you."

The Guildmaster nodded. "I appreciate that. Can we sit? There's a lot to talk about."

They seated themselves and Lloyd began his story.

He'd spun the tale enough times that he didn't have to think about it. Kendrick and Bevyn had heard an abridged version of it that time at the Broken Arrow, only to hear the entire thing later when he explained himself to the Guildmaster. Despite its familiarity, they listened raptly as if hearing it for the first time. Henry however, wasn't content with listening; he questioned and listened closely to the answers, perhaps comparing them with the information gleaned from Douglas.

Finally, he was done with the tale, leaving Henry frowning and the others waiting upon him. The silence stretched out, threatening to become uncomfortable.

Bevyn broke it. "Might I meet Lloyd's friends do you suppose, your Grace?"

"Call me Henry."

"Henry then. I've heard Lloyd's story three times now, and each retelling makes me more eager to meet them."

Henry nodded and headed for the door. "We need to plan a rescue, and Tomas at least needs to be a part of that," he said over his shoulder. He opened the door and ducked his head out to speak to one of his men before returning to his seat.

"Why only Tomas?" Bevyn asked.

"Michael is more than welcome to come along, but Tomas will prove the more useful I think. You mentioned the guns that Karel's men carry. Tomas has one. It should prove useful."

Lloyd had a sudden thought that made Tomas essential to their planning. "Before leaving the city, Bevyn and Kendrick were speculating about your men's armour. Tomas' gun will be needed to test the theory."

Henry turned to the archivist. "What do you have in mind?"

"Merely some rune craft on their breastplates."

The Guildmaster snorted. "There's nothing mere about it, but I agree it must be done. If Lloyd's guns are as dangerous as he insists, they'll need protection."

"They are," Henry said grimly. "I've had a demonstration. Quick, easy to learn, and deadly accurate."

"Armour won't make them completely safe. Can you work on their helmets too?" Lloyd said, and Bevyn nodded.

"That will help. There's nothing to be done about their arms and legs I suppose?"

"I'm sure I could come up with something, given time to study the problem."

"We don't have that luxury," Henry said as the door opened to reveal Tomas and Michael. "Come on in. Look who came for a visit!"

Lloyd turned just in time to see the fist that clipped him on the jaw. Ow! He ducked the follow up, surprised but glad it was Michael attacking him, and not Tomas. The cop would have put him on the ground with one punch, but even as angry as Michael was, he wasn't a violent person. His attack was half-hearted at best.

"Enough!" Henry roared, and his guards piled into the room. He glared. "Out!"

They went.

He worked his jaw. "No harm done."

Michael growled. "Yet."

"I'm afraid I can't allow you to harm him further," Bevyn said wryly. "It would look bad. I'm his sponsor you see? I can't have him walking the halls with black eyes and bruises."

The Guildmaster snorted in amusement, but Kendrick looked concerned.

Lloyd smiled at his friend to reassure him. He'd noticed that Bevyn had allowed Michael to get a few licks in, but by his body language, he did mean what he'd said. He wouldn't allow further punishment. He wasn't sure he deserved protection.

"Is Alison around here somewhere?" Tomas asked.

No, he definitely didn't deserve it. He'd just taken a deep breathe to explain, when the door opened again and the Reverend Mother swept into the room, followed by a gaggle of women. Sandy and Alex were with them, and the huge cat he'd seen in his brazier. He stared at the ferocious looking beast in fascination. Battle cat was a good name for a giant prehistoric tiger. That's what it was all right. It was a flaming sabre-tooth tiger!

"I just learned that we have visitors," Rhiannon said. "Why am I just learning we have visitors? When the Guildmaster himself visits one of my chapterhouses, I expect to be informed. Especially when I happen to be in residence!"

Henry winced. "Now Rhiannon—"

"Don't now Rhiannon me! I rule here, not you!"

"I know but—"

Rhiannon silenced him with a withering glare. Henry grinned, but she ignored him by turning her attention to her guests. Her eyes swept imperiously over everyone and locked upon the Guildmaster. She inclined her head to him regally, and he responded in kind. Though neither considered the other their equal, they did maintain the appearance in public.

"Welcome to Stonybrook, Guildmaster."

"Thank you, Reverend Mother. You know Bevyn of course but I don't think you've ever met his nephew, Kendrick?"

"Be welcome," Rhiannon said. "And this is the infamous Lloyd Hawkridge I presume?"

He winced. "I am he, Reverend Mother."

"Where is Alison?" Michael asked impatiently. "Why isn't she with you, and what about Karel?"

Rhiannon frowned.

Lloyd hesitated, but there was no escape. "She's dead. Karel killed her that same night. There was nothing I could do. I would have stopped him if I could, Michael. I swear on my life I would have." Magic swirled about him and he stiffened, eyes widening in alarm. He hadn't meant to swear an oath; it had just been an expression! He'd forgotten where he was!

Goddess please, I didn't mean...

"Foolish boy," Bevyn muttered darkly. "Throwing oaths around as if they mean nothing. Will you never learn caution?"

The magic dissipated, leaving him unharmed, and his breath whooshed out. His knees felt suddenly weak. The Lady had looked into his heart and judged him. She had judged him, and hadn't found him wanting... *this time.* Goddess bless him for a fool. Bevyn was right. He needed to learn to keep his mouth shut.

"Karel killed her, but it's your fault," Tomas said coldly. "You untied him. You helped him escape. It's your damn fault!"

"I know," he said sadly.

Michael shook his head pityingly. "Oh, you poor fool. You know what this means, and here of all places."

He nodded. The rule of three would come home to roost one day. He did know it. Tomas looked confused. He didn't have the heart to explain it to him. Alex and Sandy looked horrified. They knew. On this world where the Lady's influence was so great, his punishment would surely be of epic proportions. One day he would pay, but that day wasn't today and he needed to explain about Douglas.

Alex's eyes narrowed suspiciously. "What about, Douglas?"

He winced again and used a mental exercise to block her out of his mind. "He's a prisoner."

Alex paled. "How?" she gasped.

"Where—" Tomas cut in.

"How do you know?" Michael said.

"Silence!" Rhiannon glared at everyone, daring them to interrupt her. Miriam and Ehlana sniffed to declare their disapproval. "I will hear your story from the beginning, if you please, and then I'll hear your news of Lord Skeldon." She turned to Henry. "Your hospitality leaves much to be desired, your Grace."

Henry smiled mockingly. "Would you care to sit, Mother?"

She nodded, ignoring the twinkle in his eye.

"And wine, Mother? Should I fetch refreshments with my own hands, Mother?"

She muttered something under her breath, and Alex laughed quietly.

They found places to sit, and Lloyd spun his tale one final time. Alex listened grimly when he described Alison's death, and Tomas looked furious. He described the journey to the capital, his first brutal lessons in rune craft, and then his arrival at Hardenburg. He described the manor where they'd stayed in detail, explained about Wallace being a prisoner at the end of the hall, and his first meeting with Fergus. He couldn't help the enthusiasm that entered his voice as he described his first meeting with Bevyn, and how he gained his sponsorship.

"And then we came out here," he finished his story and drank his wine. His throat was parched. "We need soldiers to help rescue them. We can deal with Karel's magic, but his men all have modern guns."

"How many and what kind?" Tomas said intently.

"I don't have an exact count, but there must have been at least a couple of dozen men. They all carry swords and daggers, as well as guns like your nine." He nodded to the pistol, a nine-millimetre Model 34, holstered on Tomas' hip.

"Just a Glock each? What about rifles?"

He shook his head. "I never saw any."

"That's something," Tomas muttered. "Seventeen rounds per mag though. That's still a lot of firepower. If we go charging in there, some of us are going to die."

"That's what I intend to prevent," the Guildmaster said, and turned to address Henry. "Bevyn and I will strengthen your men's armour. Perhaps Tomas will demonstrate his weapon and proof our work?"

Tomas nodded "I can do that."

"Let's get to that then," Henry said. "I want Douglas out of danger before nightfall."

"I'm going with you," Alex said abruptly, but when Henry began to protest, she drowned him out. "Don't try. I'll be going with or without you. Better with, don't you think?"

Henry cursed and appealed to Rhiannon.

She smiled tightly. "I could forbid it, but she would ignore me."

"Damn right I would," Alex said hotly. "I'm not one of your girls."

"Yet," Rhiannon muttered, and exchanged a knowing look with Ehlana before bestowing Alex with a stern glare. "Be assured that sister or not, *mine* or not, if I forbid you something, I *can* make it stick. I have over two hundred sisters here. If I decide to prevent you leaving, they'll make it happen for me."

Shieri rumbled a warning.

Rhiannon ignored the cat. "Your chosen will not attack a sister. None of them will do that, no matter the provocation."

Alex's expression turned vague as she asked Shieri about the truth of that. The answer she received didn't please her. "Don't stop me... *please*," she said, in danger of strangling upon the word.

Rhiannon laughed. "Don't try to sound humble. It doesn't suit either of us. Be yourself."

"Okay, I will then. Stop me from helping Douglas, and I'll make you very *very* sorry."

Miriam and Ehlana gasped in outrage, but they were drowned out by the Reverend Mother's laughter. "Much better. I won't stop you, but I will charge Henry's men with your protection. You might have little care for your own life, but I don't think you'll risk their lives so lightly. Will you?"

Alex bit her lip.

"Time is short," Lloyd said, bringing everyone's attention back to him. "We don't know what Karel is doing, or what his plans are. I'd feel more comfortable with the prisoners out of his reach."

"I agree," the Guildmaster said. "We need your men's armour, somewhere to work, and then somewhere for Tomas to test them."

Henry nodded and stood. "Follow me then."

The meeting adjourned.

* * *

31 ~ Rescue

Alex fidgeted and plucked at her skirts, listening intently to the menfolk planning the assault. Shieri prowled the common room, obviously sensing her building frustration, but having no outlet for it except pacing. She stalked between the empty tables, crossed the open space between them and the bar where the disgruntled tavern keeper guarded the taps, and then retraced her path. The soldiers standing around the room watched her with fascination and awe writ large upon their faces. Chosen were not unknown, but bonded battle cats were almost mythological. They were that rare.

Ding... ding... ding... she counted the chimes of the clock and sighed. Eleven already.

The tavern keeper scowled even harder, probably regretting his bargain now. He should have been serving his customers their beer long since. Henry had dropped a heavy purse on his bar as compensation when they first arrived, and weighing it in hand to calculate its worth, he'd accepted it, but he'd obviously miscalculated. She totally sympathised with him. The delay was becoming intolerable.

They'd needed the tavern to conceal themselves while the scouts did their job, but they'd returned ages ago, and here they all were, still here talking! Henry's scouts were Captain Arlen's best men, clothed to blend with other pedestrians wandering Hardenburg's streets. Their disguises must have worked, because all of them had returned safely, and she'd expected things to start happening after they made their reports, but nothing had.

Karel could literally be torturing Douglas right this minute, or killing him, or any number of other things she hated to imagine. Her frustration at Henry's lack of action was about to boil over, and Shieri had picked up on it. The great cat couldn't settle, and insisted upon prowling the room, which made Lloyd and his Guild friends very nervous. Unlike the red-coated soldiers, they were unused to chosen. Men never bonded with familiars as far as she knew.

Shieri rumbled a warning.

"Oh hush! You know very well the Guild would call you my familiar."

"And they would be wrong."

"Why can't we just call the police?" Alex grumbled. "This is taking forever."

Lloyd shrugged. Like her, he'd also been left out of the planning. "The city watch is controlled from the palace. I told you that."

"So?"

"So, we know Karel visits the palace regularly. Bevyn saw him there just this morning disguised as Wallace. We don't know who he visits, but what if it's the commander or someone close to him?"

She nodded reluctantly. The commander led the watch the way a general would lead an army. If he was in Karel's pocket, nothing the watch did could be trusted. His contact didn't even have to be the commander. It could be any of a number of bureaucrats working within the palace. If word of their rescue attempt were to leak out... well, bad things would surely result. By holding it close to the chest, Henry hoped to keep the palace ignorant until after Douglas was safe.

She understood the reasoning, even agreed with it, but it didn't make the delay easier to accept. Everyone was ready to go. Even the Guildmaster wore a shiny breastplate over his robe. Very odd he looked too, but no one cared, not after Tomas drilled holes in an old one. When he went on to prove that runes did indeed make his bullets bounce, well, everyone was positively eager to wear one. Dents were better than holes any day. She was glad to have one; though hers looked even sillier over her dress, she was certain.

She sighed.

"Patience," Lloyd murmured.

"Don't try that on me!" she said hotly. "Where was your patience when you abandoned us? None of this would be necessary if you'd waited to reach the city with the rest of us. Alison would still be alive if you had!"

"Exactly."

She frowned, not understanding his point.

"I should have waited. I might never have met Kendrick and been sponsored by Bevyn, and I would regret that, but those things aren't worth Alison's life. Is your impatience worth Doug's life? I don't think so. We need to take the time to plan, and do things right the first time. Karel doesn't give second chances."

She nodded reluctantly. It annoyed her, but he had a good point. She would wait as long as she had to; she had no choice any way. Remembering Alison's fate at Karel's hands, she was glad Michael hadn't come. Armour or not, accidents happened. She wouldn't be able to face Sandy if anything happened to her husband.

To her immense relief, things started happening and the planning session broke up. Henry's officers hurried out of the tavern to join their men, already in position for the assault. Tomas checked his gun, though she was sure it was unnecessary. What could have happened to it? It never left his belt. It wasn't as if someone could have stolen the bullets! He holstered the weapon and came over to join her, while Henry and the Guildmaster conferred about something. Bevyn stood silently nearby, listening.

"What's happening?" she said when Tomas reached her.

"Our guys will go over the wall at the same time as we assault the gate. It's a simple plan, I guess, but it should work."

"You're right, that does sound simple. Why did it take so long to think up?"

Tomas ignored her snark. "We've split Henry's men into teams. Enough of our guys should still make it over, even if one of the teams is seen scaling the wall. If all goes well, they'll hit Karel's men in the rear as we assault the main gate."

"What about me?"

Tomas hesitated. **Tie her up… leave her here? What about the fanged glutton? She won't stand for that…**

"I'm not staying behind!"

"Did I say that?"

"You didn't have to."

He scowled. "Stay out of my head, dammit!"

"Then stop shouting at me!"

"I'm not shouting—" he yelled, but then lowered his voice. "I'm not the one who is shouting."

"In your head you are," she said, lowering her voice. She was very aware of all the eyes suddenly turned her way. "I'm not staying behind, Tom. I'll just follow you. Shieri can track anything, even in a city."

"I think you'll be coming with us to the gate," Lloyd said, and shrugged at Tomas' sharp look. "Unless she can teach Shieri how to climb a rope."

"I don't need rope," Shieri said scornfully. **"Walls are easy."**

"Shieri says walls are easy," Alex said, but unlike Shieri, she couldn't climb worth a damn. "Fine. The gate it is."

Tomas' lips thinned. "You'll be the last one through. Am I clear?"

She nodded.

"I mean it."

She gave him innocent face and nodded again.

He frowned, but suddenly his face smoothed and he turned to Lloyd. "You stick to her like glue. Can I trust you with that?"

"You can trust me. I owe it to Alison."

Tomas' expression darkened at the reminder, but he nodded. "I'll tell your Guildmaster. He has Bevyn and Kendrick to help him. I'm sure he can spare you."

"I'm just a novice. I doubt I could help anyway."

Tomas went back to the others, and shortly after that, they moved out. He glanced back a few times as they navigated the little used alleys, but Lloyd was as good as his word. Too good in her opinion. She had Shieri and her magic to protect her; she didn't need him to do it for her, but he was trying to prove something she figured.

They reached their destination and waited while Henry studied the situation at the gates to Wallace's estate. She could hardly contain herself. Douglas was imprisoned just a few hundred yards away, waiting for her to rescue him. She couldn't wait to see him again. Excitement thrilled through her. When they met, she had something to say to him; something he wouldn't expect. She smiled as she imagined his reaction. Rhiannon had no say in her decision; Shieri was right about that.

"Of course I am."

She grinned at the cat and put her back to the wall. She leaned there, imagining the look on Doug's face when she confronted him. Leaving her behind in Ilsehaven, upsetting though it had been, did have one redeeming quality. It had made her consider things from his perspective. Mulling it all over with Shieri on *Amelia*, she knew what he'd been thinking behind those damnably tight and impenetrable shields of his, or she believed that she did. Shieri's thoughts on her solution confirmed her beliefs anyway.

Henry pointed at the gates and Tomas nodded. He drew his gun, keeping it down by his side to hide it as he approached the soldiers guarding the estate. She watched him for any sign that he needed help. Using her magic, she could sense his life thread very clearly. It was so strong and familiar to her that she would never mistake it for another.

He stopped before the gate and addressed the guards. She couldn't hear what he said, but it was easy to guess. Sensible or not, he would never just shoot them. He would say something like: *police, drop your weapons.* Of course they wouldn't do that and—

Crack-crack, bong! Crack!

Bullets struck Tomas' armour, the sound travelling clearly, and he stumbled back from the impacts, but he wasn't hurt. His life thread reassured her that he was safe, and that his rune-strengthened armour worked. She'd been worried about it, despite the tests they'd run at Stonybrook. What if Karel's men carried different guns; more powerful guns? What then? It was a relief to find they didn't.

Tomas returned fire expertly. Faithful to his training, he ended the brief fight with a pair of double-taps. He edged forward to check the bodies, and then waved all clear. Henry and his men ran to enter the gate.

"Wait," Lloyd said and took her arm.

Crack-crack-crack!

She was about to argue, but the gunfire interrupted her. A serious firefight had just erupted. She wanted to help, but what could she do against bullets?

Crack... crack... crack! Crack-crack-crack!

"Let go!" she snapped. Frustration gaining the upper hand as the fighting intensified. Shieri growled at him. Only then did he let go. "I can use my magic to make them give up."

"Can you? Ever done that?"

"No but—"

"Then we wait. It's safer."

She scowled. "Coward."

"Say what you like. I promised Tomas I would keep you safe. Unless you can swear to me that you really can make them give up, we wait."

She bit her lip, stumped, and he grinned at her. She couldn't swear to something she was uncertain about. Oaths had power here, and the Goddess punished oath breakers harshly. She was still trying to think of something that would sway him, when his eyes popped wide in surprise. Alarmed, she turned to see what had scared him, and spotted a man's head and shoulders sticking out of the wall. The head—it was a man's head—was looking up the road, facing the opposite direction.

"Fergus?" Lloyd squeaked. "What the fu... frig?"

"A friend of yours?"

He didn't answer. Instead, he went to greet the man who stepped through the wall to meet him. Shieri surprised her by greeting the stranger warmly, rubbing herself against his legs. He bent to stroke her and mumbled a welcome.

"Do you know him, Shieri?"

"He's a green man. Just as you're a Daughter of the Mother and chosen by her to be mine, he would be a Son and chosen by her also."

"Would be?"

"They're not called Sons, but they are chosen. Green men are bonded to places by the Goddess."

Alex had never felt happier to be born female! She couldn't imagine not having Shieri as her chosen. She hated the thought of being stuck in one place forever, though her farm might have served if she hadn't come through the gate. The web there had definitely felt different to her, and it had always reacted to her oddly. Would she have been unable to leave in a few years? She shivered; it felt right. She had always felt reluctant to go into town, and the land hadn't liked it whenever she did leave. Thank the Goddess for Douglas. If she hadn't met him, she could have been chained to the Yorke Place forever.

Crack... crack-crack-crack!

The gunfire sounded distant now. The fight had moved on. She used the web to find Tomas. He was with Henry and the Guildmaster directing the fighting. Everyone seemed fine. The only dead that she could see belonged to Karel, left where they'd fallen.

"Is Fergus bonded here, to Wallace's garden, can he help?"

"No. You can feel his grove if you try."

She remembered the grove they'd visited using the web. If not for the city that had grown around it, she had no doubt a stone circle would mark its location. It was a powerful place, a nexus in the web. Although miles away, she could feel it easily. She assumed Fergus could roam the city as long as he stayed close enough. She wondered if her own bond had a similar range, but she couldn't conceive of a reason to test it. Shieri wouldn't let her out of her sight in any case, and she was more than fine with that.

"This is Alex and Shieri," Lloyd said.

Fergus nodded as if he already knew. "You've come for Red Hand I suppose? Took you long enough."

"You know where he is? Is he all right?" she asked him eagerly.

"Follow me."

She blinked as he stepped back through the wall. She glanced at Lloyd, and he shrugged. He reached to touch the masonry and gasped when the surface rippled around his fingers. He snatched his hand back when Fergus' face appeared, as if floating just beneath the surface.

"You coming?" Fergus said.

Shieri answered by going through the wall.

Alex gasped and hurried to follow. She wouldn't let her chosen go into danger without her. She held her breath and stepped into the wall. Lloyd growled a curse at her move, but followed. She didn't know what she'd expected to feel, but she hadn't expected to feel nothing at all. Walking through solid stone should feel like something, but it didn't. She could have been stepping through an ordinary open doorway for all the difference she felt. A brief moment of darkness, and she stepped into a garden. Shieri and Fergus stood together, waiting.

Crack... crack... crack...

She flinched, but like last time, the gunfire sounded distant. She hoped everyone was all right. Motion attracted her eye, and she turned to watch Lloyd appear within the wall. He had his eyes closed, and he was holding his breath. She grinned when he opened one eye to look warily around. His breath whooshed out, and he moved to join them.

"This way," Fergus said and hurried deeper into the garden.

She hesitated; he wasn't heading for the house. Shieri bounded away, unconcerned, and she sighed. "No choice," she muttered and followed.

Lloyd kept pace.

The reason Fergus led them away from the house became obvious when she used her magic to check on Tomas again. He was fine, but the fight had reached the front door of the house. There was fighting with sword and dagger there. Henry's men were about to force their way inside. Fergus was leading her through the garden to a back way into the house.

They entered the kitchen carefully, but the staff had fled. The place was deserted. Shieri prowled around, pausing when she discovered an interesting scent. Suddenly she went still, and then padded up to a door.

"Your mate was here."

Her mate indeed! Shieri meant Douglas. "Is he in there now?"

"Who?" Lloyd said. "What did she say?"

"No, but someone is."

"Shieri says Douglas was here."

Alex hurried up to the door and pressed an ear to it. She heard whispering. It was probably the kitchen staff, hiding from the fighting. She yanked open the door.

"Dammit, Alex!" Lloyd cried. "Have a care!"

She blushed when she realised what he meant. She didn't know who was in there, or where the door led; she could have been shot. She was lucky, and her guess was correct. Frightened men and women in livery huddled together in the pantry, staring at her. Fergus appeared at her shoulder, and they relaxed a little, recognising him.

Shieri appeared beside Alex, scaring them again. She laid a hand upon the cat. "It's all right. She's my chosen and won't hurt you."

"Chosen..." they whispered. "A battle cat chosen... is there war? Is that what's happening out there? Are we at war?"

They were babbling and confused. Asking questions and not waiting for an answer before asking another. She tried to reassure them, but it took Fergus and some snark to gain some semblance of order.

"Are you children?" he said. "How would an enemy break the wards on the walls? Fools."

That calmed them, but one or two looked insulted. Before they could get their hackles up, she took over. "We're here to rescue Lord Skeldon. Did you know a man named Karel is impersonating your duke?"

They fell silent, looking guiltily at each other. They did then, but none of them had been brave enough to tell anyone. Shieri growled, sending thoughts full of derision. Alex agreed with the sentiment. She didn't expect them to confront Karel or rescue their employer, but they could have sent a message to the commander, or told someone else in authority.

"Do you know where Karel is?"

The guilty silence stretched out, until one of the younger girls tentatively raised her hand. Her friends looked aghast, and pulled her hand down.

"She doesn't know," one man said hurriedly. "Please, mistress, take no notice. She's simple-minded."

The girl looked outraged.

Alex beckoned her out of the pantry, and the girl tried, having to shrug off restraining hands to obey. Shieri snarled again, for real this time, and suddenly the girl was free. She stepped into the kitchen.

"You know where Karel is?" Alex said.

"I overheard him talking to his man. They went to see someone at the Guild."

Lloyd's stiffened. "Who, do you know?"

The girl shrugged, and then shook her head.

"It doesn't matter," Alex said. "It's good that he's not here."

"But it does matter!" Lloyd said worriedly. "If he still has contacts within the guild, he could do a lot of harm. There's stuff kept there that we don't want him getting his hands on, including another gate talisman."

"Really? That's great! We can use it to send the others home."

"It's great as long as Karel doesn't get his hands on it."

She frowned, that was true. "There's nothing we can do about it now." She turned to Fergus. "Thanks for the help, but can I ask one thing more of you?"

Fergus smiled. "Ask."

"Lead these people to safety?"

"I can do that."

"Thanks."

Fergus beckoned and led the nervous people outside and

away.

Alex watched them go and then followed Lloyd through the house. They used a route normally used by the below stairs staff to service the house. They were unembellished and dingy corridors, never meant to be seen by anyone but liveried servants. How Lloyd knew the way, she had no idea, but he seemed confident. He quickly found the right door, and they emerged on the second floor, into a plushly carpeted area of the house. The decor wasn't to her taste. Darkly painted reddish-brown walls, and gilded woodwork met her eyes. Unlit, but highly polished brass lamps decorated the walls every fifteen feet or so, their glass reservoirs well-tended and filled with a golden coloured oil.

Lloyd pointed to a door at the end of the hall. "They were in that one when I lived here."

She hurried to try the door. "Locked. Of course," she said sourly.

"Let me. I can tell it's warded as well as locked. Probably to prevent Doug from doing what I'm going to try," Lloyd said and knelt before the door. "I learned the rune for unlocking the easier wards that Karel uses. Hopefully he didn't change his habits after I left."

"Convenient."

"I suppose, but I didn't learn it for convenience. I didn't want him locking me in my room. He threatened to do it more than once."

"You thought ahead," she said, impressed despite herself.

"I planned to join the Guild the moment I learned of it, but when Karel killed Alison for no reason and so easily, I knew I had to escape as soon as I could. There was no way to do that on the journey. I was never alone. Besides, I did want him to teach me. He's an excellent teacher, Alex, but brutal. He gets off on hurting people."

"Did he...?"

"Yes, more than a few times. The oath that I forced him

to swear means he can't kill me, or even hurt me directly. He can't even order it done, but it didn't stop him from finding a way to punish me. He taught me things that hurt if done wrong. I messed up a lot."

Shieri growled, sending a feeling of disgust and sympathy to Alex through the bond. She laid a hand on the cat's back, to soothe her.

"I'm sorry he did that to you."

Lloyd carefully traced a complicated looking geometric shape around the lock with a wet finger. "I deserved it. We both know the Goddess will judge me for what happened to Alison. Maybe she'll take my pain as part payment."

Anything was possible here, though a death would surely require more than Lloyd could possibly pay. His crime, causing Alison's death, would require threefold payment. She frowned, trying to imagine something that he could do, but she couldn't think of anything big enough.

"Can we help him somehow, Shieri? I feel sorry for him."

"He alone must make amends for past mistakes, as we all must."

"But he can't make up for Alison's death, can he?"

"He didn't kill her, but some of the blame is his. If he hadn't freed Karel, your friend wouldn't have died. Only the Goddess and he knows the depth of his guilt, and only She knows the price he must pay."

She nodded thoughtfully.

Lloyd stood and frowned at the door. "*Saiii-teran-ah!*" He crooned, and the lock clicked. He grinned at her, and opened the door.

"Doug don't!" she cried, but her shout was too late.

The punch landed, and Lloyd fell, his lip bleeding profusely.

Shieri sent amusement to her through the bond, as Doug dove atop Lloyd's prone form. The two men rolled around, grappling and punching. Another figure appeared in the doorway, holding a chair raised above his head. It was obvious what he planned to do. Without needing to think, she reached out to his life thread.

"Don't," she said and pushed. His thread hummed in her head, but not discordantly, and she relaxed at this evidence of the Lady's approval.

"Not approval," Shieri said, **"but not disapproval either."**

Alex was more than okay with that. She'd compelled people in the past, knowing the Lady would disapprove even as she did it. She would take indifference over that any day.

"Not indifference. She knows what is in your heart. You did him no harm, while preventing it from being done to another. She would have approved if not for the means you used. You stole his free will, and that's wrong, but you stopped him hurting Lloyd, restoring the balance."

Balance again. She didn't have time to think about that right now, but she had a feeling that there was something in what Shieri had said that might help Lloyd one day.

The man in the doorway lowered the chair, and discarded it to one side, frowning in puzzlement. Shieri took his attention a moment later when she roared at Douglas. He looked up, startled, and Lloyd got a solid punch in.

"That's enough!" Alex said. "People are dying outside while you two act like children!"

"Alex?" Douglas said in amazement.

"It's me," she said and grinned. "Henry brought me."

"Henry is here too?"

She nodded. "Outside with Tomas and his men."

Douglas stood, and perhaps a little reluctantly, offered a hand to help Lloyd rise. Lloyd accepted without hesitation and got to his feet, mopping blood. His nose was bleeding; he'd been losing.

"We need to get to the palace," Wallace said.

Douglas nodded.

"Why the palace?" she asked. "Karel is supposedly visiting the Guild."

Wallace raised an eyebrow. "Indeed? That's good news."

"I don't think it is," Lloyd said. "Apart from murdering his way across two worlds, Karel is most known for stealing a talisman from the archives. He could be doing the same thing right now. If he gets his hands on a way to open a gate, no one and nowhere will be safe from him. He could open one into this house, and send an army through it!"

"There's another gate talisman—you're certain?" Douglas said.

Lloyd nodded. "I've seen it. I asked the Guildmaster to let Alex use it to get home. Karel can't use that one."

"Why not?"

"It needs a full coven of thirteen witches to activate. There are a lot of things in the archive that we don't know how to use, and some could be for making gates. The Guildmaster told me about some weapons stored there, that were used to destroy entire armies during the war of power."

Douglas shot an alarmed look at Wallace.

Wallace nodded grimly. "Karel will bypass the city's wards by sending his men through a gate, and then they'll attack the palace during the coronation. That must be his plan. They'll assassinate Erland, and then escape back through the gate. Simple."

"Wait, a minute. I thought gates only worked between worlds," Alex said, feeling confused. "Why would Karel want to kill the prince, and what's in it for him?"

"No time to explain that, now," Douglas said. "We need to get Erland into hiding. If Karel doesn't know where he is, he can't make a gate to reach him."

"Persuading the queen will be hard," Wallace warned, "But it must be done. We have to smuggle Erland out of the palace and take him to..." he frowned, trying to think of a safe place.

"Stonybrook!" she said. "He wouldn't expect that, would he?"

Douglas frowned. "He might. Stonybrook or the Guild are the obvious places."

She felt a little deflated hearing that. "Obvious, really?"

"Where else is so well protected by magic? Of the two, Stonybrook is the best choice; it has Henry's protection as well."

"We have our mercenary guards," Lloyd said, a little defensively. "The Guildmaster needs to hear this."

"Henry too," she agreed, and they headed downstairs to find him.

The sounds of fighting had died away while they were discussing things, but they didn't take chances. They stole through the house like thieves, but they met no one. The house was utterly still.

"You didn't tell him," Shieri accused.

"The time wasn't right," she said a little defensively.

"My chosen is not a coward. I won't have it be said that she is."

"I'll tell him, don't worry. We have to see the prince to safety, and deal with Karel first. Who have you been talking to about me?"

"The other chosen at the chapterhouse. You will tell him before we return there. You will!"

"I will," she soothed. *"Don't worry."*

"They can say what they like," Shieri said as if she hadn't heard her. **"I am Shieriraneth, the strongest and fiercest of my generation! My chosen is, and must be, better than their chosen."**

"I'm sure I will be," Alex soothed, rolling her eyes at such foolishness, and trying not to laugh. Was there anything vainer than a cat?

* * *

32 ~ Prince

Prince Erland listened quietly to his mother's conversation, not revealing his thoughts on Duke Isten's treachery. As far as Alex could tell, he wasn't concerned about the possibility of his assassination, and his life thread proved to her that his calm was no pretence. His demeanour was... well, it was very regal. She was impressed despite herself. She'd been prepared to dislike him, expecting someone overly concerned with his own importance, but he didn't give that impression at all. She had a good feeling about him.

He would be a good king.

It didn't hurt that he looked the part. He had the body of an athlete, strong, but not overly muscular for a man his age. It was easy to forget that he was only sixteen. He reminded her of a bronze-haired Douglas. He had the wide shoulders of a man who swung a heavy sword every day, and the muscular thighs of a horseman. He was about the same height as Doug as well, though a growth spurt could easily see him spring up another six inches overnight. Although he wasn't armed, he looked like a soldier, not a pampered prince.

"Are we sure this is even necessary?" Queen Isabeau said.

"Warren and Bevyn are checking the archive now,"

Henry said. "I don't think we can afford to wait for news. Karel doesn't need a gate to kill the prince."

"That's true, my queen. I've been seen walking the halls of the palace frequently," Wallace said dryly. "This very morning Bevyn saw me here. I assure you, it was not I."

"But surely that's the best evidence of all, that this isn't a credible threat," Erland said. "A dagger in the back, poison in my wine cup... even an arrow from hiding while I ride on the hunt would be easier to accomplish. None of those things have happened. If Karel is wandering the palace corridors in disguise, and he hasn't killed me yet, it must mean that killing me *isn't* his plan."

"Well reasoned, your highness," Henry said, "But there could be many reasons for his inaction. The simplest that I can think of is that his orders are to perform the deed at the coronation itself."

Erland frowned. "If so, his goal isn't my death, or it isn't my death *alone*. If time and location are important to him, we should try to discover why that is."

"May I say something?" Lloyd said, and Erland nodded his permission. "Karel's reasons are no doubt important, but we can't stay here guessing. It's a pointless exercise without a way to verify anything. We need to get you to safety."

Douglas nodded. "I agree with him, your highness. We can discuss this on the journey, and later at Stonybrook. Our priority right now should be getting you away from the palace unseen."

Lloyd nodded. "Goddess forbid it happens, but if Karel does gain a way to open gates again, you need to be out of his reach—either somewhere he wouldn't guess to look for you, or somewhere closed to him for some other reason. I understand that the chapterhouse is well defended."

"Only the Motherhouse at Dehra is more secure," Henry said. "With Rhiannon in residence, my men are on high alert, and the sisters we escorted here for the coronation easily double the number normally living there."

Isabeau frowned. "I'm not convinced this is necessary."

"Forgive me, your majesty," Henry said. "Does it matter? If Karel isn't a threat as you assume, then nothing is lost by the prince's visit to Stonybrook. If he *is* a threat...?"

The queen nodded and made her decision. "He must visit with Rhiannon," she frowned in thought. "But he mustn't be accused of running from danger. I'll not have his ascension to the throne besmirched by innuendo and rumour. His reign will be a golden age for Inari. He will be Erland the Just, or Erland the Great."

Alex grinned when the prince rolled his eyes. He was just a young boy again in that moment.

"Officially, we'll say that he's meeting with the Reverend Mother to pay his respects," the queen went on. "He can convey my invitation to Rhiannon to visit the palace at the same time."

"That's all fine and good," Henry said. "But we need to get him there undetected." He frowned at Erland. "Stand a moment if you would, laddy."

Erland looked puzzled, but did as he was bid. Meanwhile, Henry had opened the door and asked Captain Arlen to join them. He had the two men stand together. They were of similar stature.

"That should work, don't you think?" Henry said, and Wallace nodded.

Erland looked the captain over. "Red isn't really my colour."

Royal blue was the traditional colour of Dun'Harden.

Douglas pursed his lips thoughtfully. "You have your father's hair, your highness. It's very distinctive. I can use a spell, or you can use coal dust or something."

"Not magic," Lloyd said and faltered as all eyes focused upon him. "I... I mean, he'll detect it. Karel will feel it."

She nodded. "He's right. Dye would be better."

Erland winced. "Not dye, please. A helmet will cover it."

"No," Isabeau agreed. "Not dye. The coronation is too close. It would take months to grow out."

"A helmet then, as long as you keep it on," Henry said.

Erland nodded.

Henry went on. "We'll ride in column as Lady Alex's escort to Stonybrook. Such things are common enough; we won't draw attention. I shall ride beside her as is proper, and you will pose as the good captain riding directly behind me. Tomas, I want your gun beside him."

"I'll look after him," Tomas said.

Henry nodded. "Arlen?"

"Your, Grace?"

"Switch clothes with the prince, if you would. I want him in uniform and wearing our special armour as soon as possible."

"Follow me, Captain," Erland said.

Arlen followed the prince to find some privacy.

Alex rode through the city streets next to Henry, very aware of the spectacle they made. Although Daughters of the Mother were a reasonably common sight, battle cats were not. A Daughter of the Mother with a battle cat chosen, *and* one escorted by a fifty-strong detachment of soldiers, was unusual.

They drew attention.

She'd been concerned about it at first, but she quickly realised she needn't worry. All attention was on Shieri. It was perfect. No one paid the slightest attention to Erland. He was just one red-coated soldier among many, and completely anonymous. His helmet covered his hair, and its nose and chin guards obscured his face.

They rode through the city gates unmolested.

"That was easy," she said.

Henry grunted. "We're not there yet, but I really do

think Karel's plan will involve an attack upon the coronation ceremony."

"Could it be that I'm not the target after all?" Erland said. "There will be many others there."

"It's possible," Wallace agreed. He was riding next to Erland, so that the boy was sandwiched between him and Tomas. "The emperor might want all of your nobles dead alongside you, your highness. With all of us dead, he could annex Inari unopposed."

"Not unopposed," Erland protested. "Rhiannon and the Guild would unite with my father's allies against him. I have assurances that when I'm king, they'll renew their pledges and agreements with me."

Wallace nodded. "Then we're back to Karel replacing you with your sister."

"I love my sister very much. She would make a fine queen should I die, but she's too young."

"Your mother would become regent for her, as she did for you, your highness. She has proven more than capable, and she's the emperor's sister."

"What are you implying?" Erland said, his manner turning frosty.

Douglas diffused the rising tension. "If you should fall, your mother would become regent for your sister, and the empire would automatically enjoy another ten years as our most favoured trading partner. Do you see?"

Erland nodded.

"Your mother purchased the peace we enjoy with concessions to her brother's empire, but most assume that when you ascend the throne, you will tighten controls upon the borders again, and regulate the empire's access to our ports."

"I've made no such announcement," Erland said stiffly.

"Of course not. Angering your uncle sooner than you must isn't in the kingdom's best interests, but we all know that change is coming."

"Speculation and rumour."

"Rumours based upon the kingdom's needs, your highness. We've bled trade ever since your father died. Your mother has done her best, but the concessions she made to keep her brother at bay cannot continue forever. They'll bankrupt your treasury. The clans have tolerated them as necessary, but they'll expect you to redress the balance soon after you're crowned."

Erland grimaced. "They expect a lot of things."

Henry chuckled. "The crown is a heavy burden. You could refuse it."

"Very funny, your grace. I'll not disgrace myself or my father's memory."

"Well said," Wallace said, and everyone mumbled in agreement. "The trick will be redressing the balance while avoiding war—"

Crack!

The first shot rang out, and Wallace fell without a sound, hitting the road in a boneless heap. More shots erupted, and the horses screamed in panic at the noise. Alex's horse reared, but she clung on with her knees, and wrestled it under control. Others weren't so lucky. Men fell, thrown from their mounts, and their screams added themselves to that of the injured horses.

"Dismount, dammit!" Henry roared, trying to make sense of the confusion.

Crack-crack-crack!

Her horse went nuts, crow hopping and circling, trying to escape her control. She tried to use her magic to calm her, but the moment she connected with the web, she had other things on her mind. Life threads rose up all around, blazing in her mind. There were dozens of men hiding in the fields bordering the road.

Crack-crack-crack!

Impact!

She cried out, a searing agony crackling through her left shoulder and arm. Shieri screamed in outrage, as her pain transmitted itself through the bond. She tried to block it from the cat, but couldn't. The bond with her chosen was unlike others; it couldn't be blocked, or if it could, she didn't know how. She groaned at the pain, and gave up trying to control her fool horse. She let herself fall out of the saddle, and grunted with the impact upon the road. The horse bolted, not alone in fleeing. Henry's men must have had similar thoughts, and decided to let them run. Not all had. Some were down, kicking and screaming their agony, while others lay still. All too many were accompanied by their riders.

She crawled toward one of the dead mounts, intending to use it as cover, groaning at the agony in her shoulder. Blood trickled down her arm, staining the road, but it wasn't pumping out of her. The luck of the Goddess was with her, and the bullet had gone straight through without hitting an artery. She was lucky. She didn't feel lucky, but she was. It could have hit her in the head, and killed her stone dead.

She hunkered down behind the dead horse, trying not to notice its rider lying trapped beneath it. His thread was dull, dead of a broken neck.

Shieri screamed her outrage again.

"I'm okay! I'll live, Shieri!"

She flinched at the rage coming through the bond. There was no soothing the cat. Shieri roared, and charged into battle. Men screamed as she pounced and ripped them apart.

The fields became her hunting grounds.

Alex turned her attention to the wound. She ripped the sleeve from her beautiful dress, furious that she had to ruin it, and wadded it up to press against the wound. The bullet had hit her in the arm, and travelled upward at an angle to exit the top of her shoulder. No bones were broken, and it wasn't even bleeding that hard... really... she was very lucky... very...

She swayed, suddenly dizzy, and her vision tunnelled and dimmed.

She couldn't afford to pass out. She took hold of her magic, concentrating her will upon it, letting the web energise her. Its strength roared into her, filled her, and buoyed her up until the pain in her arm became nothing but a minor irritation. She flung out her will to find her friends, and found them easily.

Tomas and the prince were still together and unhurt.

Douglas was fighting! She yearned to go to him, but he was cutting Karel's men down with his sword as if they were nothing to fear. He seemed unstoppable. Wallace was unconscious on the ground where he'd fallen. His head wound looked bloody, but the bullet must have glanced off the bone, because his thread was still strong.

Henry led his men in a counterattack, and took a heavy toll upon them. The sound of clashing swords, battle cries, and the harsher screams of the dying, replaced gunfire. Shieri was fine, leaving a trail of bodies in her wake, as she stalked Karel's men through the tall stalks of wheat.

Alex staggered to her feet, not letting go of her magic, and headed for Tomas and the prince. They were circling the main battle like wolves circling wounded prey. Tomas used his gun sparingly, only shooting when he had to. He must be nearly out of ammunition by now. The prince fought well, wielding his sword expertly, though this must be his first real battle.

"What do we have here?" Karel said. "This is a pleasant surprise, I must say. Here I was, expecting to find a princeling, and instead I find Skeldon's little witchy morsel."

She spun, flinching at the pain in her shoulder. He had snuck up behind her so easily. She attacked, using a compulsion spell, but he just smiled! She'd done it right, dammit! It never failed. She tried again, and he laughed.

She backed away and bumped into Mardus. He grabbed her wounded arm, and she shrieked as pain exploded. She fumbled for her magic, but the pain made it slip from her grasp.

Oh Goddess, it hurt so much. Her vision dimmed.

Crack!

Her cheek flamed and stung. Karel had slapped her! She glared at him, reaching for Shieri. The cat was close, slinking through the tall stalks of wheat at her back. Her rage had turned to icy calm. Mardus was a dead man walking; he just didn't know it yet.

"Can't have you falling asleep," Karel muttered as he retrieved something from beneath his robe.

It looked very familiar, and she felt sick. The Guild had lost another treasure. Could anyone just wander into their vault and take whatever they wanted? Maybe Rhiannon was right. If the Guild couldn't be trusted to guard such dangerous things, the sisterhood should do it.

"I think a quick retreat might be in order," Karel muttered.

"The men?" Mardus said.

"There are plenty more where they came from," Karel said, but before he could begin his gate spell, everything went to hell.

Shieri leapt upon Mardus' back, riding him screaming to the ground. Alex staggered and landed painfully at Karel's feet, just as Douglas arrived. He saw her fall, and bellowed in anger. Seeing red, he swung his sword intending to bisect Karel, and put him out of everyone's misery. The wizard bent to grab Alex, and the sword swept over him, missing entirely.

He turned, eyes going wide at what had nearly happened. He gathered his magic, traced a rune in the air, and gestured toward a still snarling Douglas. Lloyd arrived at that moment, panting from his run, and skidded to an alarmed stop at the sight of Karel… right in his line of fire.

"No!" Karel shrieked in horror.

Lloyd flinched, and cried out, but magic swirled around him, and the spell bounced!

Alex gasped as she felt the hand of the Goddess protect Lloyd, and send the spell back to its maker. The hex struck, and Karel screamed. He screamed and screamed and screamed, and went on screaming, as he slowly turned to stone. Feet first.

Lloyd swallowed hard and stepped forward to take the talisman out of Karel's limp grip.

"Should I end it?" Douglas said.

Lloyd shrugged, not caring in the least, and tucked the Guild's treasure out of sight beneath his robes.

Shieri finished off Mardus and trotted up to Karel. She circled him. **"Let him scream. This is justice, and the hand of the Goddess at work."**

Alex swallowed, and relayed that.

Douglas nodded and helped her up. "You're hurt."

"Shot, but it's not too bad."

"You could have died."

She nodded, realising how close they'd come to losing each other. She hugged him one-armed, shaking in reaction. Oh Goddess, she could have lost him!

"I love you," she whispered, beginning to cry. "I do." She kissed him, putting all of her love and fear into it. When it ended, they were both gasping for breath. "I love you," she said again, this time kissing his cheek, and then the hollow beneath his jaw. "I love you," more kisses. "I love you."

"And I love you," Douglas said, his voice husky.

"Finally," Shieri said sounding satisfied. **"My chosen is not a coward. My chosen is victorious in battle, and has claimed her mate. They cannot say otherwise. They'll not dare!"**

"I'm sure they won't, Shieri," Alex said, wondering why the

other chosen would even care.

"My God," Tomas said, arriving at a run with Erland hard on his heels. "I heard the screams. What the hell did you do to him?" He looked at Alex in horror.

She shrugged. "It wasn't me."

Lloyd explained. "Karel swore an oath not to harm me. The spell was meant for Douglas, not me, but that doesn't matter. It would have killed me. That makes him an oath breaker; the Goddess made his spell bounce."

Tomas raised his gun. "No one deserves this." He fired into Karel's chest.

Crack-varoom! Crack-varoom!

She ducked as the bullets ricocheted. "Damn it, Tom! I've nearly died once today. Watch what you're doing!"

Tomas gaped at the piteously screaming man. The spell had progressed too far; he was more statue now than flesh and blood, yet still he screamed. He wasn't breathing, *couldn't* be breathing, petrified as he was, yet the spell sustained him. The hex was an evil thing, sustaining its victim through the agonising process, even as it slowly killed him.

Henry appeared with his surviving men. They had won their battle, but at a terrible cost. Less than half of his soldiers still lived, many with gunshot wounds in arms and legs. They gathered around, propping each other up in many cases, to witness the Goddess' judgement. With cold eyes and grim satisfaction, they watched him scream. Minutes later, it was over, and the screams ended. They turned silently away, leaving the statue of a screaming man behind for the crows to perch upon.

Alex walked with Douglas to the road. "I love you," she said. She couldn't say it enough. "I do. I love you."

"And I love you," Douglas said. "But—"

"No buts. I love you. That's all that matters."

"But the sisters don't—"

"Marry me," she said. "Please marry me. Don't say but.

Don't say the sisters don't marry. Don't say Rhiannon won't like it, or anything else! Just say yes! Say it!"

He grinned. "Yes."

She flung herself into his arms, kissed him deeply, and then she just hugged him again, one-armed. Over his shoulder, she found Tomas' eyes. He looked at her as if she'd just ripped his still beating heart out. She closed her eyes to hide the hurt she saw in his, and held on. Douglas was hers, and she was his. Tomas would have to get over it. He was her past, and she wouldn't live in the past.

* * *

33 ~ Full Circle

The Guild's main assembly hall could easily be mistaken for one within the palace. It was a perfectly round room encircled by massive columns supporting its dome roof. Tomas guessed it was about two hundred feet in diameter. It obviously needed them. The weight of all that stone must be huge. A million tons, two?

The Guild was an extremely wealthy organisation, and the decor at the heart of its power was lavish. Fine tapestries and portraits hung upon the walls, and there were many examples of statuary scattered around. He guessed they were famous Guild members of the past. The huge columns had gilt patterns worked into their bases, and it was all real gold, not paint. He had asked about it, and Lloyd had explained that with rune magic almost anything was possible. He didn't actually say that he could turn lead into gold now, but he'd implied it, before laughing the matter off. Tomas was almost sure he'd been joking. Almost.

The assembly hall was the ancient core of the current Guildhall. It was the original home of its founders, inherited from scholars supported by the crown in their researches long ago. The Guild was independent these days, and wealthy. It had spent that wealth on expanding its reach across the continent, but had not held back on spending here in Hardenburg. The original hall had been expanded many times over the centuries, until it became the sprawling mega structure it now was. The Guild owned many chapterhouses spread across the kingdom, but Hardenburg was its home base, just as the motherhouse at Dehra was the spiritual home of all witches. That made Dehra Alex's home too now.

He frowned at the reminder.

He watched her performing the ritual, noting how much she had changed. The clothes, her hair, the air of confidence and strength... she had grown into her role as the Reverend Mother's protege, despite her supposed dislike of Rhiannon. He thought their animosity was more for show than real. He knew that she did respect the Reverend Mother, despite her highhanded ways. A lot of the antagonism was pure stubbornness on both their parts. They were just too much alike. Despite that, Alex seemed truly happy for the first time in a long while.

A year. It had taken an entire year to figure out how to open a portal home, but he still wasn't sure he wanted to go back. He'd had time to think about it. He'd considered all his options, and he did have some good ones. Henry Moore had offered a commission in his army, but although he'd enjoyed the training Arlen had given him, and felt fitter than he had in years, he wasn't really a soldier at heart. Deep down he was still a small town sheriff. Doug had offered that exact thing to him, serving the people of Dun'Morgan as a thief catcher, but although he respected the man, he couldn't warm to him as a real friend. He couldn't look at Alex and Doug, and see anything but a travesty and lost opportunity. He certainly couldn't stomach calling Alex's husband his boss.

So here he was, still uncertain and the portal was about to open. He watched the proceedings surrounded by a full circle of thirteen sisters—another symbol of the year just gone. Everything had come full circle. From his arrival by Karel's gate to his departure via Alex's portal today... if he stepped through.

If.

What was he going to do? Any moment now, she would complete her ritual and a way home would open. He was minutes away from the rest of his life, and leaving her behind with Douglas. He sought his rival out, and found him standing with Lloyd and the Guildmaster just outside the circle. They were watching Alex intently. Everyone was, but he recognised the expression upon Doug's face easily. He knew what it felt like to love her.

The Guildmaster whispered something to Bevyn, who nodded without taking his eyes off the witches. He and his top people were watching everything with wary eyes from places all around the huge hall. They had obviously placed themselves strategically to cover all exits, as if fearing theft of the talisman that Alex was using so confidently. Allowing witches to convene a coven, and use one of the treasures that the Guild guarded, all within the heart of the Guild's headquarters, was showing the sisters unprecedented trust. Lloyd and Alex were the reason for that trust, limited though it might be. Expecting more wasn't realistic.

"Are you okay?" Michael whispered as Alex worked. She was playing the part of focus and leader of the coven, because she knew the target intimately—her farm. "You've been quiet."

He shrugged, his grip tightening upon his sword as doubt assailed him again. "I've had a lot to think about."

"You're still uncertain?"

Was he? Was he *really* considering not going back? He frowned as he tried to understand what he was feeling. "I... don't have anything to stay for," he said and realised, finally and irrevocably, that it was true.

If he stayed, it would be for sentimental reasons, not

practical ones. He'd made some friends here, but he had friends back home too, and all his family was there. His brother didn't live in Susanville, but he was on Earth not Othala. There were his nieces and nephews to think of, and his sister-in-law too. He hadn't seen them in too long. He wanted to talk with his brother, and catch up. He wanted to be part of his life again, but that would never happen if he stayed here. He watched Alex working her magic with that enormous cat of hers sitting beside her, and knew there was nothing for him here but heartache.

"I'm leaving with you."

"Good decision."

"You think?"

Michael nodded. "You don't belong here. She does."

"She does have Shieri to consider," he admitted.

"That's not what I meant. She just fits. It's like she was born here, and didn't know it."

He nodded slowly. She was the happiest he'd seen her in a long time. Whether she belonged here or not, didn't really enter into it. What really mattered was where she would be happiest living, and that was obviously here with Shieri and... and Douglas, dammit. He didn't like admitting that, but it was so obviously true that he couldn't deny it. He'd been a selfish and foolish idiot when he broke her heart all those years ago, but he was older and wiser now. He could recognise the obvious when confronted by it. She would stay here, and he would leave.

At least he knew that she was safe and happy. He wouldn't have to fear being called out to identify her body. He had feared that more than once. She had seemed tired and broken in spirit when she came home from the big city. Suicidal. It had taken her months to recover.

The chanting grew louder and more strident, and suddenly there it was! A hole in the air. The gate sprang into being out of nothing. It was just there, fully formed, but it wasn't like Karel's gate. He could see that clearly. The one he'd arrived through had been a void. This one was like an open door into another room, a room that was Alex's farm. He could see part of her truck parked not far away, and the barn beyond it.

She turned and smiled at him. "There. Are you ready?"

Sandy hurried over to hug her friend and kiss her cheek. "I'll miss you."

"But not Rhiannon I bet."

Sandy grimaced. "She's okay when she's not being the all holier than thou Reverend Mother."

Rhiannon glared from her place in the circle.

Tomas snorted. The Reverend Mother never forgot her position as the leader of the sisterhood. She had never come across to him as anything but a tyrant.

Alex glanced at him but then addressed Michael. "Look after her for me, and make some babies!"

Michael blushed and nodded. "I'll name them Alex and Douglas."

He rolled his eyes and shook his head. Michael got along well with Douglas. They were good friends, and they enjoyed each other's company.

Michael and his wife stepped before the portal. They looked back once before stepping into it hand in hand.

He looked back to find Alex studying him. "I'm going home."

"I thought you would. It's the right thing, Tom. You don't fit here. You should be wearing your uniform and smokey bear hat, and carrying a gun on your hip not a sword."

"I won't win re-election, but I agree. This place is you, not me."

Alex stepped forward and kissed him on the cheek.

He hugged her, and then looked for Douglas. "You look after her, hear?"

Douglas nodded. "I hear you most clearly, Tomas. You

have my word."

He nodded and strode resolutely toward the gate. He didn't stop, but walked straight into it, bracing himself for the disorientation he'd experienced before. To his surprise, he stepped through and into Alex's front yard with no ill effect. He turned to look back then, and Alex grinned at him. He fixed her in his memory, to look back upon in the years ahead. A beautiful fair-haired woman wearing an archaic corseted dress. Behind her stood a brooding man all in black with a sword on his hip, and love shining in his eyes.

She raised the talisman and the gate snapped shut.

"Are you okay?" Michael said. "Better than last time eh?"

He nodded and took a deep breath, putting thoughts of Alex out of his mind. That part of his life was over. He looked around for the truck, hoping he could get it started. He found the keys still in the ignition. Alex never had been one to lock it. He climbed in, and tried to start it, but he was unsurprised to find the battery dead. He headed for the house, hoping for a working phone. He used an elbow to break the glass in the door, and fumbled around inside until he could unlock it.

He stepped inside and flipped the light switch. Nothing. He hoped that didn't mean anything. If the phone company had disconnected it, they would have a long walk to town. He picked up the handset and... dial tone!

"We're in luck," he said as Michael and Sandy entered the house. "I'll have a car out here in no time."

"What are we going to tell them? You know they'll ask," Michael said. "I vote for Lloyd's idea. Amnesia."

"Me too," Sandy said.

He shrugged.

"Sheriff Hale," Jenn said sounding harried. "Meeks, if this is you again, I'll kick your butt if you don't get on with it—"

He turned his attention to the phone. "Sheriff Hale now is it? Guess who?"

"Oh my God, Tom!"

"Surprise!"

* * *

Also available from Impulse

If these books are not available from your local bookshop, send this coupon together with your check made payable to:

Impulse Books UK
At the following address:

Impulse Books UK
18, Lampits Hill Avenue,
Corringham
Essex SS177NY
United Kingdom

Please send the following great titles from Impulse Books UK

Tick as approrriate:

Hard Duty (Pb)
ISBN: 978-0-9545122-3-1 £10.99 _____ ☐

What Price Honour (Pb)
ISBN: 978-1-905380-44-2 £10.99 _____ ☐

Operation Oracle (Pb)
ISBN: 978-1-905380-52-7 £10.99 _____ ☐

Operation Breakout (Pb)
ISBN: 978-1-905380-57-2 £10.99 _____ ☐

NAME   _____

ADDRESS   _____

              _____

              _____

I have enclosed a check for the sum of £ _____

Please be sure to add £2.25 to your order to cover shipping and handling charges.